Dear Reader,

When I wrote *Mackenzie's Mountain,* one of the supporting characters was Wolf's son, Joe. I fell in love with Joe, and so did everyone else. I have never received so many letters asking for a character to have his own book as I did about Joe—until Chance Mackenzie came along.

Chance was one of those characters I didn't plan. All of a sudden he was just there, without warning. He was instantly fascinating, his past mysterious and unknown, his appeal so strong he inspired literally hundreds of readers to write asking for his full story, sometimes even suggesting plot lines if I didn't have one of my own! Thank you for your suggestions, but Chance's story was in my head from the beginning.

A Game of Chance will probably be the last of the Mackenzie books. I say "probably" because all the Mackenzie offspring are still children in my mind, and they may well stay children. I can't let them grow up without Wolf and Mary dying of old age, and I can't bear that.

There were no books on Mike and Josh, the other Mackenzie sons. Somehow I already had them settled in my mind, so their stories didn't spark for me. I wish they had.

Few readers have caught it, but all of the Mackenzie books since *Mackenzie's Mountain* have been set slightly in the future. I haven't made drastic changes, just little details here and there, to have fun and keep the time line straight. So if you catch something that doesn't seem quite right…it may be twenty years in the future!

Chance's story was written as part of the celebration for Silhouette's 20th Anniversary. I hope you enjoy him as much as I did!

Sincerely,

Linda Howard

Dear Reader,

What is there to say besides, "The wait is over!" Yes, it's true. Chance Mackenzie's story is here at last. *A Game of Chance,* by inimitable *New York Times* bestselling author Linda Howard, is everything you've ever dreamed it could be: exciting, suspenseful, and so darn sexy you're going to need to turn the air-conditioning down a few more notches! In Sunny Miller, Chance meets his match—in every way. Don't miss a single fabulous page.

The twentieth-anniversary thrills don't end there, though. A YEAR OF LOVING DANGEROUSLY continues with *Undercover Bride,* by Kylie Brant. This book is proof that things aren't always what they seem, because Rachel's groom, Caleb Carpenter, has secrets…secrets that could break—or win— her heart. *Blade's Lady,* by Fiona Brand, features another of her to-die-for heroes, and a heroine who's known him—in her dreams—for years. Linda Howard calls this author "a keeper," and she's right. Barbara McCauley's SECRETS! miniseries has been incredibly popular in Silhouette Desire, and now it moves over to Intimate Moments with *Gabriel's Honor*, about a heroine on the run with her son and the irresistible man who becomes her protector. Pat Warren is back with *The Lawman and the Lady,* full of suspense and emotion in just the right proportions. Finally, Leann Harris returns with *Shotgun Bride,* about a pregnant heroine forced to seek safety—and marriage—with the father of her unborn child.

And as if all that isn't enough, come back next month for more excitement—including the next installment of A YEAR OF LOVING DANGEROUSLY and the in-line return of our wonderful continuity, 36 HOURS.

Leslie J. Wainger
Executive Senior Editor

Please address questions and book requests to:
Silhouette Reader Service
U.S.: 3010 Walden Ave., P.O. Box 1325, Buffalo, NY 14269
Canadian: P.O. Box 609, Fort Erie, Ont. L2A 5X3

LINDA HOWARD

A GAME OF CHANCE

Silhouette®
INTIMATE™MOMENTS®

Published by Silhouette Books

America's Publisher of Contemporary Romance

For the readers

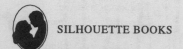 SILHOUETTE BOOKS

ISBN 0-373-27091-7

A GAME OF CHANCE

This edition published by arrangement with Harlequin Books S.A.

® and TM are trademarks of Harlequin Books S.A., used under license. Trademarks indicated with ® are registered in the United States Patent and Trademark Office, the Canadian Trade Marks Office and in other countries.

Visit Silhouette at www.eHarlequin.com

Printed in U.S.A.

Books by Linda Howard

LINDA HOWARD

says that whether she's reading them or writing them, books have long played a profound role in her life. She cut her teeth on Margaret Mitchell and from then on continued to read widely and eagerly. In recent years her interest has settled on romantic fiction, because she's "easily bored by murder, mayhem and politics." After twenty-one years of penning stories for her own enjoyment, Ms. Howard finally worked up the courage to submit a novel for publication—and met with success! Happily, the Alabama author has been steadily publishing ever since.

IT'S OUR 20th ANNIVERSARY!
We'll be celebrating all year,
Continuing with these fabulous titles,
On sale in August 2000.

The Beginning

Coming back to Wyoming—coming home—always evoked in Chance Mackenzie such an intense mixture of emotions that he could never decide which was strongest, the pleasure or the acute discomfort. He was, by nature and nurture—not that there had been any nurturing in the first fourteen or so years of his life—a man who was more comfortable alone. If he was alone, then he could operate without having to worry about anyone but himself, and, conversely, there was no one to make him uncomfortable with concern about his own well-being. The type of work he had chosen only reinforced his own inclinations, because covert operations and anti-terrorist activities predicated he be both secretive and wary, trusting no one, letting no one close to him.

And yet... And yet, there was his family. Sprawling, brawling, ferociously overachieving, refusing to let him withdraw, not that he was at all certain he could even if they would allow it. It was always jolting, alarming, to step back into that all-enveloping embrace, to be teased and questioned—*teased,* him, whom some of the most deadly people on earth justifiably feared—hugged and kissed, fussed over and yelled at and…loved, just as if he were like everyone else. He knew he wasn't; the knowledge was always there, in the back of his mind, that he was *not* like them. But he was drawn back, again and again, by something deep inside hungering for the very things that so alarmed him. Love was scary; he had learned early and hard how little he could depend on anyone but himself.

The fact that he had survived at all was a testament to his toughness and intelligence. He didn't know how old he was, or where he had been born, what he was named as a child, or if he even had a name—nothing. He had no memory of a mother, a father, anyone who had taken care of him. A lot of people simply didn't remember their childhoods, but Chance couldn't comfort himself with that possibility, that there had been someone who had loved him and taken care of him, because he remembered too damn many other details.

He remembered stealing food when he was so small he had to stand on tiptoe to reach apples in a bin in a small-town supermarket. He had been around so many kids now that, by comparing what he remembered to the sizes they were at certain ages, he could estimate he had been no more than three years old at the time, perhaps not even that.

He remembered sleeping in ditches when it was warm, hiding in barns, stores, sheds, whatever was handy, when it was cold or raining. He remembered stealing clothes to wear, sometimes by the simple means of catching a boy playing alone in a yard, overpowering him and taking the clothes off his back. Chance had always been

much stronger physically than other boys his size, because of the sheer physical difficulty of staying alive—
and he had known how to fight, for the same reason.

He remembered a dog taking up with him once, a
black-and-white mutt that tagged along and curled up
next to him to sleep, and Chance remembered being
grateful for the warmth. He also remembered that when
he reached for a piece of steak he had stolen from the
scraps in back of a restaurant, the dog bit him and stole
the steak. Chance still had two scars on his left hand
from the dog's teeth. The dog had gotten the meat, and
Chance had gone one more day without food. He didn't
blame the dog; it had been hungry, too. But Chance ran
it off after that, because stealing enough food to keep
himself alive was difficult enough, without having to
steal for the dog, too. Besides, he had learned that when
it came to survival, it was every dog for himself.

He might have been five years old when he learned
that particular lesson, but he had learned it well.

Of course, learning how to survive in both rural and
urban areas, in all conditions, was what made him so
good at his job now, so he supposed his early childhood
had its benefits. Even considering that, though, he
wouldn't wish his childhood on a dog, not even the
damn mutt that had bitten him.

His real life had begun the day Mary Mackenzie found
him lying beside a road, deathly ill with a severe case
of flu that had turned into pneumonia. He didn't remember much of the next few days—he had been too ill—
but he had known he was in a hospital, and he had been
wild with fear, because that meant he had fallen into the
hands of the system, and he was now, in effect, a prisoner. He was obviously a minor, without identification,
and the circumstances would warrant the child welfare

services being notified. He had spent his entire life avoiding just such an event, and he had tried to make plans to escape, but his thoughts were vague, hard to get ordered, and his body was too weak to respond to his demands.

But through it all he could remember being soothed by an angel with soft blue-gray eyes and light, silvery brown hair, cool hands and a loving voice. There had also been a big, dark man, a half-breed, who calmly and repeatedly addressed his deepest fear. "We won't let them take you," the big man had said whenever Chance briefly surfaced from his fever-induced stupor.

He didn't trust them, didn't believe the big half-breed's reassurances. Chance had figured out that he himself was part American Indian, but big deal, that didn't mean he could trust these people any more than he could trust that damn thieving, ungrateful mutt. But he was too sick, too weak, to escape or even struggle, and while he was so helpless Mary Mackenzie had somehow hog-tied him with devotion, and he had never managed to break free.

He hated being touched; if someone was close enough to touch him, then they were close enough to attack him. He couldn't fight off the nurses and doctors who poked and prodded and moved him around as if he were nothing more than a mindless piece of meat. He had endured it, gritting his teeth, struggling with both his own panic and the almost overpowering urge to fight, because he knew if he fought them he would be restrained. He had to stay free, so he could run when he recovered enough to move under his own power.

But *she* had been there for what seemed like the entire time, though logically he knew she had to have left the hospital sometimes. When he burned with fever, she washed his face with a cold cloth and fed him slivers of ice. She brushed his hair, stroked his forehead when his head ached so bad he thought his skull would crack; and took over bathing him when she saw how alarmed he became when the nurses did it. Somehow he could bear it better when she bathed him, though even in his illness he had been puzzled by his own reaction.

She touched him constantly, anticipating his needs so that his pillows were fluffed before he was aware of any discomfort, the heat adjusted before he became too hot or too cold, his legs and back massaged when the fever made him ache from head to toe. He was swamped by maternal fussing, enveloped by it. It terrified him, but Mary took advantage of his weakened state and ruthlessly overwhelmed him with her mothering, as if she were determined to pack enough loving care into those few days to make up for a lifetime of nothing.

Sometime during those fever-fogged days, he began to like the feel of her cool hand on his forehead, to listen for that sweet voice even when he couldn't drag his heavy eyelids open, and the sound of it reassured him on some deep, primitive level. Once he dreamed, he didn't know what, but he woke in a panic to find her arms around him, his head pillowed on her narrow shoulder as if he were a baby, her hand gently stroking his hair while she murmured reassuringly to him—and he drifted back to sleep feeling comforted and somehow…safe.

He was always startled, even now, by how small she was. Someone so relentlessly iron-willed should have been seven feet tall and weighed three hundred pounds; at least then it would have made sense that she could bulldoze the hospital staff, even the doctors, into doing what she wanted. She had estimated his age at fourteen, but even then he was over a full head taller than the dainty woman who took over his life, but in this case size didn't matter; he was as helpless against her as was the hospital staff.

There was nothing at all he could do to fight off his growing addiction to Mary Mackenzie's mothering, even though he knew he was developing a weakness, a vulnerability, that terrified him. He had never before cared for anyone or anything, instinctively knowing that to do so would expose his emotional underbelly. But knowledge and wariness couldn't protect him now; by the time he was well enough to leave the hospital, he loved the woman who had decided she was going to be his mother, loved her with all the blind helplessness of a small child.

When he left the hospital it had been with Mary and the big man, Wolf. Because he couldn't bear to leave her just yet, he braced himself to endure her family. Just for a little while, he had promised himself, just until he was stronger.

They had taken him to Mackenzie's Mountain, into their home, their arms, their hearts. A nameless boy had died that day beside the road, and Chance Mackenzie had been born in his place. When Chance had chosen a birthday—at his new sister Maris's insistence—he chose the day Mary found him, rather than the perhaps more logical date that his adoption was final.

He had never had anything, but after that day he had been flooded with…everything. He had always been hungry, but now there was food. He had been starved, too, for learning, and now there were books everywhere, because Mary was a teacher down to her fragile bones, and she had force-fed him knowledge as fast as he could gulp it down. He was accustomed to bedding down wherever and whenever he could, but now he had his own room, his own bed, a routine. He had clothes, new ones, bought specifically for him. No one else had ever worn them, and he hadn't had to steal them.

But most of all, he had always been alone, and abruptly he was surrounded by family. Now he had a mother and a father, *four* brothers, a little sister, a sister-in-law, an infant nephew, and all of them treated him as if he had been there from the beginning. He could still barely tolerate being touched, but the Mackenzie family touched *a lot*. Mary—Mom—was constantly hugging him, tousling his hair, kissing him good-night, fussing over him. Maris, his new sister, pestered the living hell out of him just the way she did her other brothers, then would throw her skinny arms around his waist and fiercely hug him, saying, "I'm so glad you're ours!"

He was always taken aback on those occasions, and would dart a wary glance at Wolf, the big man who was the head of the Mackenzie pack and who was now Chance's dad, too. What did he think, seeing his innocent little daughter hug someone like Chance? Wolf Mackenzie was no innocent; if he didn't know exactly what experiences had molded Chance, he still recognized the dangerous vein in the half-wild boy. Chance always wondered if those knowing eyes could see clear through him, see the blood on his hands, find in his mind the memory of the man he had killed when he was about ten.

Yes, the big half-breed had known very well the type of wild animal he had taken into his family and called son, had known and, like Mary, had loved him, anyway.

His early years had taught Chance how risky life was, taught him not to trust anyone, taught him that love would only make him vulnerable and that vulnerability could cost him his life. He had known all that, and still he hadn't been able to stop himself from loving the Mackenzies. It never stopped scaring him, this weakness in his armor, and yet when he was in the family bosom was the only time he was completely relaxed, because he knew he was safe with them. He couldn't stay away, couldn't distance himself now that he was a man who was more than capable of taking care of himself, because their love for him, and his for them, fed his soul.

He had stopped even trying to limit their access to his heart and instead turned his considerable talents to doing everything he could to make their world, their lives, as safe as possible. They kept making it tougher for him; the Mackenzies constantly assaulted him with expansions: his brothers married, giving him sisters-in-law to love, because his brothers loved them and they were part of the family now. Then there were the babies. When he first came into the family there was only John, Joe and Caroline's first son, newly born. But nephew had followed nephew, and somehow Chance, along with everyone else in the Mackenzie family, found himself rocking infants, changing diapers, holding bottles, letting a dimpled little hand clutch one of his fingers while tottering first steps were made…and each one of those dimpled hands had clutched his heart, too. He had no defense against them. There were twelve nephews now, and one niece against whom he was particularly helpless, much to everyone else's amusement.

Going home was always nerve-racking, and yet he yearned for his family. He was afraid for them, afraid for himself, because he didn't know if he could live now without the warmth the Mackenzies folded about him. His mind told him he would be better off if he gradually severed the ties and isolated himself from both the pleasure and the potential for pain, but his heart always led him home again.

Chapter 1

Chance loved motorcycles. The big beast between his legs throbbed with power as he roared along the narrow winding road, the wind in his hair, leaning his body into the curves with the beast so they were one, animal and machine. No other motorcycle in the world sounded like a Harley, with that deep, coughing rumble that vibrated through his entire body. Riding a motorcycle always gave him a hard-on, and his own visceral reaction to the speed and power never failed to amuse him.

Danger was sexy. Every warrior knew it, though it wasn't something people were going to read about in their Sunday newspaper magazines. His brother Josh freely admitted that landing a fighter on a carrier deck had always turned him on. "It falls just short of orgasm," was the way Josh put it. Joe, who could fly any jet built, refrained from commenting but always smiled a slow, knowing smile.

As for both Zane and himself, Chance knew there

were times when each had emerged from certain tense situations, usually involving bullets, wanting nothing more than to have a woman beneath him. Chance's sexual need was ferocious at those times; his body was flooded with adrenaline and testosterone, he was *alive,* and he desperately needed a woman's soft body in which he could bury himself and release all the tension. Unfortunately, that need always had to wait: wait until he was in a secure position, maybe even in a different country entirely; wait until there was an available, willing woman at hand; and, most of all, wait until he had settled down enough that he could be relatively civilized in the sack.

But for now, there was only the Harley and himself, the rush of sweet mountain air on his face, and the inner mixture of joy and fear of going home. If Mom saw him riding the Harley without a helmet she would tear a strip off his hide, which was why he had the helmet with him, securely fastened behind the seat. He would put it on before sedately riding up the mountain to visit them. Dad wouldn't be fooled, but neither would he say anything, because Wolf Mackenzie knew what it was to fly high and wild.

He crested a ridge, and Zane's house came into view in the broad valley below. The house was large, with five bedrooms and four baths, but not ostentatious; Zane had instinctively built the house so it wouldn't attract undue attention. It didn't look as large as it was, because some of the rooms were underground. He had also built it to be as secure as possible, positioning it so he had an unrestricted view in all directions, but using natural formations of the land to block land access by all but the one road. The doors were steel, with state-of-the-art locks; the windows were shatterproof, and had cost a small fortune. Strategic walls had interior armor, and an emergency generator was installed in the basement. The basement also concealed another means of escape, if escape became necessary. Motion sensors were installed around the house, and as Chance wheeled the motorcycle into the driveway, he knew his arrival had already been signaled.

Zane didn't keep his family locked in a prison, but the security provisions were there if needed. Given their jobs, prudence demanded caution, and Zane had always prepared for emergencies, always had a backup plan.

Chance cut off the motor and sat for a minute, letting his senses return to normal while he ran a hand through his windswept hair. Then he kicked the stand down and leaned the Harley onto it, and dismounted much the way he would a horse. Taking a thin file from the storage compartment, he went up on the wide, shady porch.

It was a warm summer day, mid-August, and the sky was a cloudless clear blue. Horses grazed contentedly in the pasture, though a few of the more curious had come to the fence to watch with huge, liquid dark eyes as the noisy machine roared into the driveway. Bees buzzed around Barrie's flowers, and birds sang continuously in the trees. Wyoming. Home. It wasn't far away, Mackenzie's Mountain, with the sprawling house on the mountaintop where he had been given...life and everything else in this world that was important to him.

"The door's open." Zane's low, calm voice issued from the intercom beside the door. "I'm in the office."

Chance opened the door and went inside, his booted feet silent as he walked down the hall to Zane's office. With small clicks, the door locks automatically engaged behind him. The house was quiet, meaning Barrie and the kids weren't at home; if Nick was anywhere in the house she would have run squealing to him, hurling herself into his arms, chattering nonstop in her mangled English while holding his face clasped between both her little hands, making certain his attention didn't wander from her—as if he would dare look away. Nick was like a tiny package of unstable explosives; it was best to keep a weather eye on her.

The door to Zane's office was unexpectedly closed. Chance paused a moment, then opened it without knocking.

Zane was behind the desk, computer on, windows open to the warm, fresh air. He gave his brother one of his rare, warm smiles. "Watch where you step," he advised. "Munchkins on deck."

Automatically Chance looked down, checking out the floor, but he didn't see either of the twins. "Where?"

Zane leaned back in his chair a little, looking around for his offspring. Spotting them, he said, "Under the desk. When they heard me let you in, they hid."

Chance raised his eyebrows. To his knowledge, the ten-month-old twins weren't in the habit of hiding from anyone or anything. He looked more carefully and saw four plump, dimpled baby hands peeping from under the cover of Zane's desk. "They aren't very good at it," he observed. "I can see their hands."

"Give them a break, they're new at this stuff. They've only started doing it this week. They're playing Attack."

"Attack?" Fighting the urge to laugh, Chance said, "What am I supposed to do?"

"Just stand there. They'll burst from cover as fast as they can crawl and grab you by the ankles."

"Any biting involved?"

"Not yet."

"Okay. What are they going to do with me once they have me captured?"

"They haven't gotten to that part yet. For now, they just pull themselves up and stand there giggling." Zane scratched his jaw, considering. "Maybe they'll sit on your feet to hold you down, but for the most part they like standing too much to settle for sitting."

The attack erupted. Even with Zane's warning, Chance was a little surprised. They were remarkably quiet, for babies. He had to admire their precision; they launched themselves from under the desk at a rapid crawl, plump little legs pumping, and with identical triumphant crows attached themselves to his ankles. Dimpled hands clutched his jeans. The one on the left plopped down on his foot for a second, then thought better of the tactic and twisted around to begin hauling himself to an upright position. Baby arms wrapped around his knees, and the two little conquerors squealed with delight, their bubbling chuckles eliciting laughter from both men.

"Cool," Chance said admiringly. "Predator babies." He tossed the file onto Zane's desk and leaned down to scoop the little warriors into his arms, settling each diapered bottom on a muscular forearm. Cameron and Zack grinned at him, six tiny white baby teeth shining in each identical dimpled face, and immediately they began patting his face with their fat little hands, pulling his ears, delving into his shirt pockets. It was like being attacked by two squirming, remarkably heavy marshmallows.

"Good God," he said in astonishment. "They weigh a ton." He hadn't expected them to have grown so much in the two months since he had seen them.

"They're almost as big as Nick. She still outweighs

them, but I swear they feel heavier.'' The twins were
sturdy and strongly built, the little boys already showing
the size of the Mackenzie males, while Nick was as
dainty as her grandmother Mary.

''Where are Barrie and Nick?'' Chance asked, missing
his pretty sister-in-law and exuberant, cheerfully diabolic
niece.

''We had a shoe crisis. Don't ask.''

''How do you have a shoe crisis?'' Chance asked,
unable to resist. He sat down in a big, comfortable chair
across from Zane's desk, setting the babies more comfortably in his lap. They lost interest in pulling his ears
and began babbling to each other, reaching out, entwin-
ing their arms and legs as if they sought the closeness
they had known while forming in the womb. Chance
unconsciously stroked them, enjoying the softness of
their skin, the feel of squirming babies in his arms. All
the Mackenzie babies grew up accustomed to being constantly, lovingly touched by the entire extended family.

Zane laced his hands behind his head, his big, powerful body relaxed. ''First you have a three-year-old who
loves her shiny, black, patent leather Sunday shoes. Then
you make the severe tactical error of letting her watch
The Wizard of Oz.'' His stern mouth twitched, and his
pale eyes glittered with amusement.

Chance's agile mind immediately made the connection, and his acquaintance with the three-year-old in
question allowed him to make a logical assumption:
Nick had decided she had to have a pair of red shoes.
''What did she use to try to dye them?''

Zane sighed. ''Lipstick, what else?'' Each and every
young Mackenzie had had an incident with lipstick. It
was a family tradition, one John had started when, at the
age of two, he had used his mother's favorite lipstick to

recolor the impressive rows of fruit salad on Joe's dress uniform. Caroline had been impressively outraged, because the shade had been discontinued and finding a new tube had been much more difficult than replacing the small colored bars that represented medals Joe had earned and services he had performed.

"You couldn't just wipe it off?" The twins had discovered his belt buckle and zipper, and Chance moved the busy little hands that were trying to undress him. They began squirming to get down, and he leaned over to set them on the floor.

"Close the door," Zane instructed, "or they'll escape."

Leaning back, Chance stretched out a long arm and closed the door, just in time. The two diaper-clad escape artists had almost reached it. Deprived of freedom, they plopped down on their padded bottoms and considered the situation, then launched themselves in crawling patrol of the perimeters of the room.

"I *could* have wiped it off," Zane continued, his tone bland, "if I had known about it. Unfortunately, Nick cleaned the shoes herself. She put them in the dishwasher."

Chance threw back his head with a shout of laughter.

"Barrie bought her a new pair of shoes yesterday. Well, you know how Nick's always been so definite about what she wants to wear. She took one look at the shoes, said they were ugly, *even though they were just like the ones she ruined,* and refused to even try them on."

"To be accurate," Chance corrected, "what she said was that they were 'ugwy.'"

Zane conceded the point. "She's getting better with

her *L*s, though. She practices, saying the really important words, like lollipop, over and over to herself.''

''Can she say 'Chance' yet, instead of 'Dance'?'' Chance asked, because Nick stubbornly refused to even acknowledge she couldn't say his name. She insisted everyone else was saying it wrong.

Zane's expression was totally deadpan. ''Not a chance.''

Chance groaned at the pun, wishing he hadn't asked. ''I gather Barrie has taken my little darling shopping, so she can pick out her own shoes.''

''Exactly.'' Zane glanced over to check on his roaming offspring. As if they had been waiting for his parental notice, first Cam and then Zack plopped down on their butts and gave brief warning cries, all the while watching their father expectantly.

''Feeding time,'' Zane said, swiveling his chair around so he could fetch two bottles from a small cooler behind the desk. He handed one to Chance. ''Grab a kid.''

''You're prepared, as always,'' Chance commented as he went over to the twins and leaned down to lift one in his arms. Holding the baby up, he peered briefly at the scowling little face to make sure he had the one he thought he had. It was Zack, all right. Chance couldn't say exactly how he knew which twin was which, how anyone in the family knew, because the babies were so identical their pediatrician had suggested putting ID anklets on them. But they each had such definite personalities, which were reflected in their expressions, that no one in the family ever confused one twin for the other.

''I have to be prepared. Barrie weaned them last month, and they don't take kindly to having to wait for dinner.''

Zack's round blue eyes were fiercely focused on the bottle in Chance's hand. "Why did she wean them so early?" Chance asked as he resumed his seat and settled the baby in the crook of his left arm. "She nursed Nick until she was a year old."

"You'll see," Zane said dryly, settling Cam on his lap.

As soon as Chance brought the bottle within reach of Zack's fat little hands the baby made a grab for it, guiding it to his rapacious, open mouth. He clamped down ferociously on the nipple. Evidently deciding to let his uncle hold the bottle, he nevertheless made certain the situation was stabilized by clutching Chance's wrist with both hands, and wrapping both chubby legs around Chance's forearm. Then he began to growl as he sucked, pausing only to swallow.

An identical growling noise came from Zane's lap. Chance looked over to see his brother's arm captured in the same manner as the two little savages held on to their meals.

Milk bubbled around Zack's rosebud mouth, and Chance blinked as six tiny white teeth gnawed on the plastic nipple.

"Hell, no wonder she weaned you!"

Zack didn't pause in his gnawing, sucking and growling, but he did flick an absurdly arrogant glance at his uncle before returning his full attention to filling his little belly.

Zane was laughing softly, and he lifted Cam enough that he could nuzzle one of the chubby legs so determinedly wrapped around his arm. Cam paused to scowl at the interruption, then changed his mind and instead favored his father with a dimpled, milky smile. The next second the smile was gone and he attacked the bottle again.

Zack's fuzzy black hair was as soft as silk against Chance's arm. Babies were a pure tactile pleasure, he thought, though he hadn't been of that opinion the first time he'd held one. The baby in question had been John, screaming his head off from the misery of teething.

Chance hadn't been with the Mackenzies long, only a few months, and he had still been extremely wary of all these people. He had managed—barely—to control his instinct to attack whenever someone touched him, but he still jumped like a startled wild animal. Joe and Caroline came to visit, and from the expressions on their faces when they entered the house, it had been a very long trip. Even Joe, normally so controlled and unflappable, was frustrated by his futile efforts to calm his son, and Caroline had been completely frazzled by a situation she couldn't handle with her usual impeccable logic. Her blond hair had been mussed, and her green eyes expressed an amazing mixture of concern and outrage.

As she had walked by Chance, she suddenly wheeled and deposited the screaming baby in his arms. Startled, alarmed, he tried to jerk back, but before he knew it he was in sole possession of the wiggling, howling little human. "Here," she said with relief and utmost confidence. "You get him calmed down."

Chance had panicked. It was a wonder he hadn't dropped the baby. He'd never held one before, and he didn't know what to do with it. Another part of him was astounded that Caroline would entrust her adored child to *him,* the mongrel stray Mary—Mom—had brought home with her. Why couldn't these people see what he was? Why couldn't they figure out he had lived wild in a kill-or-be-killed world, and that they would be safer if they kept their distance from him?

Instead, no one seemed to think it unusual or alarming that he was holding the baby, even though in his panic he held John almost at arm's length, clutched between his two strong young hands.

But blessed quiet fell in the house. John was startled out of his screaming. He stared interestedly at this new person and kicked his legs. Automatically Chance changed his grip on the baby, settling him in the cradle of one arm as he had seen the others do. The kid was drooling. A tiny bib was fastened around his neck, and Chance used it to wipe away most of the slobber. John saw this opportunity and grabbed Chance by the thumb, immediately carrying the digit to his mouth and chomping down. Chance had jumped at the force of the hard little gums, with two tiny, sharp teeth already breaking the surface. He grimaced at the pain, but hung in there, letting John use his thumb as a teething ring until Mom rescued him by bringing a cold wet washcloth for the baby to chew.

Chance had expected then to be relieved of baby duty, because Mom usually couldn't wait to get her hands on her grandson. But that day everyone had seemed content to leave John in his hands, even the kid himself, and after a while Chance calmed down enough to start walking around and pointing out things of interest to his little pal, all of which John obediently studied while gnawing on the relief-giving washcloth.

That had been his indoctrination to the ways of babies, and from that day on he had been a sucker for the parade of nephews his virile brothers and fertile sisters-in-law had produced on a regular basis. He seemed to be getting even worse, because with Zane's three he was total mush.

"By the way, Maris is pregnant."

Chance's head jerked up, and a wide grin lit his tanned face. His baby sister had been married nine whole months and had been fretting because she hadn't immediately gotten pregnant.

"When is it due?" He always ruthlessly arranged things so he could be home when a new Mackenzie arrived. Technically, this one would be a MacNeil, but that was a minor point.

"March. She says she'll be crazy before then, because Mac won't let her out of his sight."

Chance chuckled. Other than her father and brothers, Mac was the only man Maris had ever met whom she couldn't intimidate, which was one of the reasons she loved him so much. If Mac had decided he was going to ride herd on Maris during her pregnancy, she had little hope of escaping on one of those long, hard rides she so loved.

Zane nodded toward the file on his desk. "You going to tell me about it?"

Chance knew Zane was asking about more than the contents of the file. He was asking why it hadn't been transmitted by computer, instead of Chance personally bringing a hard copy. Zane knew his brother's schedule; he was the only person, other than Chance himself, who did, so he knew Chance was currently supposed to be in France. He was also asking why he hadn't been notified of Chance's change in itinerary, why his brother hadn't made a simple phone call to let him know he was coming.

"I didn't want to risk even a hint of this leaking out."

Zane's eyebrows rose. "We have security problems?"

"Nothing that I know of," Chance said. "It's what I don't know about that worries me. But, like I said, no one else can hear even a whisper of this. It's between us."

"Now you've made me curious." Zane's cool blue eyes gleamed with interest.

"Crispin Hauer has a daughter."

Zane didn't straighten from his relaxed position, but his expression hardened. Crispin Hauer had been number one on their target list for years, but the terrorist was as elusive as he was vicious. They had yet to find any way to get close to him, any vulnerability they could exploit or bait they could use to lure him into a trap. There was a record of a marriage in London some thirty-five years ago, but Hauer's wife, formerly Pamela Vickery, had disappeared, and no trace of her had ever been found. Chance, along with everyone else, had assumed the woman died soon after the marriage, either by Hauer's hand or by his enemies'.

"Who is she?" Zane asked. "*Where* is she?"

"Her name is Sonia Miller, and she's here, in America."

"I know that name," Zane said, his gaze sharpening.

Chance nodded. "Specifically, she's the courier who was supposedly robbed of her package last week in Chicago."

Zane didn't miss the "supposedly," but then, he never missed anything. "You think it was a setup?"

"I think it's a damn good possibility. I found the link when I checked into her background."

"Hauer would have known she'd be investigated after losing a package, especially one containing aerospace documents. Why take the risk?"

"He might not have thought we would find anything.

She was adopted. Hal and Eleanor Miller are listed as her parents, and they're clean as a whistle. I wouldn't have known she was adopted if I hadn't tried to pull up her birth certificate on the computer. Guess what—Hal and Eleanor never had any children. Little Sonia Miller didn't have a birth certificate. So I did some digging and found the adoption file—''

Zane's eyebrows rose. Open adoptions had caused so many problems that the trend had veered sharply back to closed files, which, coupled with electronic privacy laws and safeguards, had made it damn difficult to even locate those closed files, much less get into them. ''Did you leave any fingerprints?''

''Nothing that will lead back to us. I went through a couple of relays, then hacked into the Internal Revenue and accessed the file from their system.''

Zane grinned. If anyone did notice the electronic snooping, it likely wouldn't even be mentioned; no one messed with the tax people.

Zack had finished his bottle; his ferocious grip on it slackened, and his head lolled against Chance's arm as he briefly struggled against sleep. Automatically Chance lifted the baby to his shoulder and began patting his back. ''Ms. Miller has been employed as a courier for a little over five years. She has an apartment in Chicago, but her neighbors say she's seldom there. I have to think this is a long-term setup, that she's been working with her father from the beginning.''

Zane nodded. They had to assume the worst, because it was their job to do so. Only by anticipating the worst could they be prepared to handle it.

''Do you have anything in mind?'' he asked, taking the bottle from Cam's slackened grip and gently lifting the sleeping baby to his own shoulder.

"Getting next to her. Getting her to trust me."

"She's not going to be the trusting sort."

"I have a plan," Chance said, and grinned, because that was usually Zane's line.

Zane grinned in return, then paused as a small security console in the wall dinged a soft alarm. He glanced at the security monitor. "Brace yourself," he advised. "Barrie and Nick are home."

Seconds later the front door opened and a shriek filled the house. "Unca *Dance*! UncaDanceUncaDance-Unca*Dance!*" The chant was punctuated by the sound of tiny feet running and jumping down the hall as Nick's celebration of his visit came closer. Chance leaned back in his chair and opened the office door a bare second before Nick barreled through it, her entire little body quivering with joy and eagerness.

She hurled herself at him, and he managed to catch her with his free arm, dragging her onto his lap. She paused to bestow a big-sisterly kiss and a pat on the back of Zack's head—never mind that he was almost as big as she was—then turned all her fierce attention to Chance.

"Are you staying dis time?" she demanded, even as she lifted her face for him to kiss. He did, nuzzling her soft cheek and neck and making her giggle, inhaling the faint sweet scent of baby that still clung to her.

"Just for a few days," he said, to her disappointment. She was old enough now to notice his long and frequent absences, and whenever she saw him she tried to convince him to stay.

She scowled; then, being Nick, she decided to move on to more important matters. Her face brightened. "Den can I wide your moborcycle?"

Alarm flared through him. "No," he said firmly.

"You can't ride it, sit on it, lean on it, or put any of your toys on it *unless I'm with you.*" With Nick, it was best to close all the loopholes. She seldom disobeyed a direct order, but she was a genius at finding cracks to slip through. Another possibility occurred to him. "You can't put Cam or Zack on it, either." He doubted she could lift either of them, but he wasn't taking any risks.

"Thank you," Barrie said dryly, entering the office in time to catch his addendum. She leaned down to kiss him on the cheek, at the same time lifting Zack from his arms so he could protect himself from Nick's feet. All the Mackenzie males, at one time or another, had fallen victim to a tiny foot in the crotch.

"Mission accomplished?" Zane asked, leaning back in his chair and smiling at his wife with that lazy look in his pale eyes that said he liked what he was seeing.

"Not without some drama and convincing, but, yes, mission accomplished." She pushed a feather lock of red hair out of her eyes. As always, she looked stylish, though she was wearing nothing dressier than beige slacks and a white sleeveless blouse that set off her slim, lightly tanned arms. You could take the girl out of the finishing school, Chance thought admiringly, but you could never take the finishing school out of the girl, and Barrie had gone to the most exclusive one in the world.

Nick was still focused on negotiating riding rights on the motorcycle. She caught his face between her hands and leaned down so her nose practically touched his, insuring his complete attention. He nearly laughed aloud at the fierce intent in her expression. "I wet you wide my twicycle," she said, evidently deciding to cajole instead of demand.

"Somehow I missed that," Zane murmured in amusement, while Barrie laughed softly.

"You *offered* to let me ride your tricycle," Chance corrected. "But I'm too big to ride a tricycle, and you're too little to ride a motorcycle."

"Den when *can* I wide it?" She made her blue eyes wide and winsome.

"When you get your driver's license."

That stymied her. She had no idea what a driver's license was, or how to get it. She stuck a finger in her mouth while she pondered this situation, and Chance tried to divert her interest. "Hey! Aren't those new shoes you're wearing?"

Like magic, her face brightened again. She wriggled around so he could hold one foot up so close to his face she almost kicked him in the nose. "Dey're so *pwetty*," she crooned in delight.

He caught the little foot in his big hand, admiring the shine of the black patent leather. "Wow, that's so shiny I can see my face in it." He pretended to inspect his teeth, which set her to giggling.

Zane rose to his feet. "We'll put the boys down for their naps while you have her occupied."

Keeping Nick occupied wasn't a problem; she was never at a loss for something to say or do. He curled one silky black strand of her hair around his finger while she chattered about her new shoes, Grampa's new horses, and what Daddy had said when he hit his thumb with a hammer. She cheerfully repeated exactly what Daddy had said, making Chance choke.

"But I'm not 'posed to say dat," she said, giving him a solemn look. "Dat's a weally, weally bad word."

"Yeah," he said, his voice strained. "It is."

"I'm not 'posed to say 'damn,' or 'hell,' or 'ass,' or—"

"Then you shouldn't be saying them now." He managed to inject a note of firmness in his tone, though it was a struggle to keep from laughing.

She looked perplexed. "Den how can I tell you what dey are?"

"Does Daddy know what the bad words are?"

The little head nodded emphatically. "He knows dem *all*."

"I'll ask him to tell me, so I'll know which words not to say."

"Otay." She sighed. "But don't hit him too hard."

"Hit him?"

"Dat's de only time he says *dat* word, when he hits his dumb wid de hammer. He said so."

Chance managed to turn his laugh into a cough. Zane was an ex-SEAL; his language was as salty as the sea he was so at home in, and Chance had heard "dat word," and worse, many times from his brother. But Mom had also instilled strict courtesy in all her children, so their language was circumspect in front of women and children. Zane must not have known Nick was anywhere near him when he hit his thumb, or no amount of pain could have made him say that in her hearing. Chance only hoped she forgot it before she started kindergarten.

"Aunt Mawis is goin' to have a baby," Nick said, scrambling up to stand in his lap, her feet braced on his thighs. Chance put both hands around her to steady her, though his aid probably wasn't needed; Nick had the balance of an acrobat.

"I know. Your daddy told me."

Nick scowled at not being the first to impart the news. "She's goin' to foal in de spwing," she announced.

He couldn't hold back the laughter this time. He gathered the little darling close to him and stood, whirling her around and making her shriek with laughter as she clung to his neck. He laughed until his eyes were wet. God, he loved this child, who in the three short years of her life had taught them all to be on their toes at all times, because there was no telling what she was going to do or say. It took the entire Mackenzie family to ride herd on her.

Suddenly she heaved a sigh. "When's de spwing? Is it a wong, wong time away?"

"Very long," he said gravely. Seven months was an eternity to a three-year-old.

"Will I be old?"

He put on a sympathetic face and nodded. "You'll be four."

She looked both horrified and resigned. "Four," she said mournfully. "Whodadunkit?"

When he stopped laughing this time, he wiped his eyes and asked, "Who taught you to say *whoda-thunkit?*"

"John," she said promptly.

"Did he teach you anything else?"

She nodded.

"What? Can you remember it?"

She nodded.

"Will you tell me what they are?"

She rolled her eyes up and studied the ceiling for a moment, then gave him a narrow-eyed look. "Will you wet me wide your moborcycle?"

Damn, she was bargaining! He trembled with fear at the thought of what she would be like when she was sixteen. "No," he said firmly. "If you got hurt, your mommy and daddy would cry, Grampa and Gamma would cry, *I* would cry, Aunt Maris would cry, Mac would cry, Unca Mike would cry—"

She looked impressed at this litany of crying and interrupted before he could name everyone in the family. "I can wide a horse, Unca Dance, so why can't I wide your moborcycle?"

God, she was relentless. Where in the hell were Zane and Barrie? They'd had plenty of time to put the twins down for their naps. If he knew Zane, his brother was taking advantage of having a baby-sitter for Nick to get in some sexy time with his wife; Zane was always prepared to use a fluid situation to his advantage.

It was another ten minutes before Zane strolled back into the office, his eyes slightly heavy-lidded and his hard face subtly relaxed. Chance scowled at his brother. He'd spent the ten minutes trying to talk Nick into telling him what John had taught her, but she wasn't budging from her initial negotiation. "It's about time," he groused.

"Hey, I hurried," Zane protested mildly.

"Yeah, right."

"As much as possible," he added, smiling. He smoothed his big hand over his daughter's shining black hair. "Have you kept Uncle Chance entertained?"

She nodded. "I told him de weally, weally bad word you said when you hit your dumb."

Zane looked pained, then stern. "How did you tell him when you aren't supposed to say the word?"

She stuck her finger in her mouth and began studying the ceiling again.

"Nick." Zane plucked her from Chance's arms. "Did you say the word?"

Her lower lip stuck out a little, but she nodded, owning up to her transgression.

"Then you can't have a bedtime story tonight. You promised you wouldn't say it."

"I'm sowwy," she said, winding her arms around his neck and laying her head on his shoulder.

Gently he rubbed his hand up and down her back. "I know you are, sweetheart, but you have to keep your promises." He set her on her feet. "Go find Mommy."

When she was gone, out of curiosity Chance asked, "Why didn't you tell her that she couldn't watch television, instead of taking away the bedtime story?"

"We don't want to make television attractive by using it as a treat or a privilege. Why? Are you taking notes on being a parent?"

Appalled, Chance said, "Not in this lifetime."

"Yeah? Fate has a way of jumping up and biting you on the ass when you least expect it."

"Well, my ass is currently bite-free, and I intend to keep it that way." He nodded at the file on Zane's desk. "We have some planning to do."

Chapter 2

This whole assignment was a tribute to Murphy's Law, Sunny Miller thought in disgust as she sat in the Salt Lake City airport, waiting for her flight to be called—if it were called at all, which she was beginning to doubt. This was her fifth airport of the day, and she was still almost a thousand miles from her destination, which was Seattle. She was *supposed* to have been on a direct flight from Atlanta to Seattle, but that flight had been canceled due to mechanical problems and the passengers routed on to other flights, none of which were direct.

From Atlanta she had gone to Cincinnati, from Cincinnati to Chicago, from Chicago to Denver, and from Denver to Salt Lake City. At least she was moving west instead of backtracking, and the flight from Salt Lake City, assuming it ever started boarding, was supposed to actually land in Seattle.

The way her day had gone, she expected it to crash instead.

She was tired, she had been fed nothing but peanuts all day, and she was afraid to go get anything to eat in case her flight was called and the plane got loaded and in the air in record time, leaving her behind. When Murphy was in control, anything was possible. She made a mental note to find this Murphy guy and punch him in the nose.

Her normal good humor restored by the whimsy, she resettled herself in the plastic seat and took out the paperback book she had been reading. She was tired, she was hungry, but she wasn't going to let the stress get to her. If there was one thing she was good at, it was making the best of a situation. Some trips were smooth as silk, and some were a pain in the rear; so long as the good and the bad were balanced, she could cope.

Out of ingrained habit, she kept the strap of her soft leather briefcase looped around her neck, held across her body so it couldn't easily be jerked out of her grasp. Some couriers might handcuff the briefcase or satchel to their wrists, but her company was of the opinion that handcuffs drew unwanted attention; it was better to blend in with the horde of business travelers than to stand out. Handcuffs practically shouted ''Important stuff inside!''

After what had happened in Chicago the month before, Sunny was doubly wary and also kept one hand on the briefcase. She had no idea what was in it, but that didn't matter; her job was to get the contents from point A to point B. When the briefcase had been jerked off her shoulder by a green-haired punk in Chicago last month, she had been both humiliated and furious. She was *always* careful, but evidently not careful enough, and now she had a big blotch on her record.

On a very basic level, she was alarmed that she had

been caught off guard. She had been taught from the cradle to be both prepared and cautious, to be alert to what was going on around her; if a green-haired punk could get the best of her, then she was neither as prepared nor alert as she had thought. When one slip could mean the difference between life and death, there was no room for error.

Just remembering the incident made her uneasy. She returned the book to her carry-on bag, preferring to keep her attention on the people around her.

Her stomach growled. She had food in her carry-on, but that was for emergencies, and this didn't qualify. She watched the gate, where the two airline reps were patiently answering questions from impatient passengers. From the dissatisfied expressions on the passengers' faces as they returned to their seats, the news wasn't good; logically, she should have enough time to find something to eat.

She glanced at her watch: one-forty-five p.m., local time. She had to have the contents of the briefcase in Seattle by nine p.m. Pacific time tonight, which should have been a breeze, but the way things were going, she was losing faith the assignment could be completed on time. She hated the idea of calling the office to report another failure, even one that wasn't her fault. If the airline didn't get on the ball soon, though, she would have to do something. The customer needed to know if the packet wasn't going to arrive as scheduled.

If the news on the flight delay hadn't improved by the time she returned from eating, she would see about transferring to another airline, though she had already considered that option and none of the possibilities looked encouraging; she was in flight-connection hell. If she couldn't work out something, she would have to make that phone call.

Taking a firm grip on the briefcase with one hand and her carry-on bag with the other, she set off down the concourse in search of food that didn't come from a vending machine. Arriving passengers were pouring out of a gate to her left, and she moved farther to the right to avoid the crush. The maneuver didn't work; someone jostled her left shoulder, and she instinctively looked around to see who it was.

No one was there. A split-second reaction, honed by years of looking over her shoulder, saved her. She automatically tightened her grip on the briefcase just as she felt a tug on the strap, and the leather fell limply from her shoulder.

Damn it, not again!

She ducked and spun, swinging her heavy carry-on bag at her assailant. She caught a glimpse of feral dark eyes and a mean, unshaven face; then her attention locked on his hands. The knife he had used to slice the briefcase strap was in one hand, and he already had his other hand on the briefcase, trying to jerk it away from her. The carry-on bag hit him on the shoulder, staggering him, but he didn't release his grip.

Sunny didn't even think of screaming, or of being scared; she was too angry for either reaction, and both would have splintered her concentration. Instead, she wound up for another swing, aiming the bag for the hand holding the knife.

Around her she heard raised voices, full of confused alarm as people tried to dodge around the disturbance, and jostled others instead. Few, if any, of them would have any idea what the ruckus was about. Vision was hampered; things were happening too fast. She couldn't rely on anyone coming to help, so she ignored the noise, all her attention centered on the cretin whose dirty hand clutched her briefcase.

Whap! She hit him again, but still he held on to the knife.

"Bitch," he snarled, his knife-hand darting toward her.

She jumped back, and her fingers slipped on the leather. Triumphantly he jerked it away from her. Sunny grabbed for the dangling strap and caught it, but the knife made a silver flash as he sliced downward, separating the strap from the briefcase. The abrupt release of tension sent her staggering back.

The cretin whirled and ran. Catching her balance, Sunny shouted, "Stop him!" and ran in pursuit. Her long skirt had a slit up the left side that let her reach full stride, but the cretin not only had a head start, he had longer legs. Her carry-on bag banged against her legs, further hampering her, but she didn't dare leave it behind. Doggedly she kept running, even though she knew it was useless. Despair knotted her stomach. Her only prayer was that someone in the crowd would play hero and stop him.

Her prayer was abruptly answered.

Up ahead, a tall man standing with his back to the concourse turned and glanced almost negligently in the direction of the ruckus. The cretin was almost abreast of him. Sunny drew breath to yell out another "Stop him," even though she knew the cretin would be past before the man could react. She never got the words out of her mouth.

The tall man took in with one glance what was happening, and in a movement as smooth and graceful as a ballet pirouette, he shifted, pivoted and lashed out with one booted foot. The kick landed squarely on the cretin's right knee, taking his leg out from under him. He cart-wheeled once and landed flat on his back, his arms flung over his head. The briefcase skidded across the concourse before bouncing against the wall, then back into the path of a stream of passengers. One man hopped over the briefcase, while others stepped around it.

Sunny immediately swerved in that direction, snatching up the briefcase before any other quick-fingered thief could grab it, but she kept one eye on the action.

In another of those quick, graceful movements, the tall man bent and flipped the cretin onto his stomach, then wrenched both arms up high behind his back and held them with one big hand.

"Owww!" the cretin howled. "You bastard, you're breaking my arms!"

The name-calling got his arms roughly levered even higher. He howled again, this time wordlessly and at a much higher pitch.

"Watch your language," said his captor.

Sunny skidded to a halt beside him. "Be careful," she said breathlessly. "He had a knife."

"I saw it. It landed over there when he fell." The man didn't look up but jerked his chin to the left. As he spoke he efficiently stripped the cretin's belt from its loop and wound the leather in a simple but effective snare around his captive's wrists. "Pick it up before someone grabs it and disappears. Use two fingers, and touch only the blade."

He seemed to know what he was doing, so Sunny obeyed without question. She took a tissue out of her skirt pocket and gingerly picked up the knife as he had directed, being careful not to smear any fingerprints on the handle.

"What do I do with it?"

"Hold it until Security gets here." He angled his dark head toward the nearest airline employee, a transportation escort who was hovering nervously as if unsure what to do. "Security *has* been called, hasn't it?"

"Yes, sir," said the escort, his eyes round with excitement.

Sunny squatted beside her rescuer. "Thank you," she said. She indicated the briefcase, with the two dangling pieces of its strap. "He cut the strap and grabbed it away from me."

"Any time," he said, turning his head to smile at her and giving her her first good look at him.

Her first look was almost her last. Her stomach fluttered. Her heart leaped. Her lungs seized. *Wow,* she thought, and tried to take a deep breath without being obvious about it.

He was probably the best-looking man she had ever seen, without being pretty in any sense of the word. *Drop-dead handsome* was the phrase that came to mind. Slightly dazed, she took in the details: black hair, a little too long and a little too shaggy, brushing the collar at the back of his battered brown leather jacket; smooth, honey-tanned skin; eyes of such a clear, light brown that they looked golden, framed by thick black lashes. As if that wasn't enough, he had also been blessed with a thin, straight nose, high cheekbones, and such clearly delineated, well-shaped lips that she had the wild impulse to simply lean forward and kiss him.

She already knew he was tall, and now she had the time to notice the broad shoulders, flat belly and lean hips. Mother Nature had been in a *really* good mood when he was made. He should have been too perfect and pretty to be real, but there was a toughness in his expression that was purely masculine, and a thin, crescent-shaped scar on his left cheekbone only added to the impression. Looking down, she saw another scar slashing across the back of his right hand, a raised line that was white against his tanned skin.

The scars in no way detracted from his attractiveness; the evidence of rough living only accentuated it, stating unequivocally that this was a *man*.

She was so bemused that it took her several seconds to realize he was watching her with mingled amusement and interest. She felt her cheeks heat in embarrassment at being caught giving him a blatant once-over. Okay, twice-over.

But she didn't have time to waste in admiration, so she forced her attention back to more pressing concerns. The cretin was grunting and making noises designed to show he was in agony, but she doubted he was in any great pain, despite his bound hands and the way her hero had a knee pressed into the small of his back. She had the briefcase back, but the cretin still presented her with a dilemma: It was her civic duty to stay and press charges against him, but if her flight left any time soon, she might very well miss it while she was answering questions and filling out forms.

"Jerk," she muttered at him. "If I miss my flight..."

"When is it?" asked her hero.

"I don't know. It's been delayed, but they could begin boarding at any time. I'll check at the gate and be right back."

He nodded with approval. "I'll hold your friend here and deal with Security until you get back."

"I'll only be a minute," she said, and walked swiftly back to her gate. The counter was now jammed with angry or upset travelers, their mood far more agitated than when she had left just a few moments before. Swiftly she glanced at the board, where CANCELED had been posted in place of the DELAYED sign.

"Damn," she said, under her breath. "Damn, damn, damn." There went her last hope for getting to Seattle in time to complete her assignment, unless there was another miracle waiting for her. Two miracles in one day was probably too much to ask for, though.

She needed to call in, she thought wearily, but first she could deal with the cretin and airport security. She retraced her steps and found that the little drama was now mobile; the cretin was on his feet, being frog-marched under the control of two airport policemen into an office where they would be out of the view of curious passersby.

Her hero was waiting for her, and when he spotted her, he said something to the security guys, then began walking to meet her.

Her heart gave a little flutter of purely feminine appreciation. My, he was good to look at. His clothes were nothing special: a black T-shirt under the old leather jacket, faded jeans and scuffed boots, but he wore them with a confidence and grace that said he was utterly comfortable. Sunny allowed herself a moment of regret that she would never see him again after this little contretemps was handled, but then she pushed it away. She couldn't take the chance of letting anything develop into a relationship—assuming there was anything there to develop—with him or anyone else. She never even let anything start, because it wouldn't be fair to the guy, and she didn't need the emotional wear and tear, either. Maybe one day she would be able to settle down, date, eventually find someone to love and marry and maybe have kids, but not now. It was too dangerous.

When he reached her, he took her arm with old-fashioned courtesy. "Everything okay with your flight?"

"In a way. It's been canceled," she said ruefully. "I have to be in Seattle tonight, but I don't think I'm going to make it. Every flight I've had today has either been delayed or rerouted, and now there's no other flight that would get me there in time."

"Charter a plane," he said as they walked toward the office where the cretin had been taken.

She chuckled. "I don't know if my boss will spring for that kind of money, but it's an idea. I have to call in, anyway, when we're finished here."

"If it makes any difference to him, I'm available right now. I was supposed to meet a customer on that last flight in from Dallas, but he wasn't on the plane, and he hasn't contacted me, so I'm free."

"You're a charter pilot?" She couldn't believe it. It—*he*—was too good to be true. Maybe she did qualify for two miracles in one day after all.

He looked down at her and smiled, making a tiny dimple dance in his cheek. God, he had a dimple, too! Talk about overkill! He held out his hand. "Chance McCall— pilot, thief-catcher, jack-of-all-trades—at your service, ma'am."

She laughed and shook his hand, noticing that he was careful not to grip her fingers too hard. Considering the strength she could feel in that tough hand, she was grateful for his restraint. Some men weren't as considerate. "Sunny Miller, tardy courier and target of thieves. It's nice to meet you, Mr. McCall."

"Chance," he said easily. "Let's get this little problem taken care of, then you can call your boss and see if he thinks a charter flight is just what the doctor ordered."

He opened the door of the unmarked office for her, and she stepped inside to find the two security officers, a woman dressed in a severe gray suit and the cretin, who had been handcuffed to his chair. The cretin glared at her when she came in, as if all this were her fault instead of his.

"You lyin' bitch—" the cretin began.

Chance McCall reached out and gripped the cretin's shoulder. "Maybe you didn't get the message before," he said in that easy way of his that in no way disguised the iron behind it, "but I don't care for your language. Clean it up." He didn't issue a threat, just an order— and his grip on the cretin's shoulder didn't look gentle.

The cretin flinched and gave him an uneasy look, perhaps remembering how effortlessly this man had manhandled him before. Then he looked at the two airport policemen, as if expecting them to step in. The two men crossed their arms and grinned. Deprived of allies, the cretin opted for silence.

The gray-suited woman looked as if she wanted to protest the rough treatment of her prisoner, but she evidently decided to get on with the business at hand. "I'm Margaret Fayne, director of airport security. I assume you're going to file charges?"

"Yes," Sunny said.

"Good," Ms. Fayne said in approval. "I'll need statements from both of you."

"Any idea how long this will take?" Chance asked. "Ms. Miller and I are pressed for time."

"We'll try to hurry things along," Ms. Fayne assured him.

Whether Ms. Fayne was super-efficient or yet another small miracle took place, the paperwork was completed in what Sunny considered to be record time. Not much more than half an hour passed before the cretin was taken away in handcuffs, all the paperwork was prepared and signed, and Sunny and Chance McCall were free to go, having done their civic duty.

He waited beside her while she called the office and explained the situation. The supervisor, Wayne Beesham, wasn't happy, but bowed to reality.

"What's this pilot's name again?" he asked.

"Chance McCall."

"Hold on, let me check him out."

Sunny waited. Their computers held a vast database of information on both commercial airlines and private charters. There were some unsavory characters in the charter business, dealing more in drugs than in passengers, and a courier company couldn't afford to be careless.

"Where's his home base?"

Sunny repeated the question to Chance.

"Phoenix," he said, and once again she relayed the information.

"Okay, got it. He looks okay. How much is his fee?" Sunny asked.

Mr. Beesham grunted at the reply. "That's a bit high."

"He's here, and he's ready to go."

"What kind of plane is it? I don't want to pay this price for a crop-duster that still won't get you there in time."

Sunny sighed. "Why don't I just put him on the line? It'll save time." She handed the receiver to Chance. "He wants to know about your plane."

Chance took the receiver. "McCall." He listened a moment. "It's a Cessna Skylane. The range is about eight hundred miles at seventy-five percent power, six hours flying time. I'll have to refuel, so I'd rather it be around the midway point, say at Roberts Field in Redmond, Oregon. I can radio ahead and have everything rolling so we won't spend much time on the ground.'' He glanced at his wristwatch. ''With the hour we gain when we cross into the Pacific time zone, she can make it—barely.''

He listened for another moment, then handed the receiver back to Sunny. ''What's the verdict?'' she asked.

''I'm authorizing it. For God's sake, get going.''

She hung up and grinned at Chance, her blood pumping at the challenge. ''It's a go! How long will it take to get airborne?''

''If you let me carry that bag, and we run...fifteen minutes.''

Sunny never let the bag out of her possession. She hated to repay his courtesy with a refusal, but caution was so ingrained in her that she couldn't bring herself to take the risk. ''It isn't heavy,'' she lied, tightening her grip on it. ''You lead, I'll follow.''

One dark eyebrow went up at her reply, but he didn't argue, just led the way through the busy concourse. The private planes were in a different area of the airport, away from the commercial traffic. After several turns and a flight of stairs, they left the terminal and walked across the concrete, the hot afternoon sun beating down on their heads and making her squint. Chance slipped on a pair of sunglasses, then shrugged out of the jacket and carried it in his left hand.

Sunny allowed herself a moment of appreciation at the way his broad shoulders and muscled back filled out the black T-shirt he wore. She might not indulge, but she could certainly admire. If only things were different—but they weren't, she thought, reining in her thoughts. She had to deal with reality, not wishful thinking.

He stopped beside a single-engine airplane, white with gray-and-red striping. After storing her bag and briefcase and securing them with a net, he helped her into the co-pilot's seat. Sunny buckled herself in and looked around with interest. She'd never been in a private plane before, or flown in anything this small. It was surprisingly comfortable. The seats were gray leather, and behind her was a bench seat with individual backs. Carpet covered the metal floor.

There were two sun visors, just like in a car. Amused, she flipped down the one in front of her and laughed aloud when she saw the small mirror attached to it.

Chance walked around the plane, checking details one last time before climbing into the seat to her left and buckling himself in. He put on a set of headphones and began flipping switches while he talked to the air traffic control tower. The engine coughed, then caught, and the propeller on the nose began to spin, slowly at first, then gaining speed until it was an almost invisible blur.

He pointed to another set of headphones, and Sunny put them on. "It's easier to talk using the headphones," came his voice in her ear, "but be quiet until we get airborne."

"Yes, sir," she said, amused, and he flashed a quick grin at her.

They were airborne within minutes, faster than she had ever experienced on a commercial carrier. Being in the small plane gave her a sense of speed that she had never before felt, and when the wheels left the ground the lift was incredible, as if she had sprouted wings and jumped into the air. The ground quickly fell away below, and the vast, glistening blue lake spread out before her, with the jagged mountains straight ahead.

"Wow," she breathed, and brought one hand up to shield her eyes from the sun.

"There's an extra pair of sunglasses in the glove box," he said, indicating the compartment in front of her. She opened it and dug out a pair of inexpensive but stylish Foster Grants with dark red frames. They were obviously some woman's sunglasses, and abruptly she wondered if he was married. He would have a girlfriend, of course; not only was he very nice to look at, he seemed to be a nice person. It was a combination that was hard to find and impossible to beat.

"Your wife's?" she asked as she put on the glasses and breathed a sigh of relief as the uncomfortable glare disappeared.

"No, a passenger left them in the plane."

Well, that hadn't told her anything. She decided to be blunt, even while she wondered why she was bothering, since she would never see him again after they arrived in Seattle. "Are you married?"

Again she got that quick grin. "Nope." He glanced at her, and though she couldn't see his eyes through the dark glasses, she got the impression his gaze was intense. "Are you?"

"No."

"Good," he said.

Chapter 3

Chance watched her from behind the dark lenses of his sunglasses, gauging her reaction to his verbal opening. The plan was working better than he'd hoped; she was attracted to him and hadn't been trying very hard to hide it. All he had to do was take advantage of that attraction and win her trust, which normally might take some doing, but what he had planned would throw her into a situation that wasn't *normal* in any sense of the word. Her life and safety would depend on him.

To his faint surprise, she faced forward and pretended she hadn't heard him. Wryly, he wondered if he'd misread her and she wasn't attracted to him after all. No, she had been watching him pretty blatantly, and in his experience, a woman didn't stare at a man unless she found him attractive.

What was *really* surprising was how attractive he found *her*. He hadn't expected that, but sexual chemistry was an unruly demon that operated outside logic. He had

known she was pretty, with brilliant gray eyes and
golden-blond hair that swung smoothly to her shoulders,
from the photographs in the file he had assembled on
her. He just hadn't realized how damn *fetching* she was.

He slanted another glance at her, this time one of pure
male assessment. She was of average height, maybe,
though a little more slender than he liked, almost delicate. Almost. The muscles of her bare arms, revealed by
a white sleeveless blouse, were well-toned and lightly
tanned, as if she worked out. A good agent always stayed
in good physical condition, so he had to expect her to
be stronger than she looked. Her delicate appearance
probably took a lot of people off guard.

She sure as hell had taken Wilkins off guard. Chance
had to smother a smile. While Sunny had gone back to
her gate to check on the status of her flight, which
Chance had arranged to be cancelled, Wilkins had told
him how she had swung her carry-on bag at him, one-
armed, and that the damn thing had to weigh a ton, because it had almost knocked him off his feet.

By now, Wilkins and the other three, "Ms. Fayne"
and the two security "policemen," would have vanished
from the airport. The real airport security had been
briefed to stay out of the way, and everything had
worked like a charm, though Wilkins had groused at
being taken down so roughly. "First that little witch
damn near breaks my arm with that bag, then you try to
break my back," he'd growled, while they all laughed
at him.

Just what was in that bag, anyway? She had held on
to it as if it contained the crown jewels, not letting him
carry it even when she was right there with him, and
only reluctantly letting him take it to stow in the luggage
compartment behind them. He'd been surprised at how

heavy it was, too heavy to contain the single change of clothes required by an overnight trip, even with a vast array of makeup and a hairdryer thrown in for good measure. The bag had to weigh a good fifty pounds, maybe more. Well, he would find out soon enough what was in it.

"What were you going to do with that guy if you'd caught him?" he asked in a lazy tone, partly to keep her talking, establishing a link between them, and partly because he was curious. She had been chasing after Wilkins with a fiercely determined expression on her face, so determined that, if Wilkins were still running, she would probably still be chasing him.

"I don't know," she said darkly. "I just knew I couldn't let it happen again."

"Again?" Damn, was she going to tell him about Chicago?

"Last month, a green-haired cretin snatched my briefcase in the airport in Chicago." She slapped the arm of the seat. "That's the first time anything like that has ever happened on one of my jobs, then to have it happen again just a month later—I'd have been fired. Heck, *I* would fire me, if I were the boss."

"You didn't catch the guy in Chicago?"

"No. I was in Baggage Claims, and he just grabbed the briefcase, zipped out the door and was gone."

"What about security? They didn't try to catch him?"

She peered at him over the top of the oversize sunglasses. "You're kidding, right?"

He laughed. "I guess I am."

"Losing another briefcase would have been a catastrophe, at least to me, and it wouldn't have done the company any good, either."

"Do you ever know what's in the briefcases?"

"No, and I don't want to. It doesn't matter. Someone could be sending a pound of salami to their dying uncle Fred, or it could be a billion dollars worth of diamonds—not that I think anyone would ever ship diamonds by a courier service, but you get the idea."

"What happened when you lost the briefcase in Chicago?"

"My company was out a lot of money—rather, the insurance company was. The customer will probably never use us again, or recommend us."

"What happened to you? Any disciplinary action?" He knew there hadn't been.

"No. In a way, I would have felt better if they had at least fined me."

Damn, she was good, he thought in admiration—either that, or she was telling the truth and hadn't had anything to do with the incident in Chicago last month. It was possible, he supposed, but irrelevant. Whether or not she'd had anything to do with losing that briefcase, he was grateful it had happened, because otherwise she would never have come to his notice, and he wouldn't have this lead on Crispin Hauer.

But he didn't think she was innocent; he thought she was in this up to her pretty neck. She was better than he had expected, an actress worthy of an Oscar—so good he might have believed she didn't know anything about her father, if it wasn't for the mystery bag and her deceptive strength. He was trained to put together seemingly insignificant details and come up with a coherent picture, and experience had made him doubly cynical. Few people were as honest as they wanted you to believe, and the people who put on the best show were often the ones with the most to hide. He should know—he was an expert at hiding the black secrets of his soul.

He wondered briefly what it said about him that he was willing to sleep with her as part of his plan to gain her trust, but maybe it was better not to think about it. Someone had to be willing to work in the muck, to do things from which ordinary people would shrink, just to protect those ordinary people. Sex was…just sex. Part of the job. He could even divorce his emotions to the point that he actually looked forward to the task.

Task? Who was he kidding? He couldn't wait to slide into her. She intrigued him, with her toned, tight body and the twinkle that so often lit her clear gray eyes, as if she was often amused at both herself and the world around her. He was fascinated by her eyes, by the white striations that made her eyes look almost faceted, like the palest of blue diamonds. Most people thought of gray eyes as a pale blue, but when he was close to her, he could see that they were, very definitely, brilliantly gray. But most of all he was intrigued by her expression, which was so open and good-humored she could almost trademark the term "Miss Congeniality." How could she look like that, as sweet as apple pie, when she was working hand in glove with the most-wanted terrorist in his files?

Part of him, the biggest part, despised her for what she was. The animal core of him, however, was excited by the dangerous edge of the game he was playing, by the challenge of getting her into bed with him and convincing her to trust him. When he was inside her, he wouldn't be thinking about the hundreds of innocent people her father had killed, only about the linking of their bodies. He wouldn't let himself think of anything else, lest he give himself away with some nuance of expression that women were so good at reading. No, he would make love to her as if he had found his soul mate, because that was the only way he could be certain of fooling her.

But he was good at that, at making a woman feel as if he desired her more than anything else in the world. He knew just how to make her aware of him, how to push hard without panicking her—which brought him back to the fact that she had totally ignored his first opening. He smiled slightly to himself. Did she really think that would work?

"Will you have dinner with me tonight?"

She actually jumped, as if she had been lost in her thoughts. "What?"

"Dinner. Tonight. After you deliver your package."

"Oh. But—I'm supposed to deliver it at nine. It'll be late, and—"

"And you'll be alone, and I'll be alone, and you have to eat. I promise not to bite. I may lick, but I won't bite."

She surprised him by bursting into laughter.

Of all the reactions he had anticipated, laughter wasn't one of them. Still, her laugh was so free and genuine, her head tilted back against the seat, that he found himself smiling in response.

"'I may lick, but I won't bite.' That was good. I'll have to remember it," she said, chuckling.

After a moment, when she said nothing else, he realized that she was ignoring him again. He shook his head. "Does that work with most men?"

"Does what work?"

"Ignoring them when they ask you out. Do they slink away with their tails tucked between their legs?"

"Not that I've ever noticed." She grinned. "You make me sound like a femme fatale, breaking hearts left and right."

"You probably are. We guys are tough, though. We can be bleeding to death on the inside and we'll put up such a good front that no one ever knows." He smiled at her. "Have dinner with me."

"You're persistent, aren't you?"

"You still haven't answered me."

"All right—no. There, I've answered you."

"Wrong answer. Try again." More gently, he said, "I know you're tired, and with the time difference, nine o'clock is really midnight to you. It's just a meal, Sunny, not an evening of dancing. That can wait until our second date."

She laughed again. "Persistent *and* confident." She paused, made a wry little face. "The answer is still no. I don't date."

This time he was more than surprised, he was stunned. Of all the things he had expected to come out of her mouth, that particular statement had never crossed his mind. Damn, had he so badly miscalculated? "At all? Or just men?"

"At all." She gestured helplessly. "See, this is why I tried to ignore you, because I didn't want to go into an explanation that you wouldn't accept, anyway. No, I'm not gay, I like men very much, but I don't date. End of explanation."

His relief was so intense, he felt a little dizzy. "If you like men, why don't you date?"

"See?" she demanded on a frustrated rush of air. "You didn't accept it. You immediately started asking questions."

"Damn it, did you think I'd just let it drop? There's something between us, Sunny. I know it, and you know it. Or are you going to ignore that, too?"

"That's exactly what I'm going to do."

He wondered if she realized what she had just admitted. "Were you raped?"

"No!" she half shouted, goaded out of control. "I just…don't…date."

She was well on her way to losing her temper, he thought, amused. He grinned. "You're pretty when you're mad."

She sputtered, then began laughing. "How am I supposed to stay mad when you say things like that?"

"You aren't. That's the whole idea."

"Well, it worked. What it didn't do was change my mind. I'm sorry," she said gently, sobering. "It's just…I have my reasons. Let it drop. Please."

"Okay." He paused. "For now."

She gave an exaggerated groan that had him smiling again. "Why don't you try to take a nap?" he suggested. "You have to be tired, and we still have a long flight ahead of us."

"That's a good idea. You can't badger me if I'm asleep."

With that wry shot, she leaned her head back against the seat. Chance reached behind her seat and produced a folded blanket. "Here. Use this as a pillow, or you'll get a stiff neck."

"Thanks." She took off the headset and tucked the blanket between her head and shoulder, then shifted around in her seat to get more comfortable.

Chance let silence fall, occasionally glancing at her to see if she really fell asleep. About fifteen minutes later, her breathing deepened and evened out into a slow rhythm. He waited a few minutes longer, then eased the plane into a more westerly direction, straight into the setting sun.

Chapter 4

"Sunny." The voice was insistent, a little difficult to hear, and accompanied by a hand on her shoulder, shaking her. "Sunny, wake up."

She stirred and opened her eyes, stretching a little to relieve the kinks in her back and shoulders. "Are we there?"

Chance indicated the headset in her lap, and she slipped it on. "We have a problem," he said quietly.

The bottom dropped out of her stomach, and her heartbeat skittered. No other words, she thought, could be quite as terrifying when one was in an airplane. She took a deep breath, trying to control the surge of panic. "What's wrong?" Her voice was surprisingly steady. She looked around, trying to spot the problem in the cluster of dials in the cockpit, though she had no idea what any of them meant. Then she looked out of the window at the rugged landscape below them, painted in stark reds and blacks as the setting sun threw shadows over jagged rock. "Where are we?"

"Southeastern Oregon."

The engine coughed and sputtered. Her heart felt as if it did, too. As soon as she heard the break in the rhythm, she became aware that the steady background whine of the motor had been interrupted several times while she slept. Her subconscious had registered the change in sound but not put it in any context. Now the context was all too clear.

"I think it's the fuel pump," he added, in answer to her first question.

Calm. She had to stay calm. She pulled in a deep breath, though her lungs felt as if they had shrunk in size. "What do we do?"

He smiled grimly. "Find a place to set it down before it falls down."

"I'll take setting over falling any day." She looked out the side window, studying the ground below. Jagged mountain ridges, enormous boulders and sharp-cut arroyos slicing through the earth were all she could see. "Uh-oh."

"Yea. I've been looking for a place to land for the past half hour."

This was not good, not good at all. In the balance of good and bad, this weighed heavily on the bad side.

The engine sputtered again. The whole frame of the aircraft shook. So did her voice, when she said, "Have you radioed a Mayday?"

Again that grim smile. "We're in the middle of a great big empty area, between navigational beacons. I've tried a couple of times to raise someone, but there haven't been any answers."

The scale tipped even more out of balance. "I knew

it,'' she muttered. ''The way today has gone, I *knew* I'd crash if I got on another plane.''

The grouchiness in her voice made him chuckle, despite the urgency of their situation. He reached over and gently squeezed the back of her neck, startling her with his touch, his big hand warm and hard on her sensitive nape. ''We haven't crashed yet, and I'm going to try damn hard to make sure we don't. The landing may be rough, though.''

She wasn't used to being touched. She had accustomed herself to doing without the physical contact that it was human nature to crave, to keep people at a certain distance. Chance McCall had touched her more in one afternoon than she had been touched in the past five years. The shock of pleasure almost distracted her from their situation—almost. She looked down at the unforgiving landscape again. ''How rough does a landing have to get before it qualifies as a crash?''

''If we walk away from it, then it was a landing.'' He put his hand back on the controls, and she silently mourned that lost connection.

The vast mountain range spread out around them as far as she could see in any direction. Their chances of walking away from this weren't good. How long would it be before their bodies were found, if ever? Sunny clenched her hands, thinking of Margreta. Her sister, not knowing what had happened, would assume the worst— and dying in an airplane crash was *not* the worst. In her grief, she might well abandon her refuge and do something stupid that would get her killed, too.

She watched Chance's strong hands, so deft and sure on the controls. His clear, classic profile was limned against the pearl and vermillion sky, the sort of sunset one saw only in the western states, and likely the last sunset she would ever see. He would be the last person she ever saw, or touched, and she was suddenly, bitterly angry that she had never been able to live the life most women took for granted, that she hadn't been free to accept his offer of dinner and spend the trip in a glow of anticipation, free to flirt with him and maybe see the glow of desire in his golden-brown eyes.

She had been denied a lot, but most of all she had been denied opportunity, and she would never, never forgive her father for that.

The engine sputtered, caught, sputtered again. This time the reassuring rhythm didn't return. The bottom dropped out of her stomach. God, oh God, they were going to crash. Her nails dug into her palms as she fought to contain her panic. She had never before felt so small and helpless, so fragile, with soft flesh and slender bones that couldn't withstand such battering force. She was going to die, and she had yet to live.

The plane jerked and shuddered, bucking under the stress of spasmodic power. It pitched to the right, throwing Sunny against the door so hard her right arm went numb.

"That's it," Chance said between gritted teeth, his knuckles white as he fought to control the pitching aircraft. He brought the wings level again. "I have to take it down now, while I have a little control. Look for the best place."

Best place? There *was* no best place. They needed somewhere that was relatively flat and relatively clear; the last location she had seen that fit that description had been in Utah.

He raised the right wingtip, tilting the plane so he had a better side view.

"See anything?" Sunny asked, her voice shaking just a little.

"Nothing. Damn."

"Damn is the wrong word. Pilots are supposed to say something else just before they crash." Humor wasn't much of a weapon with which to face death, but it was how she had always gotten herself through the hard times.

Unbelievably, he grinned. "But I haven't crashed yet, sweetheart. Have a little faith. I promise I'll say the right word if I don't find a good-looking spot pretty soon."

"If you don't find a good-looking spot, I'll say it for you," she promised fervently.

They crossed a jagged, boulder-strewn ridge, and a long, narrow black pit yawned beneath them like a doorway to hell. "There!" Chance said, nosing the plane down.

"What? Where?" She sat erect, desperate hope flaring inside her, but all she could see was that black pit.

"The canyon. That's our best bet."

The black pit was a canyon? Weren't canyons supposed to be big? That looked like an arroyo. How on earth would the plane ever fit inside it? And what difference did it make, when this was their only chance? Her heart lodged itself in her throat, and she gripped the edge of the seat as Chance eased the pitching aircraft lower and lower.

The engine stopped.

For a moment all she heard was the awful silence, more deafening than any roar.

Then she became aware of the air rushing past the metal skin of the plane, air that no longer supported them. She heard her own heart beating, fast and heavy, heard the whisper of her breath. She heard everything except what she most wanted to hear, the sweet sound of an airplane engine.

Chance didn't say anything. He concentrated fiercely on keeping the plane level, riding the air currents down, down, aiming for that long, narrow slit in the earth. The plane spiraled like a leaf, coming so close to the jagged mountainside on the left that she could see the pits in the dark red rock.

Sunny bit her lip until blood welled in her mouth, fighting back the terror and panic that threatened to erupt in screams. She couldn't distract him now, no matter what. She wanted to close her eyes, but resolutely kept them open. If she died now, she didn't want to do it in craven fear. She couldn't help the fear, but she didn't have to be craven. She would watch death come at her, watch Chance as he fought to bring them down safely and cheat the grim horseman.

They slipped below the sunshine, into the black shadows, deeper and deeper. It was colder in the shadows, a chill that immediately seeped through the windows into her bones. She couldn't see a thing. Quickly she snatched off the sunglasses and saw that Chance had done the same. His eyes were narrowed, his expression hard and intent as he studied the terrain below.

The ground was rushing at them now, a ground that was pocked and scored with rivulets, and dotted with boulders. It was flat enough, but not a nice, clear landing spot at all. She braced her feet against the floor, her body rigid as if she could force the airplane to stay aloft.

"Hold on." His voice was cool. "I'm going to try to make it to the stream bed. The sand will help slow us down before we hit one of those rocks."

A stream bed? He was evidently much better at reading the ground than she was. She tried to see a ribbon of water, but finally realized the stream was dry; the bed was that thin, twisting line that looked about as wide as the average car.

She started to say "Good luck," but it didn't seem appropriate. Neither did "It was nice knowing you." In the end, all she could manage was "Okay."

It happened fast. Suddenly they were no longer skimming above the earth. The ground was *there,* and they hit it hard, so hard she pitched forward against the seat belt, then snapped back. They went briefly airborne again as the wheels bounced, then hit again even harder. She heard metal screeching in protest; then her head banged against the side window, and for a chaotic moment she didn't see or hear anything, just felt the tossing and bouncing of the plane. She was boneless, unable to hold on, flopping like a shirt in a clothes dryer.

Then there came the hardest bounce of all, jarring her teeth. The plane spun sideways in a sickening motion, then lurched to a stop. Time and reality splintered, broke apart, and for a long moment nothing made any sense; she had no grasp on where she was or what had happened.

She heard a voice, and the world jolted back into place.

"Sunny? Sunny, are you all right?" Chance was asking urgently.

She tried to gather her senses, tried to answer him. Dazed, battered, she realized that the force of the landing had turned her inside the confines of the seat belt, and she was facing the side window, her back to Chance. She felt his hands on her, heard his low swearing as he unclipped the seat belt and eased her back against his chest, supporting her with his body.

She swallowed, and managed to find her voice. "I'm

okay.'' The words weren't much more than a croak, but if she could talk at all that meant she was alive. They were both alive. Joyful disbelief swelled in her chest. He had actually managed to land the plane!

"We have to get out. There may be a fuel leak." Even as he spoke, he shoved open the door and jumped out, dragging her with him as if she was a sack of flour. She felt rather sacklike, her limbs limp and trembling.

A fuel leak. The engine had been dead when they landed, but there was still the battery, and wiring that could short out and spark. If a spark got to any fuel, the plane and everything in it would go up in a fireball.

Everything in it. The words rattled in her brain, like marbles in a can, and with dawning horror she realized what that meant. Her bag was still in the plane.

"Wait!" she shrieked, panic sending a renewed surge of adrenaline through her system, restoring the bones to her legs, the strength to her muscles. She twisted in his grasp, grabbing the door handle and hanging on. "My bag!"

"Damn it, Sunny!" he roared, trying to break her grip on the handle. "Forget the damn bag!"

"No!"

She jerked away from him and began to climb back into the plane. With a smothered curse he grabbed her around the waist and bodily lifted her away from the plane. "I'll get the damn bag! Go on—get out of here! Run!"

She was appalled that he would risk his life retrieving her bag, while sending her to safety. "I'll get it," she said fiercely, grabbing him by the belt and tugging. "*You* run!"

For a split second he literally froze, staring at her in shock. Then he gave his head a little shake, reached in for the bag and effortlessly hefted it out. Wordlessly Sunny tried to take it, but he only gave her an incendiary look and she didn't have time to argue. Carrying the bag in his left hand and gripping her upper arm with his right, he towed her at a run away from the plane. Her shoes sank into the soft grit, and sand and scrub brush bit at her ankles, but she scrambled to stay upright and keep pace with him.

They were a good fifty yards away before he judged it safe. He dropped the bag and turned on her like a panther pouncing on fresh meat, gripping her upper arms with both hands as if he wanted to shake her. "What the hell are you thinking?" he began in a tone of barely leashed violence, then cut himself off, staring at her face. His expression altered, his golden-brown eyes darkening.

"You're bleeding," he said harshly. He grabbed his handkerchief out of his pocket and pressed it to her chin. Despite the roughness of his tone, his touch was incredibly gentle. "You said you weren't hurt."

"I'm not." She raised her trembling hand and took the handkerchief, dabbing it at her chin and mouth. There wasn't much blood, and the bleeding seemed to have stopped. "I bit my lip," she confessed. "Before you landed, I mean. To keep from screaming."

He stared down at her with an expression like flint. "Why didn't you just scream?"

"I didn't want to distract you." The trembling was growing worse by the second; she tried to hold herself steady, but every limb shook as if her bones had turned to gelatin.

He tilted up her face, staring down at her for a moment in the deepening twilight. He breathed a low, savage curse, then slowly leaned down and pressed his lips to her mouth. Despite the violence she sensed in him, the kiss was light, gentle, more of a salute than a kiss. She caught her breath, beguiled by the softness of his lips, the warm smell of his skin, the hint of his taste. She fisted her hands in his T-shirt, clinging to his strength, trying to sink into his warmth.

He lifted his head. "That's for being so brave," he murmured. "I couldn't have asked for a better partner in a plane crash."

"Landing," she corrected shakily. "It was a landing."

That earned her another soft kiss, this time on the temple. She made a strangled sound and leaned into him, a different sort of trembling beginning to take hold of her. He framed her face with his hands, his thumbs gently stroking the corners of her mouth as he studied her. She felt her lips tremble a little, but then, all of her was shaking. He touched the small sore spot her teeth had made in her lower lip; then he was kissing her again, and this time there was nothing gentle about it.

This kiss rocked her to her foundation. It was hungry, rough, deep. There were reasons why she shouldn't respond to him, but she couldn't think what they were. Instead, she gripped his wrists and went on tiptoe to slant her parted lips against his, opening her mouth for the thrust of his tongue. He tasted like man, and sex, a potent mixture that went to her head faster than hundred-proof whiskey. Heat bloomed in her loins and breasts, a desperate, needy heat that brought a low moan from her throat.

He wrapped one arm around her and pulled her against him, molding her to him from knee to breast while his kisses became even deeper, even harder. She locked her arms around his neck and arched into him, wanting the feel of his hard-muscled body against her with an urgency that swept away reason. Instinctively she pushed her hips against his, and the hard length of his erection bulged into the notch of her thighs. This time she cried out in want, in need, in a desire that burned through every cell of her body. His hand closed roughly around her breast, kneading, rubbing her nipple through the layers of blouse and bra, both easing and intensifying the ache that made them swell toward his touch.

Suddenly he jerked his head back. "I don't believe this," he muttered. Reaching up, he prised her arms from around his neck and set her away from him. He looked even more savage than he had a moment before, the veins standing out in his neck. "Stay here," he barked. "Don't move an inch. I have to check the plane."

He left her standing there in the sand, in the growing twilight, suddenly cold all the way down to the bone. Deprived of his warmth, his strength, her legs slowly collapsed, and she sank to the ground.

Chance swore to himself, steadily and with blistering heat, as he checked the plane for fuel leaks and other damage. He had deliberately made the landing rougher than necessary, and the plane had a reinforced landing gear as well as extra protection for the fuel lines and tank, but a smart pilot didn't take anything for granted. He had to check the plane, had to stay in character.

He didn't want to stay in character. He wanted to back her against one of those big boulders and lift her skirt. Damn! What was wrong with him? In the past fifteen years he'd held a lot of beautiful, deadly women in his arms, and even though he let his body respond, his mind had always remained cool. Sunny Miller wasn't the most beautiful, not by a long shot; she was more gamine than goddess, with bright eyes that invited laughter rather than seduction. So why was he so hot to get into her pants?

"Why" didn't matter, he angrily reminded himself. Okay, so his attraction to her was unexpected; it was an advantage, something to be used. He wouldn't have to fake anything, which meant there was even less chance of her sensing anything off-kilter.

Danger heightened the emotions, destroying inhibitions. They had lived through a life-threatening situation together, they were alone, and there was a definite physical attraction between them. He had arranged the first two circumstances; the third was a bonus. It was a textbook situation; studies in human nature had shown that, if a man and a woman were thrown together in a dangerous situation and they had only each other to rely on, they quickly formed both sexual and emotional bonds. Chance had the advantage, in that he knew the plane hadn't been in any danger of crashing, and that they weren't in a life-and-death situation. Sunny would think they were stranded, while he knew better. Whenever he signaled Zane, they would promptly be "rescued," but he wouldn't send that signal until Sunny took him into her confidence about her father.

Everything was under control. They weren't even in Oregon, as he'd told her. They were in Nevada, in a narrow box canyon he and Zane had scouted out and selected because it was possible to land a plane in it, and, unless one had the equipment to scale vertical rock walls, impossible to escape. They weren't close to any commercial flight pattern, he had disabled the transponder so no search plane would pick up a signal, and they were far off their route. They wouldn't be found.

Sunny was totally under his control; she just didn't know it.

The growing dusk made it impossible to see very much, and it was obvious that if the plane was going to explode in flames, it would already have done so. Chance strode back to where Sunny was sitting on the ground, her knees pulled up and her arms wrapped around her legs, and that damn bag close by her side. She scrambled to her feet as he approached. "All clear?"

"All clear. No fuel leaks."

"That's good." She managed a smile. "It wouldn't do us any good for you to fix the fuel pump if there wasn't any fuel left."

"Sunny...if it's a clogged line, I can fix it. If the fuel pump has gone out, I can't."

He decided to let her know right away that they might not be flying out of here in the morning.

She absorbed that in silence, rubbing her bare arms to ward off the chill of the desert air. The temperature dropped like a rock when the sun went down, which was one of the reasons he had chosen this site. They would have to share their body heat at night to survive.

He leaned down and hefted the bag, marveling anew at its weight, then took her arm to walk with her back to the plane. "I hope you have a coat in this damn bag, since you thought it was important enough to risk your life getting it," he growled.

"A sweater," she said absently, looking up at the crystal clear sky with its dusting of stars. The black walls of the canyon loomed on either side of them, making it obvious they were in a hole in the earth. A big hole, but still a hole. She shook herself, as if dragging her thoughts back to the problem at hand. "We'll be all right," she said. "I have some food, and—"

"Food? You're carrying food in here?" He indicated the bag.

"Just some emergency stuff."

Of all the things he'd expected, food was at the bottom of the list. Hell, food wasn't even *on* the list. Why would a woman on an overnight trip put food in her suitcase?

They reached the plane, and he set the bag down in the dirt. "Let me get some things, and we'll find a place to camp for the night. Can you get anything else in there, or is it full?"

"It's full," she said positively, but then, he hadn't expected her to open it so easily.

He shrugged and dragged out his own small duffel, packed with the things a man could be expected to take on a charter flight: toiletries, a change of clothes. The duffel was unimportant, but it wouldn't look right if he left it behind.

"Why can't we camp here?" she asked.

"This is a stream bed. It's dry now, but if it rains anywhere in the mountains, we could be caught in the runoff."

As he spoke, he got a flashlight out of the dash, the blanket from the back, and a pistol from the pocket in the pilot's side door. He stuck the pistol in his belt, and draped the blanket around her shoulders. "I have some water," he said, taking out a plastic gallon milk jug that he'd refilled with water. "We'll be all right tonight." Water had been the toughest thing to locate. He and Zane had found several box canyons in which he could have landed the plane, but this was the only one with water. The source wasn't much, just a thin trickle running out of the rock at the far end of the canyon, but it was enough. He would "find" the water tomorrow.

He handed her the flashlight and picked up both bags.

"Lead the way," he instructed, and indicated the direction he wanted. The floor of the canyon sloped upward on one side; the stream bed was the only smooth ground. The going was rough, and Sunny carefully picked her way over rocks and gullies. She was conscientious about shining the light so he could see where he was going, since he was hampered by both bags.

Damn, he wished she had complained at least a little, or gotten upset. He wished she wasn't so easy to like. Most people would have been half-hysterical, or asking endless questions about their chances of being rescued if he couldn't get the plane repaired. Not Sunny. She coped, just as she had coped at the airport, with a minimum of fuss. Without *any* fuss, actually; she had bitten the blood out of her lip to keep from distracting him while he was bringing the plane down.

The canyon was so narrow it didn't take them long to reach the vertical wall. Chance chose a fairly flat section of sandy gray dirt, with a pile of huge boulders that formed a rough semi-circle. "This will give us some protection from the wind tonight."

"What about snakes?" she asked, eyeing the boulders.

"Possible," he said, as he set down the bags. Had he found a weakness he could use to bring her closer to him? "Are you afraid of them?"

"Only the human kind." She looked around as if taking stock of their situation, then kind of braced her shoulders. It was a minute movement, one he wouldn't have noticed if he hadn't been studying her so keenly. With an almost cheerful note she said, "Let's get this camp set up so we can eat. I'm hungry."

She squatted beside her bag and spun the combination dial of the rather substantial lock on her bag. With a quiet *snick* the lock opened, and she unzipped the bag.

Chance was a bit taken aback at finding out what was in the bag this easily, but he squatted beside her. "What do you have? Candy bars?"

She chuckled. "Nothing so tasty."

He took the flashlight from her and shone it into the bag as she began taking out items. The bag was as neatly packed as a salesman's sample case, and she hadn't been lying about not having any room in there for anything else. She placed a sealed plastic bag on the ground between them. "Here we go. Nutrition bars." She slanted a look at him. "They taste like you'd expect a nutrition bar to taste, but they're concentrated. One bar a day will give us all we need to stay alive. I have a dozen of them."

The next item was a tiny cell phone. She stared at it, frozen, for a moment, then looked up at him with fragile hope in her eyes as she turned it on. Chance knew there wasn't a signal here, but he let her go through the motions, something inside him aching at the disappointment he knew she would feel.

Her shoulders slumped. "Nothing," she said, and turned the phone off. Without another word she returned to her unpacking.

A white plastic box with a familiar red cross on the top came out next. "First aid kit," she murmured, reaching back into the bag. "Water purification tablets. A couple of bottles of water, ditto orange juice. Light sticks. Matches." She listed each item as she set it on the ground. "Hairspray, deodorant, toothpaste, premoistened towelettes, hairbrush, curling iron, blow dryer, two space blankets—" she paused as she reached the bottom of the bag and began hauling on something bigger than any of the other items. "—and a tent."

Chapter 5

A tent. Chance stared down at it, recognizing the type. This was survivalist stuff, what people stored in underground shelters in case of war or natural disaster—or what someone who expected to spend a lot of time in the wilderness would pack.

"It's small," she said apologetically. "Really just a one-man tent, but I had to get something light enough for me to carry. There will be enough room for both of us to sleep in it, though, if you don't mind being a little crowded."

Why would she carry a *tent* on board a plane, when she expected to spend one night in Seattle—in a hotel—then fly back to Atlanta? Why would anyone carry that heavy a bag around when she could have checked it? The answer was that she hadn't wanted it out of her possession, but he still wanted an explanation of why she was carrying it at all.

Something didn't add up here.

* * *

His silence was unnerving. Sunny looked down at her incongruous pile of possessions and automatically emptied out the bag, removing her sweater and slipping it on, sitting down to pull on a pair of socks, then stuffing her change of clothes and her grooming items back into the bag. Her mind was racing. There was something about his expression that made a chill go down her spine, a hardness that she hadn't glimpsed before. Belatedly, she remembered how easily he had caught the cretin in the airport, the deadly grace and speed with which he moved. This was no ordinary charter pilot, and she was marooned with him.

She had been attracted to him from the first moment she saw him, but she couldn't afford to let that blind her to the danger of letting down her guard. She was accustomed to living with danger, but this was a different sort of danger, and she had no idea what form it could, or would, take. Chance could simply be one of those men who packed more punch than others, a man very capable of taking care of himself.

Or he could be in her father's pay.

The thought chilled her even more, the cold going down to her bones before common sense reasserted itself. No, there was no way her father could have arranged for everything that had happened today, no way he could have known she would be in the Salt Lake City airport. Being there had been pure bad luck, the result of a fouled-up flight schedule. *She* hadn't known she would be in Salt Lake City. If her father had been involved, he would have tried to grab her in either Atlanta or Seattle. All the zig-zagging across the country she had done today had made it impossible for her father to be involved.

As her mind cleared of that silent panic, she remembered how Chance had dragged her bodily from the plane, the way he had draped the blanket around her, even the courtesy with which he had treated her in the airport. He was a strong man, accustomed to being in the lead and taking the risks. *Military training,* she thought with a sudden flash of clarity, and wondered how she had missed it before. Her life, and Margreta's, depended on how well she could read people, how prepared she was, how alert. With Chance, she had been so taken off guard by the strength of her attraction to him, and the shock of finding that interest returned, that she hadn't been thinking.

"What's this about?" he asked quietly, squatting down beside her and indicating the tent. "And don't tell me you were going to camp out in the hotel lobby."

She couldn't help it. The thought of setting up the tent in a hotel lobby was so ludicrous that she chuckled. Seeing the funny side of things was what had kept her sane all these years.

One big hand closed gently on the nape of her neck. "Sunny," he said warningly. "Tell me."

She shook her head, still smiling. "We're stranded here tonight, but essentially we're strangers. After we get out of here we'll never see each other again, so there's no point in spilling our guts to each other. You keep your secrets, and I'll keep mine."

The flashlight beam sharpened the angles of his face. He exhaled a long, exasperated breath. "Okay—for now. I don't know why it matters, anyway. Unless I can get the plane fixed, we're going to be here a long time, and the reason why you have the tent will be irrelevant."

She searched his face, trying to read his impassive expression. "That isn't reassuring."

"It's the truth."

"When we don't show up in Seattle, someone will search for us. The Civil Air Patrol, someone. Doesn't your plane have one of those beacon things?"

"We're in a canyon."

He didn't have to say more than that. Any signal would be blocked by the canyon walls, except for directly overhead. They were in a deep, narrow slit in the earth, the narrowness of the canyon limiting even more their chances of anyone picking up the signal.

"Well, darn," she said forcefully.

This time he was the one who laughed, and he shook his head as he released her neck and stood up. "Is that the worst you can say?"

"We're alive. That outcome is so good considering what *could* have happened that, in comparison, being stranded here only rates a 'darn.' You may be able to fix the plane." She shrugged. "No point in wasting the really nasty words until we know more."

He leaned down and helped her to her feet. "If I can't get us going again, I'll help you with those words. For now, let's get this tent set up before the temperature drops even more."

"What about a fire?"

"I'll look for firewood tomorrow—*if* we need it. We can get by tonight without a fire, and I don't want to waste the flashlight batteries. If we're here for any length of time, we'll need the flashlight."

"I have the lightsticks."

"We'll save those, too. Just in case."

Working together, they set up the tent. She could have done it herself; it was made for one person to handle, and she had practiced until she knew she could do it with a minimum of fuss, but with two people the job took only moments. Brushing away the rocks so they would have a smooth surface beneath the tent floor took longer, but even so, they weren't going to have a comfortable bed for the night.

When they were finished, she eyed the tent with misgivings. It was long enough for Chance, but... She visually measured the width of his shoulders, then the width of the tent. She was either going to have to sleep on her side all night long—or on top of him.

The heat that shot through her told her which option her body preferred. Her heart beat a little faster in anticipation of their enforced intimacy during the coming night, of lying against his strong, warm body, maybe even sleeping in his arms.

To his credit, he didn't make any insinuating remarks, even though when he looked at the tent he must have drawn the same conclusion as she had. Instead, he bent down to pick up the bag of nutrition bars and said smugly, ''I knew you'd have dinner with me tonight.''

She began laughing again, charmed by both his tact and his sense of humor, and fell a little in love with him right then.

She should have been alarmed, but she wasn't. Yes, letting herself care for him made her emotionally vulnerable, but they had lived through a terrifying experience together, and she *needed* an emotional anchor right now. So far she hadn't found a single thing about the man that she didn't like, not even that hint of danger she kept sensing. In this situation, a man with an edge to him was an asset, not a hindrance.

She allowed herself to luxuriate in this unaccustomed feeling as they each ate a nutrition bar—which was edible, but definitely not tasty—and drank some water. Then they packed everything except the two space blankets back in the bag, to protect their supplies from snakes and insects and other scavengers. They didn't have to worry about bears, not in this desertlike part of the country, but coyotes were possible. Her bag was supposedly indestructible; if any coyotes showed up, she supposed she would find out if the claim about the bag was true, because there wasn't room in the tent for both them and the bag.

Chance checked the luminous dial of his watch. "It's still early, but we should get in the tent to save our body heat, and not burn up calories trying to stay warm out here. I'll spread this blanket down, and we'll use your two blankets for cover."

For the first time, she realized he was in his T-shirt. "Shouldn't you get your jacket from the plane?"

"It's too bulky to wear in the tent. Besides, I don't feel the cold as much as you do. I'll be fine without it." He sat down and pulled off his boots, tossed them inside the tent, then crawled in with the blanket. Sunny slipped off her own shoes, glad she had the socks to keep her feet warm.

"Okay, come on in," Chance said. "Feet first."

She gave him her shoes, then sat down and worked herself feetfirst into the tent. He was lying on his side, which gave her room to maneuver, but it was still a chore keeping her skirt down and trying not to bunch up the blanket as she wiggled into place. Chance zipped the tent flaps shut, then pulled his pistol out of his waistband and placed it beside his head. Sunny eyed the big black automatic; she wasn't an expert on pistols, but she knew it was one of the heavier calibers, either a .45 or a 9mm. She had tried them, but the bigger pistols were too heavy for her to handle with ease, so she had opted for a smaller caliber.

He had already unfolded the space blankets and had them ready to pull in place. She could already feel his body heat in the small space, so she didn't need a blanket yet, but as the night grew colder, they would need all the covering they could get.

They both moved around, trying to get comfortable. Because he was so big, Sunny tried to give him as much room as possible. She turned on her side and curled her arm under her head, but they still bumped and brushed against each other.

"Ready?" he asked.

"Ready."

He turned off the flashlight. The darkness was complete, like being deep in a cave. "Thank God I'm not claustrophobic," she said, taking a deep breath. His scent filled her lungs, warm and...different, not musky, exactly, but earthy, and very much the way a man should smell.

"Just think of it as being safe," he murmured. "Darkness can feel secure."

She did feel safe, she realized. For the first time in her memory, she was certain no one except the man beside her knew where she was. She didn't have to check locks, scout out an alternate exit, or sleep so lightly she sometimes felt as if she hadn't slept at all. She didn't have to worry about being followed, or her phone being tapped, or any of the other things that could happen. She did worry about Margreta, but she had to think positively. Tomorrow Chance would find the problem was a clogged fuel line, he would get it cleared, and they would finish their trip. She would be too late to deliver the package in Seattle, but considering they had landed safely instead of crashing, she didn't really care about the package. The day's outcome could have been so much worse that she was profoundly grateful they were all in one piece and relatively comfortable—"relatively" being the key word, she thought, as she tried to find a better position. The ground was as hard as a rock. For all she knew the ground *was* a rock, covered by a thin layer of dirt.

She was suddenly exhausted. The events of the day— the long flight and fouled-up connections, the lack of food, the stress of being mugged, then the almost unbearable tension of those last minutes in the plane— finally took their toll on her. She yawned and unconsciously tried yet again to find a comfortable position, turning over to pillow her head on her other arm. Her elbow collided with something very solid, and he grunted.

"I'm sorry," she mumbled. She squirmed a little more, inadvertently bumping him with her knee. "This is so crowded I may have to sleep on top."

She heard the words and in shock realized that she had actually said them aloud. She opened her mouth to apologize again.

"Or I could be the one on top."

His words stopped her apology cold. Her breath tangled in her lungs and didn't escape. His deep voice seemed to echo in the darkness, that single sentence reverberating through her consciousness. She was suddenly, acutely, aware of every inch of him, of the sensual promise in his tone. The kiss—the kiss she could write off as reaction; danger was supposed to be an aphrodisiac, and evidently that was true. But this wasn't reaction; this was desire, warm and curious, seeking.

"Is that a 'no' I'm hearing?"

Her lungs started working again, and she sucked in a breath. "I haven't said anything."

"That's my point." He sounded faintly amused. "I guess I'm not going to get lucky tonight."

Feeling more certain of herself with his teasing, she said dryly, "I guess not. You've already used up your quota of luck for the day."

"I'll try again tomorrow."

She stifled a laugh.

"Does that snicker mean I haven't scared you?"

She should be scared, she thought, or at least wary. She had no idea why she wasn't. The fact was, she felt tempted. Very tempted. "No, I'm not scared."

"Good." He yawned. "Then why don't you pull off that sweater and let me use it as a pillow, and you can use my shoulder. We'll both be more comfortable."

Common sense said he was right. Common sense also said she was asking for trouble if she slept in his arms. She trusted him to behave, but she wasn't that certain of herself. He was sexy, with a capital SEX. He made her laugh. He was strong and capable, with a faintly wicked edge to him. He was even a little dangerous. What more could a woman want?

That was perhaps the most dangerous thing about him, that he made her want him. She had easily resisted other men, walking away without a backward look or a second thought. Chance made her long for all the things she had denied herself, made her aware of how lonely and alone she was.

"Are you sure you can trust me to behave?" she asked, only half joking. "I didn't mean to say that about being on top. I was half-asleep, and it just slipped out."

"I think I can handle you if you get fresh. For one thing, you'll be sound asleep as soon as you stop talking."

She yawned. "I know. I'm crashing hard, if you'll pardon the terminology."

"We didn't crash, we landed. Come on, let's get that sweater off, then you can sleep."

There wasn't room to fully sit up, so he helped her struggle out of the garment. He rolled it up and tucked it under his head, then gently, as if worried he might frighten her, drew her against his right side. His right arm curled around her, and she nestled close, settling her head in the hollow of his shoulder.

The position was surprisingly comfortable, and comforting. She draped her right arm across his chest, because there didn't seem to be any other place to put it. Well, there were other places, but none that seemed as safe. Besides, she liked feeling his heartbeat under her hand. The strong, even thumping satisfied some primitive instinct in her, the desire not to be alone in the night.

"Comfortable?" he asked in a low, soothing tone.

"Um-hmm."

With his left arm he snagged one of the space blankets and pulled it up to cover her to the shoulders, keeping the chill from her bare arms. Cocooned in warmth and darkness, she gave in to the sheer pleasure of lying so close to him. Sleepy desire hummed just below the surface, warming her, softening her. Her breasts, crushed against his side, tightened in delight, and her nipples felt achy, telling her they had hardened. Could he feel them? she wondered. She wanted to rub herself against him like a cat, intensifying the sensation, but she lay very still and concentrated on the rhythm of his heartbeat.

He had touched her breasts when he kissed her. She wanted to feel that again, feel his hard hand on her bare flesh. She wanted him, wanted his touch and his taste and the feel of him inside her. The force of her physical yearning was so strong that she actually ached from the emptiness.

If we don't get out of here tomorrow, she thought in faint despair just before she went to sleep, I'll be under him before the sun goes down again.

Sunny was accustomed to waking immediately when anything disturbed her; once, a car had backfired out in the street and she had grabbed the pistol from under the pillow and rolled off the bed before the noise had completely faded. She had learned how to nap on demand, because she never knew when she might have to run for her life. She could count on one hand the number of nights since she had stopped being a child that she had slept through undisturbed.

But she woke in Chance's arms aware that she had slept all night long, that not only had lying next to him not disturbed her, in a very basic way his presence had been reassuring. She was safe here, safe and warm and unutterably relaxed. His hand was stroking slowly down her back, and that was what had awakened her.

Her skirt had ridden up during the night, of course, and was twisted at midthigh. Their legs were tangled together, her right leg thrown over his; his jeans were old and soft, but the denim was still slightly rough against the inside of her thigh. She wasn't lying completely on top of him, but it was a near thing. Her head lay pillowed on his chest instead of his shoulder, with the steady thumping of his heart under her ear.

The slow motion of his hand continued. "Good morning," he said, his deep voice raspy from sleep.

"Good morning." She didn't want to get up, she realized, though she knew she should. It was after dawn; the morning light seeped through the brown fabric of the tent, washing them with a dull gold color. Chance should get started on the fuel pump, so they could get airborne and in radio contact with someone as soon as possible, to let the FAA know they hadn't crashed. She knew what she should do, but instead she continued to lie there, content with the moment.

He touched her hair, lifting one strand and watching it drift back down. "I could get used to this," he murmured.

"You've slept with women before."

"I haven't slept with *you* before."

She wanted to ask how she was different, but she was better off not knowing. Nothing could come of this fast-deepening attraction, because she couldn't let it. She had to believe that he could repair the plane, that in a matter of hours they would be separating and she would never see him again. That was the only thing that gave her the strength, finally, to pull away from him and straighten her clothes, push her hair out of her face and unzip the tent.

The chill morning air rushed into their small cocoon. "Wow," she said, ignoring his comment. "Some hot coffee would be good, wouldn't it? I don't suppose you have a jar of instant in the plane?"

"You mean you don't have coffee packed in that survival bag of yours?" Taking his cue from her, he didn't push her to continue their provocative conversation.

"Nope, just water." She crawled out of the tent, and he handed her shoes and sweater out through the opening. Quickly she slipped them on, glad she had brought a heavy cardigan instead of a summer-weight one.

Chance's boots came out next, then him. He sat on the ground and pulled on his boots. "Damn, it's cold. I'm going to get my jacket from the plane. I'll take care of business there, and you go on the other side of these boulders. There shouldn't be any snakes stirring around this early, but keep an eye out.''

Sunny dug some tissues out of her skirt pocket and set off around the boulders. Ten minutes later, nature's call having been answered, she washed her face and hands with one of the pre-moistened towelettes, then brushed her teeth and hair. Feeling much more human and able to handle the world, she took a moment to look around at their life-saving little canyon.

It was truly a slit in the earth, no more than fifty yards wide where he had landed the plane. About a quarter of a mile farther down it widened some, but the going was much rougher. The stream bed was literally the only place they could have safely landed. Just beyond the widest point, the canyon made a dog leg to the left, so she had no idea how long it was. The canyon floor was littered with rocks big and small, and a variety of scrub brush. Deep grooves were cut into the ground where rain had sluiced down the steep canyon walls and arrowed toward the stream.

All the different shades of red were represented in the dirt and rock, from rust to vermillion to a sandy pink The scrub brush wasn't a lush green; the color was dry, as if it had been bleached by the sun. Some of it was silvery, a bright contrast against the monochromatic tones of the earth.

They seemed to be the only two living things there. She didn't hear any birds chirping, or insects rustling. There had to be small wildlife such as lizards and snakes, she knew, which meant there had to be something for them to eat, but at the moment the immense solitude was almost overwhelming.

Looking at the plane, she saw that Chance was already

poking around in its innards. Shoving her cold hands into the sweater pockets, she walked down to him.

"Don't you want to eat something?"

"I'd rather save the food until I see what the problem is." He gave her a crooked grin. "No offense, but I don't want to eat another one of those nutrition bars unless I absolutely have to."

"And if you can fly us out of here, you figure you can hold out until we get to an airport."

"Bingo."

She grinned as she changed positions so she could see what he was doing. "I didn't eat one, either," she confessed.

He was checking the fuel lines, his face set in that intent expression men got when they were doing anything mechanical. Sunny felt useless; she could have helped if he was working on a car, but she didn't know anything about airplanes. "Is there anything I can do to help?" she finally asked.

"No, it's just a matter of taking off the fuel lines and checking them for clogs."

She waited a few more minutes, but the process looked tedious rather than interesting, and she began getting restless. "I think I'll walk around, explore a bit."

"Stay within yelling distance," he said absently.

The morning, though still cool, was getting warmer by the minute as the sun heated the dry desert air. She walked carefully, watching where she placed each step, because a sprained ankle could mean the difference between life and death if she had to run for it. Someday, she thought, a sprain would be an inconvenience, nothing more. One day she would be free.

She looked up at the clear blue sky and inhaled the clean, crisp air. She had worked hard to retain her enjoyment of life, the way she had learned to rely on a sense of humor to keep her sane. Margreta didn't handle things nearly as well, but she already had to deal with a heart condition that, while it could be controlled with medication, nevertheless meant that she had to take certain precautions. If she were ever found, Margreta lacked Sunny's ability to just drop out of sight. She had to have her medication refilled, which meant she had to occasionally see her doctor so he could write a new prescription. If she had to find a new doctor, that would mean being retested, which would mean a lot more money.

Which meant that Sunny never saw her sister. It was safer if they weren't together, in case anyone was looking for sisters. She didn't even have Margreta's phone number. Margreta called Sunny's cell phone once a week at a set time, always from a different pay phone. That way, if Sunny was captured, she had no information her captors could get by any means, not even drugs.

She had four days until Margreta called, Sunny thought. If she didn't answer the phone, or if Margreta didn't call, then each had to assume the other had been caught. If Sunny didn't answer the phone, Margreta would bolt from her safe hiding place, because with the phone records her location could be narrowed down to the correct city. Sunny couldn't bear to think what would happen then; Margreta, in her grief and rage, might well throw caution to the wind in favor of revenge.

Four days. The problem *had* to be a clogged fuel line. It just had to be.

Chapter 6

Mindful of Chance's warning, Sunny didn't wander far. In truth, there wasn't much to look at, just grit and rocks and scraggly bushes, and those vertical rock walls. The desert had a wild, lonely beauty, but she was more appreciative when she wasn't stranded in it. When rain filled the stream this sheltered place probably bloomed with color, but how often did it rain here? Once a year?

As the day warmed, the reptiles began to stir. She saw a brown lizard dart into a crevice as she approached. A bird she didn't recognize swooped down for a tasty insect, then flew back off to freedom. The steep canyon walls didn't mean anything to a bird, while the hundred feet or so were unscalable to her.

She began to get hungry, and a glance at her watch told her she had been meandering through the canyon for over an hour. What was taking Chance so long? If there was a clog in the lines he should have found it by now.

She began retracing her steps to the plane. She could see Chance still poking around the engine, which meant he probably hadn't found anything. A chilly finger of fear prodded her, and she pushed it away. She refused to anticipate trouble. She would deal with things as they happened, and if Chance couldn't repair the plane, then they would have to find some other way out of the canyon. She hadn't explored far; perhaps the other end was open, and they could simply walk out. She didn't know how far they were from a town, but she was willing to make the effort. Anything was better than sitting and doing nothing.

As she approached, Chance lifted his hand to show he saw her, then turned back to the engine. Sunny let her gaze linger, admiring the way his T-shirt clung to the muscles of his back and shoulders. The fit of his jeans wasn't bad, either, she thought, eyeing his butt and long legs.

Something moved in the sand near his feet.

She thought she would faint. Her vision dimmed and narrowed until all she saw was the snake, perilously close to his left boot. Her heart leaped, pounding against her ribcage so hard she felt the thuds.

She had no sensation or knowledge of moving; time took on the viscosity of syrup. All she knew was that the snake was getting bigger and bigger, closer and closer. Chance looked around at her and stepped back from the plane, almost on the coiling length. The snake's head drew back and her hand closed on a coil, surprisingly warm and smooth, and she threw the awful thing as far as she could. It was briefly outlined against the stark rock, then sailed beyond a bush and dropped from sight.

"Are you all right? Did it bite you? Are you hurt?"

She couldn't stop babbling as she went down on her knees and began patting his legs, looking for droplets of blood, a small tear in his jeans, anything that would show if he had been bitten.

"I'm all right. I'm all right. Sunny! It didn't bite me." His voice overrode hers, and he hauled her to her feet, shaking her a little to get her attention. "Look at me!" The force of his tone snagged her gaze with his and he said more quietly, "I'm okay."

"Are you sure?" She couldn't seem to stop touching him, patting his chest, stroking his face, though logically she knew there was no way the snake could have bitten him up there. Neither could she stop trembling. "I hate snakes," she said in a shaking voice. "They terrify me. I saw it—it was right under your feet. You almost *stepped* on it."

"Shh," he murmured, pulling her against him and rocking her slowly back and forth. "It's all right. Nothing happened."

She clutched his shirt and buried her head against his chest. His smell, already so familiar and now with the faint odor of grease added, was comforting. His heartbeat was steady, as if he hadn't almost been snakebitten. *He* was steady, rock solid, his body supporting hers.

"Oh my God," she whispered. "That was awful." She raised her head and stared at him, an appalled expression on her face. "Yuk! I *touched* it!" She snatched her hand away from him and held it at arm's length. "Let me go, I have to wash my hand. Now!"

He released her, and she bolted up the slope to the tent, where the towelettes were. Grabbing one, she scrubbed furiously at her palm and fingers.

Chance was laughing softly as he came up behind her.

"What's the matter? Snakes don't have cooties. Besides, yesterday you said you weren't afraid of them."

"I lied. And I don't care what they have, I don't want one anywhere near me." Satisfied that no snake germs lingered on her hand, she blew out a long, calming breath.

"Instead of swooping down like a hawk," he said mildly, "why didn't you just yell out a warning?"

She gave him a blank look. "I couldn't." Yelling had never entered her mind. She had been taught her entire life not to yell in moments of tension or danger, because to do so would give away her position. Normal people could scream and yell, but she had never been allowed to be normal.

He put one finger under her chin, lifting her face to the sun. He studied her for a long moment, something dark moving in his eyes; then he tugged her to him and bent his head.

His mouth was fierce and hungry, his tongue probing. She sank weakly against him, clinging to his shoulders and kissing him in return just as fiercely, with just as much hunger. More. She felt as if she had always hungered, and never been fed. She drank life itself from his mouth, and sought more.

His hands were all over her, on her breasts, her bottom, lifting her into the hard bulge of his loins. The knowledge that he wanted her filled her with a deep need to know more, to feel everything she had always denied herself. She didn't know if she could have brought herself to pull away, but he was the one who broke the kiss, lifting his head and standing there with his eyes closed and a grim expression on his face.

"Chance?" she asked hesitantly.

He growled a lurid word under his breath. Then he

opened his eyes and glared down at her. "I can't believe I'm stopping this a second time," he said with a raw, furious frustration. "Just for the record, I'm *not* that noble. Damn it all to hell and back—" He broke off, breathing hard. "It isn't a clogged fuel line. It must be the pump. We have other things we need to do. We can't afford to waste any daylight."

Margreta. Sunny bit her lip to hold back a moan of dismay. She stared up at him, the knowledge of the danger of their situation lying like a stark shadow between them.

She wasn't licked yet. She had four days. "Can we walk out?"

"In the desert? In August?" He looked up at the rim of the canyon. "Assuming we can even get out of here, we'd have to walk at night and try to find shelter during the day. By afternoon, the temperature will be over a hundred."

The temperature was probably already well into the seventies, she thought; she was dying of heat inside her heavy sweater, or maybe that was just frustrated lust, since she hadn't noticed how hot it was until now. She peeled off the sweater and dropped it on top of her bag. "What do we need to do?"

His eyes gleamed golden with admiration, and he squeezed her waist. "I'll reconnoiter. We can't get out on this end of the canyon, but maybe there's a way farther down."

"What do you want me to do?"

"Look for sticks, leaves, anything that will burn. Gather as much as you can in a pile."

He set off in the direction she had gone earlier, and she went in the opposite direction. The scrub brush grew heavier at that end of the canyon, and she would find more wood there. She didn't like to think about how limited the supply would be, or that they might be here for a long, long time. If they couldn't get out of the canyon, they would eventually use up their meager resources and die.

He hated lying to her. Chance's expression was grim as he stalked along the canyon floor. He had lied to terrorists, hoodlums and heads of state alike without a twinge of conscience, but it was getting harder and harder to lie to Sunny. He fiercely protected a hard core of honesty deep inside, the part of him that he shared only with his family, but Sunny was getting to him. She wasn't what he had expected. More and more he was beginning to suspect she wasn't working with her father. She was too... *gallant* was the word that sprang to mind. Terrorists weren't gallant. In his opinion, they were either mad or amoral. Sunny was neither.

He was more shaken by the episode with the snake than he had let her realize. Not by the snake itself—he had on boots, and since he hadn't heard rattles he suspected the snake hadn't been poisonous—but by her reaction. He would never forget the way she had looked, rushing in like an avenging angel, her face paper-white and utterly focused. By her own admission she was terrified of snakes, yet she hadn't hesitated. What kind of courage had it taken for her to pick up the snake with her bare hand?

Then there was the way she had patted him, looking for a bite. Except with certain people, or during sex, he had to struggle to tolerate being touched. He had learned how to accept affection in his family, because Mom and Maris would *not* leave him alone. He unabashedly loved playing with all his nephews—and niece—but his family had been the only exception. Until now. Until Sunny. He not only hadn't minded, he had, for a moment, allowed himself the pure luxury of enjoying the feel of her hands on his legs, his chest. And that didn't even begin to compare to how much he had enjoyed sleeping with her, feeling those sweet curves all along his side. His hand clenched as he remembered the feel of her breast in his palm, the wonderful resilience that was both soft and firm. He ached to feel her bare skin, to taste her. He wanted to strip her naked and pull her beneath him for a long hard ride, and he wanted to do it in broad daylight so he could watch her brilliant eyes glaze with pleasure.

If she wasn't who she was he would take her to the south of France, maybe, or a Caribbean island, any place where they could lie naked on the beach and make love in the sunshine, or in a shaded room with fingers of sunlight slipping through closed blinds. Instead, he had to keep lying to her, because whether or not she was working with her father didn't change the fact that she was the key to locating him.

He couldn't change the plan now. He couldn't suddenly "repair" the plane. He thanked God she didn't know anything about planes, because otherwise she would never have fallen for the fuel pump excuse; a Skylane had a backup fuel pump, for just such an emergency. No, he had to play out the game as he had planned it, because the goal was too damned important to abandon, and he couldn't take the risk that she was involved up to her pretty ears, after all.

He and Zane had walked a fine line in planning this out. The situation had to be survivable but grim, so nothing would arouse her suspicion. There was food to be had, but not easily. There was water, but not a lot. He

hadn't brought any provisions that might make her wonder why he had them, meaning he had limited himself
to the blanket, the water and the pistol, plus the expected
items in the plane, such as flares. Hell, she was a lot
more prepared than he was, and that made him wary.
She wasn't exactly forthcoming about her reason for tot-
ing a damn tent around, either. The lady had secrets of
her own.

He reached the far end of the canyon and checked to
make certain nothing had changed since he and Zane
had been here. No unexpected landslide had caved in a
wall, allowing a way out. The thin trickle of water still
ran down the rock. He saw rabbit tracks, birds, things
they could eat. Shooting them would be the easy way,
though; he would have to build some traps, to save his
ammunition for emergencies.

Everything was just as he had left it. The plan was
working. The physical attraction between them was
strong; she wouldn't resist him much longer, maybe not
at all. She certainly hadn't done anything to call a halt
earlier. And after he was her lover—well, women were
easily beguiled by sexual pleasure, the bonds of the
flesh. He knew the power of sex, knew how to use it to
make her trust him. He wished he could trust *her*—this
would be a lot easier if he could—but he knew too much
about the human soul's capability of evil, and that a
pretty face didn't necessarily mean a pretty person was
behind it.

When he judged enough time had passed for him to
completely reconnoiter the canyon, he walked back. She
was still gathering sticks, he saw, going back and forth
between the bushes and the growing pile next to the tent.
She looked up when he got closer, hope blazing in her
expression.

He shook his head. "It's a box canyon. There's no way out," he said flatly. "The good news is, there's water at the far end."

She swallowed. Her eyes were huge with distress, almost eclipsing her face. "We can't climb out, either?"

"It's sheer rock." He put his hands on his hips, looking around. "We need to move closer to the water, for convenience. There's an overhang that will give us shade from the sun, and the ground underneath is sandier, so it'll be more comfortable."

Or as comfortable as they could get, sleeping in that small tent.

Wordlessly she nodded and began folding the tent. She did it briskly, without wasted movement, but he saw she was fighting for control. He stroked her upper arm, feeling her smooth, pliant skin, warm and slightly moist from her exertion. "We'll be okay," he reassured her. "We just have to hold out until someone sees our smoke and comes to investigate."

"We're in the middle of nowhere," she said shakily. "You said so yourself. And I only have four days until—"

"Until what?" he asked, when she stopped.

"Nothing. It doesn't matter." She stared blindly at the sky, at the clear blue expanse that was turning whiter as the hot sun climbed upward.

Four days until what? he wondered. What was going to happen? Was she supposed to do something? Was a terrorist attack planned? Would it go forward without her?

The dogleg of the canyon was about half a mile long, and the angle gave it more shade than where they had landed. They worked steadily, moving their camp, with

Chance hauling the heaviest stuff. Sunny tried to keep her mind blank, to not think about Margreta, to focus totally on the task at hand.

It was noon, the white sun directly overhead. The heat was searing, the shade beneath the overhang so welcome she sighed with relief when they gained its shelter. The overhang was larger than she had expected, about twelve feet wide and deep enough, maybe eight feet, that the sunshine would never penetrate its depths. The rock sloped to a height of about four feet at the back, but the opening was high enough that Chance could stand up without bumping his head.

"I'll wait until it's cooler to get the rest," he said. "I don't know about you, but I'm starving. Let's have half of one of your nutrition bars now, and I'll try to get a rabbit for dinner."

She rallied enough to give him a look of mock dismay. "You'd eat Peter Cottontail?"

"I'd eat the Easter Bunny right now, if I could catch him."

He was trying to make her laugh. She appreciated his effort, but she couldn't quite shake off the depression that had seized her when her last hope of getting out of here quickly had evaporated.

She had lost her appetite, but she dug out one of the nutrition bars and halved it, though she hid the fact that Chance's "half" was bigger than hers. He was bigger; he needed more. They ate their spartan little meal standing up, staring out at the bleached tones of the canyon. "Drink all the water you want," he urged. "The heat dehydrates you even in the shade."

Obediently she drank a bottle of water; she needed it to get the nutrition bar down. Each bite felt as if it was getting bigger and bigger in her mouth, making it difficult to swallow. She resorted to taking only nibbles, and got it down that way.

After they ate, Chance made a small circle of rocks, piled in some sticks and leaves, both fresh and dead, and built a fire. Soon a thin column of smoke was floating out of the canyon. It took him no more than five minutes to accomplish, but when he came back under the overhang his shirt was damp with sweat.

She handed him a bottle of water, and he drank deeply, at the same time reaching out a strong arm and hooking it around her waist. He drew her close and pressed a light kiss to her forehead, nothing more, just held her comfortingly. She put her arms around him and clung, desperately needing his strength right now. She hadn't had anyone to lean on in a long time; she had always had to be the strong one. She had tried so hard to stay on top of things, to plan for every conceivable glitch, but she hadn't thought to plan for this, and now she had no idea what to do.

"I have to think of something," she said aloud.

"Shh. All we have to do is stay alive. That's the most important thing."

He was right, of course. She couldn't do anything about Margreta now. This damn canyon had saved their lives yesterday, but it had become a prison from which she couldn't escape. She had to play the hand with the cards that had been dealt to her and not let depression sap her strength. She had to hope Margreta wouldn't do anything foolish, just go to ground somewhere. How she would ever find her again she didn't know, but she could deal with that if she just knew her sister was alive and safe somewhere.

"Do you have family who will worry?" he asked.

God, that went to the bone! She shook her head. She

had family, but Margreta wouldn't worry; she would simply assume the worst.

"What about you?" she asked, realizing she had fallen halfway in love with the man and didn't know a thing about him.

He shook his head. "C'mon, let's sit down." With nothing to use for a seat, they simply sat on the ground. "I'll take two of the seats out of the plane this afternoon, so we'll be more comfortable," he said. "In answer to your question, no, I don't have anyone. My folks are dead, and I don't have any brothers or sisters. There's an uncle somewhere, on my dad's side, and my mom had some cousins, but we never kept in touch."

"That's sad. Family should stay together." *If they could,* she added silently. "Where did you grow up?"

"All over. Dad wasn't exactly known for his ability to keep a job. What about your folks?"

She was silent for a moment, then sighed. "I was adopted. They were good people. I still miss them." She drew a design in the dirt with her finger. "When we didn't show up in Seattle last night, would someone have notified the FAA?"

"They're probably already searching. The problem is, first they'll search the area I should have been over when I filed my flight plan."

"We were off course?" she asked faintly. It just kept getting worse and worse.

"We went off course looking for a place to land. But if anyone is searching this area, eventually he'll see our smoke. We just have to keep the fire going during the day."

"How long will they look? Before they call off the search?"

He was silent, his golden eyes narrowed as he

searched the sky. "They'll look as long as they think we might be alive."

"But if they think we've crashed—"

"Eventually they'll stop looking," he said softly. "It might be a week, a little longer, but they'll stop."

"So if no one finds us within, say, ten days—" She couldn't go on.

"We don't give up. There's always the possibility a private plane will fly over."

He didn't say that the possibility was slight, but he didn't have to. She had seen for herself the kind of terrain they'd flown over, and she knew how narrow and easily missed this canyon was.

She drew up her knees and wrapped her arms around her legs, staring wistfully at the languid curls of gray smoke. "I used to wish I could go someplace where no one could find me. I didn't realize there wouldn't be room service."

He chuckled as he leaned back on one elbow and stretched out his long legs. "Nothing gets you down for long, does it?"

"I try not to let it. Our situation isn't great, but we're alive. We have food, water and shelter. Things could be worse."

"We also have entertainment. I have a deck of cards in the plane. We can play poker."

"Do you cheat?"

"Don't need to," he drawled.

"Well, I do, so I'm giving you fair warning."

"Warning taken. You know what happens to cheaters, don't you?"

"They win?"

"Not if they get caught."

"If they're any good, they don't get caught."

He twirled a finger in her hair and lightly tugged. "Yeah, but if they get caught they're in big trouble. You can take that as my warning."

"I'll be careful," she promised. A yawn took her by surprise. "How can I be sleepy? I got plenty of sleep last night."

"It's the heat. Why don't you take a nap? I'll watch the fire."

"Why aren't you sleepy?"

He shrugged. "I'm used to it."

She really was sleepy, and there was nothing else to do. She didn't feel like setting up the tent, so she dragged her bag into position behind her and leaned back on it. Silently Chance tossed her sweater into her lap. Following his example, she rolled up the sweater and stuffed it under her head. She dozed within minutes. It wasn't a restful sleep, being one of those light naps in which she was aware of the heat, of Chance moving around, of her worry about Margreta. Her muscles felt heavy and limp, though, and completely waking up was just too much trouble.

The problem with afternoon naps was that one woke feeling both groggy and grungy. Her clothes were sticking to her, which wasn't surprising considering the heat. When she finally yawned and sat up, she saw that the sun was beginning to take on a red glow as it sank, and though the temperature was still high, the heat had lost its searing edge.

Chance was sitting cross-legged, his long, tanned fingers deftly weaving sticks and string into a cage. There was something about the way he looked there in the shadow of the overhang, his attention totally focused on the trap he was building while the light reflected off the sand outside danced along his high cheekbones, that made recognition click in her brain. "You're part Native American, aren't you?"

"American Indian," he corrected absently. "Everyone born here is a native American, or so Dad always told me." He looked up and gave her a quick grin. "Of course, 'Indian' isn't very accurate, either. Most labels aren't. But, yeah, I'm a mixed breed."

"And ex-military." She didn't know why she said that. Maybe it was his deftness in building the trap. She wasn't foolish enough to attribute that to any so-called Native American skills, not in this day and age, but there was something in the way he worked that bespoke survival training.

He gave her a surprised glance. "How did you know?"

She shook her head. "Just a guess. The way you handled the pistol, as if you were very comfortable with it. What you're doing now. And you used the word 'reconnoiter.'"

"A lot of people are familiar with weapons, especially outdoorsmen, who would also know how to build traps."

"Done in by your vocabulary," she said, and smirked. "You said 'weapons' instead of just 'guns,' the way most people—even outdoorsmen—would have."

Again she was rewarded with that flashing grin. "Okay, so I've spent some time in a uniform."

"What branch?"

"Army. Rangers."

Well, that certainly explained the survival skills. She didn't know a lot about the Rangers, or any military group, but she did know they were an elite corps.

He set the finished trap aside and began work on another one. Sunny watched him for a moment, feeling useless. She would be more hindrance than help in building traps. She sighed as she brushed the dirt from her skirt. Darn, stranded only one day and here she was, smack in the middle of the old sexual stereotypes.

She surrendered with good grace. "Is there enough water for me to wash out our clothes? I've lived in these for two days, and that's long enough."

"There's enough water, just nothing to collect it in." He unfolded his legs and stood with easy grace. "I'll show you."

He led the way out of the overhang. She clambered over rocks in his wake, feeling the heat burn through the sides of her shoes and trying not to touch the rocks with her hands. When they reached more shade, the relief was almost tangible.

"Here." He indicated a thin trickle of water running down the face of the wall. The bushes were heavier here, because of the water, and the temperature felt a good twenty degrees cooler. Part of it was illusion, because of the contrast, but the extra greenery did have a cooling effect.

Sunny sighed as she looked at the trickle. Filling their water bottles would be a snap. Washing off would be easy. But washing clothes—well, that was a different proposition. There wasn't a pool in which she could soak them, not even a puddle. The water was soaked immediately into the dry, thirsty earth. The ground was damp, but not saturated.

The only thing she could do was fill a water bottle over and over, and rinse the dust out. "This will take forever," she groused.

An irritating masculine smirk was on his face as he peeled his T-shirt off over his head and handed it to her. "We aren't exactly pressed for time, are we?"

She almost thrust the shirt back at him and demanded he put it on, but not because of his comment. She wasn't a silly prude, she had seen naked chests more times than she could count, but she had never before seen *his* naked chest. He was smoothly, powerfully muscled, with pectorals that looked like flesh-covered steel and a hard, six-pack abdomen. A light patch of black hair stretched from one small brown nipple to the other. She wanted to touch him. Her hand actually ached for the feel of his skin, and she clenched her fingers hard on his shirt.

The smirk faded, his eyes darkening. He touched her face, curving his fingers under her chin and lifting it. His expression was hard with pure male desire. "You know what's going to happen between us, don't you?" His voice was low and rough.

"Yes." She could barely manage a whisper. Her throat had tightened, her body responding to his touch, his intent.

"Do you want it?"

So much she ached with it, she thought. She looked up into those golden-brown eyes and trembled from the enormity of the step she was taking.

"Yes," she said.

Chapter 7

She had lived her entire life without ever having lived at all, Sunny thought as she mechanically rinsed out his clothes and draped them over the hot rocks to dry. She and Chance might never get out of this canyon alive, and even if they did, it could take a long time. Weeks, perhaps months, or longer. Whatever Margreta did, she would long since have done it, and there wasn't a damn thing Sunny could do about the situation. For the first time in her life, she had to think only about herself and what *she* wanted. That was simple; what she wanted was Chance.

She had to face facts. She was good at it; she had been doing it her entire life. The fact that had been glaring her in the face was that they could very well die here in this little canyon. If they didn't survive, she didn't want to die still clinging to the reasons for not getting involved that, while good and valid in civilization, didn't mean spit here. She already *was* involved with him, in a battle for their very lives. She certainly didn't want to die without having known what it was like to be loved by him, to feel him inside her and hold him close, and to tell him that she loved him. She had a whole world of love dammed up inside her, drying up because she hadn't had anyone to whom she could give it, but now she had this opportunity, and she wasn't going to waste it.

A psych analyst would say this was just propinquity: the "any port in a storm" type of attraction, or the Adam and Eve syndrome. That might be part of it, for him. If she had to guess, Sunny would say that Chance was used to having sex whenever he wanted it. He had that look about him, a bone-deep sexual confidence that would draw women like flies. She was currently the only fly available.

But it wasn't just that. He had been attracted to her before, just as she had been to him. If they had made it to Seattle without trouble, she would have been strong enough to refuse his invitation and walk away from him. She would never have allowed herself to get to know him. Maybe they had met only twenty-four hours before, but those hours had been more intense than anything else she had ever known. She imagined it was as if they had gone into battle together; the danger they had faced, and were still facing, had forged a bond between them like soldiers in a war. She had learned things about him that it would have taken her weeks to learn in a normal situation, weeks that she would never have given herself.

Of all the things she had learned about him in those twenty-four hours, there wasn't one she didn't like. He was a man willing to step forward and take a risk, get involved, otherwise he wouldn't have stopped the cretin in the airport. He was calm in a crisis, self-sufficient and capable, and he was more considerate of her than anyone else she had ever known. On top of all that, he was so sexy he made her mouth water.

Most men, after hearing something like what she had told him, would have immediately gone for the sex. Chance hadn't. Instead, he had kissed her very sweetly and said, "I'll get the rest of the things from the plane, so I can change clothes and give you my dirty ones to wash."

"Gee, thanks," she had managed to say.

He had winked at her. "Any time."

He was a man who could put off his personal pleasure in order to take care of business. So here she was, scrubbing his underwear. Not the most romantic thing in the world to be doing, yet it was an intimate chore that strengthened the link forming between them. He was working to feed her; she was working to keep their clothes clean.

So far, Chance was everything that was steadfast and reliable. So why did she keep sensing that edge of danger in him? Was it something his army training had given him that was just *there* no matter what he was doing? She had never met anyone else who had been a ranger, so she had no means of comparison. She was just glad of that training, if it helped keep them alive.

After his clothes were as clean as she could get them, she hesitated barely a second before stripping out of her own, down to her skin. She couldn't tolerate her grimy clothes another minute. The hot desert air washed over her bare skin, a warm, fresh caress on the backs of her knees, the small of her back, that made her nipples pinch into erect little nubs. She had never before been outside in the nude, and she felt positively decadent.

What if Chance saw her? If he was overcome with

lust by the sight of her naked body, nothing would happen that hadn't been going to happen, anyway. Not that it was likely he would be overcome, she thought wryly, smiling to herself, her curves were a long way from voluptuous. Still, if a man was faced with a naked, available woman—it could happen.

She poured a bottle of water over herself, then scooped up a handful of sand and began scrubbing. Rinsing off the sand was a matter of refilling the bottle several times. When she was finished she felt considerably refreshed and her skin was baby smooth. Maybe the skin-care industry should stop grinding up shells and rock for body scrubs, she thought, and just go for the sand.

Naked and wet, she could feel a slight breeze stirring the hot air, cooling her until she was actually comfortable. She didn't have a towel, so she let herself dry naturally while she washed her own clothes, then quickly dressed in the beige jeans and green T-shirt that she always carried. They were earth colors, colors that blended in well with vegetation and would make her more difficult to see if she had to disappear into the countryside. She would have opted for actual camouflage-patterned clothing, if that wouldn't have made her more noticeable in public. Her bra was wet from its scrubbing, so she hadn't put it back on, and the soft cotton of the T-shirt clung to her breasts, clearly revealing their shape and their soft jiggle when she walked, and the small peaks of her nipples. She wondered if Chance would notice.

"Hey," he said from behind her, his voice low and soft.

Startled, she whirled to face him. It was as if she had conjured him from her thoughts. He stood motionless about ten yards away, his eyes narrowed, his expression focused. His whiskey-coloured gaze went straight to her breasts. Oh, he noticed all right.

Her nipples got even harder, as if he had touched them.

She swallowed, trying to control a ridiculous twinge of her nerves. After all, he had already touched her breasts, and she had given him permission to do more. "How long have you been there?"

"A while." His eyelids were heavy, his voice a little rough. "I kept waiting for you to turn around, but you never did. I enjoyed the view, anyway."

Her breath hitched. "Thank you."

"You have the sweetest little ass I've ever seen."

Liquid heat moved through her. "You sweet talker, you," she said, not even half kidding. "When do I get a peep show?"

"Any time, honey." His tone was dark with sensual promise. "Any time." Then he smiled ruefully. "Any time except now. We need to move these clothes so I can set the trap up here. Since this is where the water is, this is where the game will come. I'll set the traps now and try to catch something for supper, then wash up after I clean whatever we catch—if we catch anything at all."

He wasn't exactly swept away with lust, but there was that reassuring steadfastness again, the ability to keep his priorities straight. In this situation, she didn't want Gonad the Barbarian; she wanted a man on whom she could depend to do the smart thing.

He began gathering the wet clothes off the rocks, and Sunny moved to help him. "Let me guess," she said. "The clothes still smell like humans."

"There's that, plus they're something different. Wild

animals are skittish whenever something new invades their territory.''

As they walked back to the overhang she asked, ''How long does it normally take to catch something in a trap?''

He shrugged. ''There's no 'normal' to it. I've caught game before within ten minutes of putting out the trap. Sometimes it takes days.''

She wasn't exactly looking forward to eating Peter Cottontail, but neither did she want another nutrition bar. It would be nice if some big fat chicken had gotten lost in the desert and just happened to wander into their trap. She wouldn't mind eating a chicken. After a moment of wishful thinking she resigned herself to rabbit—if they were lucky, that is. They would have to eat whatever Chance could catch.

When they reached ''home,'' which the overhang had become, they spread their clothes out on another assortment of hot rocks. The first items she had washed were already almost dry; the dry heat of the desert was almost as efficient as an electric clothes dryer.

When they had finished, Chance collected his two handmade traps and examined them one last time. Sunny watched him, seeing the same intensity in his eyes and body that she had noticed before. ''You're enjoying this, aren't you?'' she asked, only mildly surprised. This was, after all, the ultimate in primitive guy stuff.

He didn't look at her, but a tiny smile twitched the corners of his mouth. ''I guess I'm not all that upset. We're alive. We have food, water and shelter. I'm alone with a woman I've wanted from the first minute I saw her.'' He produced a badly crushed Baby Ruth candy bar from his hip pocket and opened the wrapper, then pinched off small pieces of it and put them in the traps.

Sunny was instantly diverted. "You're using a candy bar as bait?" she demanded in outraged tones. "Give me that! You can use my nutrition bar in the traps."

He grinned and evaded her as she tried to swipe the remainder of the candy bar. "The nutrition bar wouldn't be a good bait. No self-respecting rabbit would touch it."

"How long have you been hiding that Baby Ruth?"

"I haven't been hiding it. I found it in the plane when I got the rest of the stuff. Besides, it's melted from being in the plane all day."

"Melted, schmelted," she scoffed. "That doesn't affect chocolate."

"Ah." He nodded, still grinning. "You're one of those."

"One of those *what?*"

"Chocoholics."

"I am not," she protested, lifting her chin at him. "I'm a sweetaholic."

"Then why didn't you pack something sweet in that damn survival bag of yours, instead of something that tastes like dried grass?"

She scowled at him. "Because the idea is to stay alive. If I had a stash of candy, I'd eat it all the first day, then I'd be in trouble."

The golden brown gaze flicked at her, lashing like the tip of a whip. "When are you going to tell me why you packed survival gear for an overnight plane trip to Seattle?" He kept his tone light, but she felt the change of mood. He was dead serious about this, and she wondered why. What did it matter to him why she lugged that stuff everywhere she went? She could understand why he would be curious, but not insistent.

"I'm paranoid," she said, matching his tone in lightness. "I'm always certain there will be some sort of emergency, and I'm terrified of being unprepared."

His eyes went dark and flat. "Bull. Don't try to blow me off with lies."

Sunny might be good-natured almost to a fault, but she didn't back down. "I was actually trying to be polite and avoid telling you it's none of your business."

To her surprise, he relaxed. "That's more like it."

"What? Being rude?"

"Honest," he corrected. "If there are things you don't want to tell me, fine. I don't like it, but at least it was the truth. Considering our situation, we need to be able to totally rely on each other, and that demands trust. We have to be up front with each other, even when the truth isn't all sweetness and light."

She crossed her arms and narrowed her eyes, giving him an "I'm not buying this" look. "Even when you're just being nosy? I don't think so." She sniffed. "You're trying to psych me into spilling my guts."

"Is it working?"

"I felt a momentary twinge of guilt, but then logic kicked in."

She sensed he tried to fight it, but a smile crinkled his eyes, then moved down to curl the corners of that beautifully cut mouth. He shook his head. "You're going to cause me a lot of trouble," he said companionably as he picked up the traps and started back to their little water hole, if a trickle could be called a hole.

"Why's that?" she called to his back.

"Because I'm afraid I'm going to fall in love with you," he said over his shoulder as he walked around a jutting curve of the canyon wall and disappeared from sight.

Sunny's legs felt suddenly weak; her knees actually

wobbled, and she reached out to brace her hand on the wall. Had he really said that? Did he mean it? Would a man admit to something like that if he wasn't already emotionally involved?

Her heart was pounding as if she had been running. She could handle a lot of things most people never even thought of having to do, such as running for her life, but when it came to a romantic relationship she was a babe in the woods—or in the desert, to be accurate. She had never let a man get close enough to her to matter, because she had to be free to disappear without a moment's notice or regret. But this time she couldn't disappear; she couldn't go anywhere. This time she was in a lot more trouble than Chance was, because she was already in love—fully, falling-down-a-mine-shaft, terrifyingly in love.

The feeling was a stomach-tightening mixture of ecstasy and horror. The last thing she wanted to do was love him, but it was way too late to worry about that now. What had already begun had blossomed into full flower when he *didn't* make love to her after she had said he could. Something very basic and primal had recognized him then as her mate. He was everything she had ever wanted in a man, everything she had ever dreamed about in those half-formed thoughts she had never let fully surface into her consciousness, because she had always known that life wasn't for her.

But those circumstances held sway up in the world, not down here in this sunlit hole where they were the only two people alive. She felt raw inside, as if all her nerve endings and emotions had been stripped of their protective coverings, leaving her vulnerable to feelings she had always before been able to keep at bay. Those emotions kept sweeping over her in exhilarating waves, washing her into unknown territory. She wanted very much to protect herself, yet all the shields she had used over the years were suddenly useless.

Tonight they would become lovers, and one last protective wall would be irrevocably breached. Sex wasn't just sex to her; it was a commitment, a dedication of self, that would be part of her for the rest of her life.

She wasn't naive about what else making love with him could mean. She wasn't on any form of birth control, and while he might have a few condoms with him, they would quickly be used. The bell couldn't be unrung, and once they had made love they couldn't go back to a chaste relationship. What would she do if she got pregnant and they weren't rescued? She had to hold out hope that they wouldn't be down here forever, yet a small kernel of logic told her that it was possible they wouldn't be found. What would she do if she got pregnant even if they *were* rescued? A baby would be a major complication. How would she protect it? Somehow she couldn't see herself and Chance and a baby making a normal little all-American family; she would still be running, because that was the only way to be safe.

Keeping him at a distance, remaining platonic, was the only safe, sane thing to do. Unfortunately, she didn't seem to have a good grip on her sanity any longer. She felt as if those waves had carried her too far from shore for her to make it back now. For better or worse, all she could do was ride the current where it would take her.

Nevertheless, she tried. She tried to tell herself how stupidly irresponsible it was to risk getting pregnant under any circumstances, but particularly in *this* circumstance. Yes, women all over the world conceived and gave birth in primitive conditions, but for whatever reasons, cultural, economic or lack of brain power, they didn't have a choice. She did. All she had to do was say "no" and ignore all her feminine instincts shrieking "yes, yes."

When Chance returned she was still standing in the same spot she had been when he left, her expression stricken. He was instantly alert, reaching for the pistol tucked into his waistband at the small of his back. "What's wrong?"

"What if I get pregnant?" she asked baldly, indicating their surroundings with a sweep of her hand. "That would be stupid."

He looked surprised. "Aren't you on birth control?"

"No, and even if I was, I wouldn't have an unlimited supply of pills."

Chance rubbed his jaw, trying to think of a way around this one without tipping his hand. He knew they wouldn't be here for long, only until she gave him the information he needed on her father, but he couldn't tell her that. And why in the hell wasn't she on some form of birth control? All of the female agents he knew were on long-term birth control, and Sunny's circumstances weren't that different. "I have some condoms," he finally said.

She gave him a wry smile. "How many? And what will we do when they're gone?"

The last thing he wanted to do now was make her hostile. Deciding to gamble a little, to risk not being able to make love to her in exchange for keeping her trust, he put his arms around her and cradled her against his chest. She felt good in his arms, he thought, firm with muscle and yet soft in all the right places. He hadn't been able to stop thinking about the way she looked naked: her slender, graceful back and small waist, and the tight, heart-shaped—and heart-stopping—curve of her butt. Her legs were as slim and sleekly muscled as he had expected, and the thought of them wrapping around his waist brought him to full, instant arousal. He held her so close there was no way she could miss his condition, but he didn't thrust himself at her; let her think he was a gentleman. *He* knew better, but it was essential she didn't.

He kissed the top of her head and took that gamble. "We'll do whatever you want," he said gently. "I want you—you know that. I have about three dozen condoms—"

She jerked back, glaring at him. *"Three dozen?"* she asked, horrified. "You carry around three dozen condoms?"

There it was again, that urge to laugh. She could get to him faster than any other woman he knew. "I had just stocked up," he explained, keeping his tone mild.

"They have an expiration date, you know!"

He bit the inside of his jaw—hard. "Yeah, but they don't go bad as fast as milk. They're good for a couple of years."

She gave him a suspicious look. "How long will thirty-six condoms keep you supplied?"

He sighed. "Longer than you evidently think."

"Six months?"

He did some quick math. Six months, thirty-six condoms…he would have to have sex more than once a week. If he were in a monogamous relationship, that would be nothing, but for an unattached bachelor…

"Look," he said, letting frustration creep into both his voice and his expression, "with you, three dozen might last a week."

She looked startled, and he could see her doing some

quick math now. As she arrived at the answer and her eyes widened, he thrust his hand into her hair, cupping the back of her head and holding her still while he kissed her, ruthlessly using all his skill to arouse her. Her hands fluttered against his chest as if she wanted to push him away, but her hands wouldn't obey. He stroked his tongue into her mouth, slow and deep, feeling the answering touch of her tongue and the pressure of her lips. She tasted sweet, and the fresh smell of her was pure woman. He felt her nipples peak under the thin fabric of her T-shirt, and abruptly he had to touch them, feel them stabbing into his palm. He had his hand under her shirt almost before the thought formed. Her breasts were firm and round, her skin cool silk that warmed under his touch. Her nipples were hard little nubs that puckered even tighter when he touched them. She arched in his arms, her eyes closed, a low moan humming in her throat.

He had intended only to kiss her out of her sudden attack of responsibility. Instead, the pleasure of touching her went to his head like old whiskey, and suddenly he had to see her, taste her. With one swift motion he pulled her shirt up, baring her breasts, and tilted her back over his arm so the firm mounds were offered up to him in a sensual feast. He bent his dark head and closed his mouth over one tight, reddening nipple, rasping his tongue over it before pressing it against the roof of his mouth and sucking. He heard the sound she made this time, the cry of a sharply aroused woman, a wild, keening sound that went straight to his loins. He was dimly aware of her nails biting into his shoulders, but the pain was small, and nothing in comparison with the urgency that had seized him. Blood thundered in his ears, roared through his veins. He wanted her with a savage intensity that rode him with sharp spurs, urging him to take instead of seduce.

Grimly he reached for his strangely elusive self-control. Only the experience and training of his entire adulthood, spent in the trenches of a dirty, covert, ongoing war, gave him the strength to rein himself in. Reluctantly he eased his clamp on her nipple, giving the turgid little bud an apologetic lick. She quivered in his arms, whimpering, her golden hair spilling back as she hung helplessly in his grasp, and he almost lost it again.

Damn it all, he couldn't wait.

Swiftly he dipped down and snagged the blanket from the ground, then hooked his right arm under her knees and lifted her off her feet, carrying her out into the sunlight. The golden glow of the lowering sun kissed her skin with a subtle sheen, deepened the glitter of her hair. Her breasts were creamy, with the delicate blue tracery of her veins showing through the pale skin, and her small nipples were a sweet rosy color, shining wetly, standing out in hard peaks. "God, you're beautiful," he said in a low, rough voice.

He set her on her feet; she swayed, her lovely eyes dazed with need. He spread out the blanket and reached for her before that need began to cool. He wanted her scorching hot, so ready for him that she would fight him for completion.

He stripped the T-shirt off over her head, dropped it on the blanket, and hooked his fingers in the waistband of her jeans. A quick pop of the snap, a jerk on the tab of the zipper, and the jeans slid down her thighs.

Her hands gripped his forearms. "Chance?" She sounded strangely uncertain, a little hesitant. If she changed her mind now—

He kissed her, slow and deep, and thumbed her nipplcs. She made that little humming sound again, rising on her toes to press against him. He pushed her jeans down to her ankles, wrapped both arms around her and carried her down to the blanket.

She gasped, her head arching back. "Here? Now?"

"I can't wait." That was nothing more than the hard truth. He couldn't wait until dark, until they had politely crawled into the tent together as if they were following some script. He wanted her now, in the sunlight, naked and warm and totally spontaneous. He stripped her panties down and freed her ankles from the tangle of jeans and underwear.

It seemed she didn't want to wait, either. She tugged at his shirt, pushing it up. Impatiently he gripped the hem and wrenched the garment off over his head, then spread her legs and eased his weight down on her, settling into the notch of her open thighs.

She went very still, her eyes widening as she stared up at him. He fished in his pocket for the condom he'd put there earlier, then lifted himself enough to unfasten his jeans and shove them down. He donned the condom with an abrupt, practiced motion. When he came back down to her, she braced her hands against his shoulders as if she wanted to preserve some small distance between them. But any distance was too much; he grasped her hands in one of his and pulled them over her head, pinning them to the blanket and arching her breasts against him. With his free hand he reached between them and guided his hard length to the soft, wet entrance of her body.

Sunny quivered, helpless in his grasp. She had never before felt so vulnerable, or so alive. His passion wasn't controlled and gentle, the way she had expected; it was fierce and tumultuous, buffeting her with its force. He held her down, dwarfed her with his big muscular body, and she trembled as she waited for the hard thrust of penetration. She was ready for him, oh, so ready. She ached with need; she burned with it. She wanted to beg him to hurry, but she couldn't make her lungs work. He reached down, and she felt the brush of his knuckles between her legs, then the stiff, hot length of him pushing against her opening.

Everything in her seemed to tighten, coiling, focusing on that intimate intrusion. The soft flesh between her legs began to burn and sting as the blunt pressure stretched her. He pushed harder, and the pressure became pain. Wild frustration filled her. She wanted him *now,* inside her, easing the ache and tension, stroking her back into feverish pleasure.

He started to draw back, but she couldn't let him, couldn't bear losing what his touch had promised. She had denied herself so many things, but not this, not now. She locked her legs around his and lifted her hips, fiercely impaling herself, thrusting past the resistance of her body.

She couldn't hold back the thin cry that tore from her throat. Shock robbed her muscles of strength, and she went limp on the blanket.

Chance moved over her, his broad shoulders blotting out the sun. He was a dark, massive silhouette, his shape blurred by her tears. He murmured a soft reassurance even as he probed deeper, and deeper still, until his full length was inside her.

He released her hands to cradle her in both arms. Sunny clung to his shoulders, holding as tight as she could, because without his strength she thought she might fly apart. She hadn't realized this would hurt so much, that he would feel so thick and hot inside her, or go so deep. He was invading all of her, taking over her body and commanding its responses, even her breathing, her heartbeat, the flow of blood through her veins.

He moved gently at first, slowly, angling his body so he applied pressure where she needed it most. He did things to her with his hands, stroking her into a return of pleasure. He kissed her, leisurely exploring her with his tongue. He touched her nipples, sucked them, nibbled on the side of her neck. His tender attention gradually coaxed her into response, into an instinctive motion as her hips rose and fell in time with his thrusts. She still clung to his shoulders, but in need rather than desperation. An overwhelming heat swept over her, and she heard herself panting.

He pushed her legs farther apart and thrust deeper, harder, faster. Sensation exploded in her, abruptly convulsing her flesh. She writhed beneath him, unable to hold back the short, sharp cries that surged upward, past her constricted throat. The pounding rhythm wouldn't let the spasms abate; they kept shuddering through her until she was sobbing, fighting him, wanting release, wanting more, and finally—when his hard body stiffened and began shuddering wanting nothing.

Chapter 8

A virgin. Sunny Miller had been a *virgin*. He tried to think, when he could think at all, what the possible ramifications were, but none of that seemed important right now. Of far more immediate urgency was how to comfort a woman whose first time had been on a blanket spread over the rough ground, in broad daylight, with a man who hadn't even taken off his boots.

He lay sprawled on his back beside her on the blanket. She had turned on her side away from him, curling in on herself while visible tremors shook her slender, naked body. Moving was an effort—*breathing* was an effort— as he pulled off the condom and tossed it away. He had climaxed so violently that he felt dazed. And if it affected him so strongly, with his experience, what was she thinking? Feeling? Had she anticipated the pain, or been shocked by it?

He knew she had climaxed. She had been as aroused as he; when he had started to pull back in stunned re-

alization, she had hooked her legs around his and forced
the entry herself. He had seen the shock in her eyes as
he penetrated her, felt the reverberations in her flesh.
And he had watched her face as he carefully aroused
her, holding himself back with ruthless control until he
felt the wild clenching of her loins. Then nothing had
been able to hold him back, and he had exploded in his
own gut-wrenching release.

For a woman of twenty-nine to remain a virgin, she
had to have some strongly held reason for doing so.
Sunny had willingly, but not lightly, surrendered her
chastity to him. He felt humbled, and honored, and he
was scared as hell. He hadn't been easy with her, either
in the process or the culmination. At first glance the fact
that she had climaxed might make everything all right
with her, but he knew better. She didn't have the experience to handle the sensual violence her body and
emotions had endured. She needed holding, and reassuring, until she stopped shaking and regained her equilibrium.

He put his hand on her arm and tugged her over onto
her back. She didn't actively resist, but she was stiff,
uncoordinated. She was pale, her eyes unusually brilliant, as if she fought tears. He cradled her head on his
arm and leaned over her, giving her the attention and
the contact he knew she needed. She glanced quickly up
at him, then away, and a surge of color pinkened her
cheeks.

He was charmed by the blush. Gently he smoothed
his hand up her bare torso, stroking her belly, trailing
his fingers over her breasts. The lower curves of her
breasts bore the marks of his beard stubble. He soothed
them with his tongue, taking care not to add more abra-
sions, and made a mental note to shave when he washed.

Something needed to be said, but he didn't know what. He had talked his way into strongholds, drug dens and government offices; he had an uncanny knack for making a lightning assessment of any given person and situation, and then saying exactly the right thing to get the reaction he wanted. But from the moment he had seen Sunny, lust had gotten in the way of his usual expertise. No amount of prep work could have prepared him for the impact of her sparkling eyes and bright smile, or told him he could be so disarmed by a sense of humor. "Sunny" was a very apt nickname for her.

Just now his sunshine was very quiet, almost stricken, as if she regretted their intimacy. And he couldn't bear it. He had lost count, over the years, of the women who had tried to cling to him after the sex act was finished and he slipped away, both physically and mentally, but he couldn't bear it that this one woman wasn't trying to hold him. For some reason, whether this was simply too much too soon or for some deeper reason, she was trying to hold her distance from him. She wasn't curling in his arms, sighing with repletion; she was retreating behind an invisible wall, the one that had been there from the beginning.

Everything in him rejected the idea. A primitive, possessive rage swept over him. She was his, and he would not let her go. His muscles tightened in a renewed surge of lust, and he mounted her, sliding into the tight, swollen clasp of her sheath. She inhaled sharply, the shock of his entry jarring her out of her malaise. She wedged her hands between them and sank her nails into his chest, but she didn't try to push him away. Her legs came up almost automatically, wrapping around his hips. He caught her thighs and adjusted them higher, around his waist. "Get used to it," he said, more harshly than he'd intended. "To me. To this. To us. Because I won't let you pull away from me."

Her lips trembled, but he had her full attention now. "Even for your own sake?" she whispered, distress leaching the blue undertones from her eyes and leaving them an empty gray.

He paused for a fraction of a second, wondering if she was referring to her father. "Especially for that," he replied, and set himself to the sweet task of arousing her. This time was totally for her; he wooed her with a skill that went beyond sexual experience. His extensive training in the martial arts had taught him how to cripple with a touch, kill with a single blow, but it had also taught him all the places on the human body that were exquisitely sensitive to pleasure. The backs of her knees and thighs, the delicate arches of her feet, the lower curve of her buttocks, all received their due attention. Slowly she came alive under him, a growing inner wetness easing his way. She began to move in time with his leisurely thrusts, rising up to meet him. He stroked the cluster of nerves in the small of her back and was rewarded by the reflexive arch that took him deeper into her.

She sighed, her lips parted, her eyes closed. Her cheeks glowed; her lips were puffy and red. He saw all the signs of her arousal and whispered encouragement. Her head tossed to the side, and her hardened nipples stabbed against his chest. Gently, so gently, he bit the tender curve where her neck met her shoulder.

She cried out and began climaxing, her peak catching him by surprise. So did his own. He hadn't meant to climax, but the delicate inner clench and release of her body sent pleasure roaring through him, bursting out of control.

He tried to stop, tried to withdraw; his body simply wouldn't obey. Instead, he thrust deep and shuddered wildly as his seed spurted from him into the hot, moist depths of her. He heard his own deep, rough cry; then both time and thought stopped, and all that was left of him sank down on her in a heavy sprawl.

Shadow had crept across the canyon floor when he wrapped her in the blanket and carried her back to the sheltering overhang. The surrounding rock blocked the sun during the day, but it also absorbed its heat so that at night, when the temperature dropped, it was noticeably warmer in their snug little niche than it was outside. Sunny yawned, drowsy with satisfaction, and rested her head on his shoulder. "I can walk," she said mildly, though she made no effort to slide her feet to the ground.

"Hey, I'm doing my macho act here," he protested. "Don't ruin it."

She tilted her head back to look at him. "You aren't acting, though, are you?"

"No," he admitted, and earned a chuckle from her.

Time had gotten away from him while they drifted in the sleepy aftermath of passion. The sun was so far down in the sky that only the upper rim of the canyon was lit, the reds and golds and purples of the rock catching fire in the sunset, while the sky had taken on a deep violet hue.

"I'm going to check the traps while there's still a few minutes of light left," he said as he deposited her on the ground. "Sit tight. I won't be long."

Sunny sat tight for about two seconds after he disappeared from view, then bounced to her feet. Quickly she washed and dressed, needing the protection of her clothing. She had the uneasy feeling that nothing was the same as it had been before Chance carried her out into the sunlight. She had been prepared for the lovemaking, but not for that overwhelming assault on her senses. She had hoped for pleasure, and instead found something so much more powerful that she couldn't control it.

And most of all, Chance had revealed himself for the marauder he was.

She had seen glimpses of it before, in moments when the force of his personality broke through his control. She should have realized then; one didn't bolt a steel gate on an empty room. His control had given her the rare, luxurious feeling of safety, and she had been so beguiled that she had ignored the power that gate held constrained, or what would happen if it ever broke loose. This afternoon, she had found out.

He had said he'd been in the Army Rangers. That should have told her everything she needed to know about the kind of man he was. She could only think she'd let the stress of the situation, and her worry about Margreta, blind her to his true nature.

A shiver rippled down her spine, a totally sensual re-action as she remembered the tumultuous hour—or hours—on the blanket. She had been helpless, totally blindsided by the force of her reaction. She had known from the beginning that she responded to him as she never had before to any man, but she still hadn't been prepared for such a complete upheaval of her senses. He wasn't the only one accustomed to control; her very life had depended on her control of any given situation, and with Chance, she had found that she couldn't control either him or herself.

She had never been more terrified in her life.

The way she had felt about him before was nothing compared to now. It wasn't just the sex, which had been so much more intense and harsh than she had ever imagined. No, it was the part of his character he had revealed, the part that he had tried to keep hidden, that called to her so strongly she knew only her own death would end the love she felt for him. Chance was one of a very special breed of men, a warrior. All the little pieces of him she had sensed were now settled into place, forming the picture of a man who would always have something wild and ruthless inside him, a man willing to put himself at risk, step into the line of fire, to protect what he loved. He was the complete antithesis of her father, whose life was devoted wholly to destruction.

Sunny hadn't had a choice in a lot of the sacrifices of her life. Their mother had given her and Margreta away in an effort to save them, but hadn't been able to completely sever herself from her daughters' lives. Instead, she had taught them all her hard-learned skills, taught them how to hide, to disappear—and, if necessary, how to fight. By necessity, Pamela Vickery Hauer had become an expert in her own brand of guerrilla warfare. Whenever she thought it safe she would visit, and the kindly Millers would go out of their way to give her time with her girls.

When Sunny was sixteen, Pamela's luck had finally run out. Their father's network was extensive, and he had many more resources at his disposal than his fugitive wife could command. Logically, it had been only a matter of time before he found her. And when she was finally run to ground, Pamela had killed herself rather than take the chance he would, by either torture or drugs, be able to wring their location from her.

That was Sunny's legacy, a life living in shadows, and a courageous mother who had killed herself in order to protect her children. No one had asked her if this was the life she wanted; it was the life she had, so she had made the best of it she could.

Nor had it been her choice to live apart from Margreta; that had been her sister's decision. Margreta was older; she had her own demons to fight, her own battles to wage, and she had never been as adept at the survival skills taught by their mother as Sunny had been. So Sunny had lost her sister, and when the Millers died, first Hal and then Eleanor, she had been totally alone. The calls on her cell phone from Margreta were the only contact she had, and she knew Margreta was content to leave it at that.

She didn't think she had the strength to give up Chance, too. That was why she was terrified to the point of panic, because her very presence endangered his life. Her only solace was that because he was the man he was, he was very tough and capable, more able to look after himself.

She took a deep breath, trying not to anticipate trouble. If and when they got out of this canyon, then she would decide what to do.

Because she was too nervous to sit still, she checked the clothes she had washed out and found they were already dry. She gathered them off the various rocks where they had spread them, and though the little chore had taken only minutes, by the time she walked back to the overhang there was barely enough light for her to see.

Chance hadn't taken the flashlight with him, she remembered. It was a moonless night; if he didn't get back within the next few minutes, he wouldn't be able to see.

The fire had been kept smoldering all day, to maximize the smoke and conserve their precious store of wood, but now she quickly added more sticks to bring up a good blaze, both for her own sake and so he would have the fire as a beacon. The flickering firelight penetrated the darkness of the overhang, sending patterns dancing against the rock wall. She searched through their belongings until she found the flashlight, to have it at hand in case she had to search for him.

Total blackness came suddenly, as if Mother Nature had dropped her petticoats over the land. Sunny stepped to the front of the overhang. "Chance!" she called, then paused to listen.

The night wasn't silent. There were rustlings, the whispers of the night things as they crept about their business. A faint breeze stirred the scrub brush, sounding like dry bones rattling together. She listened carefully, but didn't hear an answering call.

"Chance!" She tried again, louder this time. Nothing. "Damn it," she muttered, and flashlight in hand set off for the deep end of the canyon where their life-giving water trickled out of a crack in the rock.

She walked carefully, checking where she put her feet. A second encounter with a snake was more than she could handle in one day. As she walked she periodically called his name, growing more irritated by the moment. Why didn't he answer her? Surely he could hear her by now; sound carried in the thin, dry air.

A hard arm caught her around the waist and swung her up against an equally hard body. She shrieked in alarm, the sound cut off by a warm, forceful mouth. Her head tilted back under the pressure, and she grabbed his shoulders for support. He took his time, teasing her with his tongue, kissing her until the tension left her body and she was moving fluidly against him.

When he lifted his head his breathing was a little ragged. Sunny felt obliged to complain about his treatment of her. "You scared me," she accused, though her voice sounded more sultry than sulky.

"You got what you deserved. I told you to sit tight." He kissed her again, as if he couldn't help himself.

"Is this part of the punishment?" she murmured when he came up for air.

"Yeah," he said, and she felt him smile against her temple.

"Do it some more."

He obliged, and she felt the magic fever begin burning again deep inside her. She ached all over from his previous lovemaking; she shouldn't feel even a glimmer of desire so soon, and yet she did. She wanted to feel all the power of his superbly conditioned body, take him inside her and hold him close, feel him shake as the pleasure overwhelmed him just as it did her.

Finally he tore his mouth from hers, but she could feel his heart pounding against her, feel the hard ridge in his jeans. "Have mercy," he muttered. "I won't have a chance to starve to death. I'm going to die of exhaustion."

Starving reminded her of the traps, because she was very hungry. "Did you catch a rabbit?" she asked, her tone full of hope.

"No rabbit, just a scrawny bird." He held up his free hand, and she saw that he held the plucked carcass of a bird that was quite a bit smaller than the average chicken.

"That isn't the Roadrunner, is it?"

"What's this thing you have with imaginary animals? No, it isn't a roadrunner. Try to be a little more grateful."

"Then what is it?"

"Bird," he said succinctly. "After I spit it and turn

it over the flames for a while, it'll be roasted bird. That's all that matters.''

Her stomach growled. "Well, okay. As long as it isn't the Roadrunner. He's my favorite cartoon character. After Bullwinkle.''

He began laughing. "When did you see those old cartoons? I didn't think they were on anywhere now.''

"They're all on disk," she said. "I rented them from my local video store.''

He took her arm, and they began walking back to camp, chatting and laughing about their favorite cartoons. They both agreed that the slick animated productions now couldn't match the older cartoons for sheer comedy, no matter how realistic the modern ones were. Sunny played the flashlight beam across their path as they walked, watching for snakes.

"By the way, why were you calling me?" Chance asked suddenly.

"It's dark, in case you didn't notice. You didn't carry the flashlight with you.''

He made a soft, incredulous sound. "You were coming to *rescue* me?''

She felt a little embarrassed. Of course, a former ranger could find his way back to camp in the dark. "I wasn't thinking," she admitted.

"You were thinking too much," he corrected, and hugged her to his side.

They reached their little camp. The fire she had built up was still sending little tongues of flame licking around the remnants of the sticks. Chance laid the bird on a rock, swiftly fashioned a rough spit from the sticks, and sharpened the end of another stick with his pocket knife. He skewered the bird with that stick, and set it in the notches of the spit, then added some small sticks to the fire. Soon the bird was dripping sizzling juice into the flames, which leaped higher in response. The delicious smell of cooking meat made her mouth water.

She shoved a flat rock closer to the fire and sat down, watching him turn the bird. She was close enough to feel the heat on her arms; as chilly as the night was already, it was difficult to remember that just a few short hours ago the heat had been scorching. She had camped out only once before, but the circumstances had been nothing like this. For one thing, she had been alone.

The amber glow of the flames lit the hard angles of his face. He had washed up while he was gone, she saw; his hair was still a little damp. He had shaved, too. She smiled to herself.

He looked up and saw her watching him, and a wealth of knowledge, of sensual awareness, flashed between them. "Are you all right?" he asked softly.

"I'm fine." She had no idea how her face glowed as she wrapped her arms around her legs and rested her chin on her drawn-up knees.

"Are you bleeding?"

"Not now. And it was only a little, at first," she added hastily when his eyes narrowed in concern.

He returned his gaze to the bird, watching as he carefully turned it. "I wish I had known."

She wished he didn't know now. The reasons for her recently lost virginity weren't something she wanted to dissect. "Why?" she asked, injecting a light note into her tone. "Would you have been noble and stopped?"

"Hell, no," he said. "I'd have gone about it a little differently, is all."

Now, that was interesting. "What would have been different?"

"How rough I was. How long I took."

"You took long enough," she assured him, smiling. "Both times."

"I could have made it better for you."

"How about for you?"

His dark gaze flashed upward, and he gave a rueful smile. "Sweetheart, if it had been any better for me, my heart would have given out."

"Ditto."

He turned the bird again. "I didn't wear a condom the second time."

"I know." The evidence had been impossible to miss.

Their gazes met and locked again, and again they were linked by that silent communication. He might have made her pregnant. He knew it, and she knew it.

"How's the timing?"

She rocked her hand back and forth. "Borderline." The odds were in their favor, she figured, but it wasn't a risk she wanted to take again.

"If we weren't stuck here—" he began, then shrugged.

"What?"

"I wouldn't mind."

Desire surged through her, and she almost jumped his bones right then. She got a tight grip on herself, literally, and fought to stay seated. Hormones were sneaky devils, she thought, ready to undermine her common sense just because he mentioned wanting to make her pregnant.

"Neither would I," she admitted, and watched to see if he had the same reaction. Color flared high on his carved cheekbones, and a muscle in his jaw flexed. His hand tightened on the spit until his knuckles were white. Yep, it went both ways, she thought, fascinated by his battle to remain where he was.

When he judged the bird was done, he took the skewer

off the spit and kicked another rock over to rest beside hers, then sat down on it. With his pocket knife he cut a strip of meat and held it out to her. "Careful, don't burn yourself," he warned as she reached eagerly for the meat.

She juggled the strip back and forth in her hands, blowing on it to cool it. When she could hold it, she took her first tentative bite. Her taste buds exploded with the taste of wood and smoke and roasted fowl. "Oh, that's good," she moaned, chewing slowly to get every ounce of flavor.

Chance cut off a strip for himself and took his first bite, looking as satisfied as she with their meal. They chewed in silence for a while. He was careful to divide the meat equally, until she was forced to stop eating way before she was satisfied. He was so much bigger than she was that if they each ate the same amount, he would be short-changed.

He knew what she was doing, of course. "You're taking care of me again," he observed. "You're hell on my image, you know that? I'm supposed to be taking care of you."

"You're a lot bigger than I am. You need larger portions."

"Let me worry about the food, sweetheart. We won't starve. There's more game to catch, and tomorrow I'll look for some edible plants to round out our diet."

"Bird and bush," she said lightly. "What all the trendy people are eating these days."

Her quip made him grin. He persuaded her to eat a little more of the meat, then they finished off one of the remaining nutrition bars. Their hunger appeased, they began getting ready to turn in for the night.

He banked the fire while she got the tent ready. They

brushed their teeth and made one last nature call, just like old married folks, she thought in amusement. Their "home" wasn't much, really nothing more than a niche in the rock, but their preparations for the night struck her as very domestic—until he said, "Do you want to wear my shirt tonight? It would be more like a nightgown on you than the shirt you're wearing."

There was nothing the least bit tamed in the way he was looking at her. Her heartbeat picked up in speed, and the now familiar heat began spreading through her. That was all he had to do, she thought; one look and she was aroused. He had taught her body well during the short time she had been sprawled beneath him on the blanket. Now that she knew exactly how it felt to take his hard length inside her, she craved the sensation. She wanted that convulsive peak of pleasure, even though it had frightened her with its intensity. She hadn't realized she would feel as if she were flying apart, as if her soul was being wrenched from her body. In a blinding, paralyzing moment of clarity, she knew that no other man in the world would be able to do that for her, to her. He was the One for her, capital *O*, big letter, underlined and italicized. The *One*. She would never again be whole without him.

She must have looked stricken, because suddenly he was by her side, supporting her with an arm around her waist as he gently but inexorably guided her to the tent. He would be considerate, she realized, but he didn't intend to be refused.

She cleared her throat, searching for her equilibrium. "You'll need your shirt to keep warm—"

"You're joking, right?" He smiled down at her, the corners of his eyes crinkling. "Or did you think we were through for the night?"

She couldn't help smiling back. "That never crossed my mind. I just thought you'd need it *afterward.*"

"I don't think so," he said, his hands busy unsnapping her jeans.

They were both naked and inside the tent in record time. He switched off the flashlight to save the batteries, and the total darkness closed around them, just as it had the night before. Making love when one was going totally by feel somehow heightened the other senses, she found. She was aware of the calluses on his hands as he stroked her, of the heady male scent of his skin, of the powerful muscles that bunched under her own exploring hands. His taste filled her; his kisses were a feast. She reveled in the smooth firmness of his lips, the sharp edges of his teeth; she rubbed his nipples and felt them contract under her fingers. She loved the harsh groan he gave when she cupped the soft, heavy sacs between his legs, and the way they tightened even as she held them.

She was shocked when she closed her hand around his pulsing erection. How on earth had she ever taken him inside her? The long, thick column ended in a smooth, bulbous flare, the tip of which was wet with fluid. Entranced, she curled down until she could take the tip in her mouth and lick the fluid away.

He let out an explosive curse and tumbled her on her back, reversing their positions. The confines of the small tent restricted their movement, but he managed the shift with his usual powerful grace.

She laughed, full of wonder at the magic between them, and draped her arms around his neck as he settled on top of her. "Didn't you like it?"

"I almost came," he growled. "What do you think?"

"I think I'll have my way with you yet. I may have

to overpower you and tie you up, but I think I can handle the job.''

"I'm positive of it. Let me know when you're going to overpower me, so I can have my clothes off.''

That afternoon, caught in the whirlpool of his love-making, she wouldn't have believed she would be so at ease with him now, that they could indulge in this sensual teasing. She wouldn't have believed how naturally her thighs parted to accommodate his hips, or how comfortable it was, as if nature had designed them to fit together just so. Actually nature had; she just hadn't realized it until now.

He gave her a taste of her own medicine, kissing his way down her body until his hair brushed the insides of her thighs and she discovered a torture so sweet she shattered. When she could breathe again, when the colored pinpoints of light stopped flashing against her closed eyelids, he kissed her belly and laid his head on the pillowing softness. "My God, you're easy," he whispered.

She managed a strangled sound that was almost a laugh. "I guess I am. For you, anyway.''

"Just for me." The dark tones of masculine possessiveness and triumph underlaid the words.

"Just for you," she whispered in agreement.

He put on a condom and slid into place between her thighs. She fought back a cry; she was sore and swollen, and he was big. He moved gently back and forth until she accepted him more easily and the discomfort faded, but gradually his thrusts quickened, became harder. Even then she sensed he was holding himself back to keep from hurting her. When he climaxed, he pulled back so only half his length was inside her, and held himself there while shudders racked his strong body.

Afterward, he tugged his T-shirt on over her head, immediately enveloping her in his scent. The roomy garment came halfway to her knees—or it would have if he hadn't bunched it around her waist. He cradled her in his arms, one big hand on her bare bottom to keep her firmly against him. He used her rolled-up cardigan for a pillow, and she used him. Oh, this was wonderful.

"Is Sunny your real name, or is it a nickname?" he asked sleepily, his lips brushing her hair.

Even as relaxed as she was, as sated, a twinge of caution made her hesitate. She never told anyone her real name. It took her a moment to remember that none of that made any difference here now. "It's a nickname," she murmured. "My real name is Sonia, but I've never used it. Sonia Ophelia Gabrielle."

"Good God." He kissed her. "Sunny suits you. So you're saddled with four names, huh?"

"Yep. I never use the middle ones, though. What about you? What's your middle name?"

"I don't have one. It's just Chance."

"Really? You aren't lying to me because it's something awful, like Eustace?"

"Cross my heart."

She settled herself more comfortably against him. "I suppose it balances out. I have four names, you have two—together, we average three."

"How about that."

She could hear a smile in his voice now. She rewarded him with a small, sneaky pinch that made him jump. His retaliation ended, a long time later, in the use of another condom.

Sunny went to sleep to the knowledge that she was happier now, with Chance, than she had ever before been in her life.

Chapter 9

The next morning the traps were empty. Sunny struggled with her disappointment. After such an idyllic, pleasure-filled night, the day should have been just as wonderful. A nice hot, filling breakfast would have been perfect.

"Could you shoot something?" she asked as she chewed half of one of the tasteless nutrition bars. "We have eight of these bars left." If they each ate a bar a day, that meant they would be out of food in four days.

In three days, Margreta would call.

Sunny pushed that thought away. Whether or not they got out of here in time for her to answer Margreta's call was something she couldn't control. Food was a more immediate problem.

Chance narrowed his eyes as he scanned the rim of the canyon, as if looking for a way out. "I have fifteen rounds in the pistol, and no extra cartridges. I'd rather save them for emergencies, since there's no telling how long we'll be here. Besides, a 9mm bullet would tear a rabbit to pieces and wouldn't leave enough left of a bird for us to eat. Assuming I could hit a bird with a pistol shot, that is.''

She wasn't worried about his marksmanship. He was probably much better with a rifle, but with his military background, he would be more than competent with the pistol. She looked down at her hands. ''Would a .38 be better?''

''It isn't as powerful, so for small game, yeah, it would be better. Not great, but better—but I have a 9mm, so it's a moot point.''

''I have one,'' she said softly.

His head whipped around. Something dangerous flashed in his eyes. ''What did you say?''

She nodded toward her bag. ''I have a .38.''

He looked in the direction of her gaze, then back at her. His expression was like flint. ''Would you like to tell me,'' he said very deliberately, ''just how you happen to have a pistol of any kind with you? You were on a commercial flight. How did you get past the scanners?''

She didn't like giving away all her secrets, not even to Chance. A lifetime on the run had ingrained caution into her very bones, and she had already given him more of herself than she ever had anyone else. Still, they were in this together. ''I have some special containers.''

''Where?'' he snapped. ''I saw you unpack everything in your bag and there weren't any—ah, hell. The hair spray can, right?''

Unease skittered along her spine. Why was he angry? Even if he was a stickler for rules and regulations, which she doubted, he should be glad they had an extra weapon, no matter how they came by it. She straightened her shoulders. ''And the blow-dryer.''

He stood over her like an avenging angel, his jaw set. ''How long have you been smuggling weapons on board airplanes?''

''Every time I've flown,'' she said coolly, standing up. She was damned if she would let him tower over her as if she was a recalcitrant child. He still towered over, just not as much. ''I was sixteen the first time.''

She walked over to the bag and removed the pertinent items. Chance leaned down and snagged the can of spray from her hands. He took the cap off and examined the nozzle, then pointed it away from him and depressed it. A powder-fine mist of spray shot out.

''It's really hair spray,'' she said. ''Just not much of it.'' She took the can and deftly unscrewed the bottom. A short barrel slid out of the can into her hands. Putting it aside, she lifted the hair-dryer and took it apart with the same deft twist, yielding the remaining parts of the pistol. She assembled it with the ease of someone who had done the task so often she could do it in her sleep, then fed the cartridges into the magazine, snapped it into place, reversed the pistol and presented it to him butt-first.

He took it, his big hand almost swallowing the small weapon. ''What in *hell* are you doing with a weapon?'' he bit out.

''The same thing you are, I imagine.'' She walked away from him and missed the look of shock that crossed his face. With her back to him she said, ''I carry it for self-protection. Why do you carry yours?''

''I charter my plane to a lot of different people, most of whom I don't know. I fly into some isolated areas sometimes. And my weapon is licensed." He hurled the words at her like rocks. "Is yours?"

"No," she said, unwilling to lie. "But I'm a single woman who travels alone, carrying packages valuable enough that a courier service is hired to deliver them. The people I deliver the packages to are strangers. Think about it. I'd have to be a fool not to carry some means of protection." That was the truth, as far as it went.

"If your reason for carrying is legitimate, then why don't you have a license?"

She felt as if she were being interrogated, and she didn't like it. The tender, teasing lover of the night was gone, and in his place was someone who sounded like a prosecutor.

She had never applied for a license to carry a concealed weapon because she didn't want any background checks in the national data system, didn't want to bring herself to the notice of anyone in officialdom.

"I have my reasons," she retorted, keeping her tone very deliberate.

"And you aren't going to tell me what they are, right?" He threw her a look that was almost sulfuric in its fury and stalked off in the direction of the traps. His stalking, like everything else he did, was utterly graceful—and completely silent.

"Good riddance, Mr. Sunshine," she hurled at his back. It was a childish jab, but she felt better afterward. Sometimes a little childishness was just what the doctor ordered.

With nothing better to do, she set off in the opposite direction, toward the plane, to gather more sticks and twigs for the all-important fire. If he tried to keep her pistol when they got out of here—and they *would* get out, she had to keep hoping—then it would be war.

* * *

Chance examined the compact pistol in his hand. It was unlike any he had ever seen before, for the simple reason that it hadn't come from any manufacturer. A gunsmith, a skilled one, had made this weapon. It bore no serial number, no name, no indication of where or when it was made. It was completely untraceable.

He couldn't think of any good reason for Sunny to have it, but he could think of several bad ones.

After yesterday, he had been more than halfway convinced she was innocent, that she was in no way involved with her father. Stupid of him, but he had equated chastity with honor. Just because a woman didn't sleep around didn't mean she was a fine, upstanding citizen. All it meant was that, for whatever reason, she hadn't had sex.

He knew better. He was far better acquainted with the blackness of the human soul than with its goodness, because he had chosen to live in the sewers. Hell, he came from the sewers; he should be right at home there, and most of the time he was. The blackness of his own soul was always there, hidden just a few layers deep, and he was always aware of it. He used to make his way in the dangerous world he had chosen, shaped it into a weapon to be used in defense of his country and, ultimately, his family. And being on such intimate terms with hell, with the twisted evil humans could visit on one another, he should know that golden hair and bright, sparkling eyes didn't necessarily belong on an angel. Shakespeare had hit the nail on the head when he warned the world against smiling villains.

It was just—*damn* it, Sunny got to him. She had slipped right past defenses he would have sworn were impregnable, and she had done it so easily they might as well not have been there at all. He wanted her, and so he had almost convinced himself that she was innocent.

Almost. There was just too much about her that didn't add up, and now there was this untraceable pistol that she smuggled on board airplanes, concealed in some very effective but simple containers. Airport scanners would show metal, but if a security guard was suspicious enough to check, he or she would find only the normal female styling aids. The hair spray can actually sprayed, and he didn't doubt the blow-dryer would work, too.

If Sunny could get a pistol on board a plane, then others could, too. He went cold at the thought of how many weapons must be flying around at any given time. Airport security wasn't his line of work, but damn if he wasn't going to make it a point to kick some asses over this.

He shoved his anger aside so he could concentrate on this assignment. He hoped he hadn't blown it by losing his temper with her, but his disillusionment had been too sharp for him to contain. The pleasure of the night they had just spent together should more than outweigh their first argument. Her inexperience with men worked against her; she would be easy to manipulate, where a seasoned veteran of the mattress wars would be more wary and blasé about their lovemaking. He still held all the trump cards, and soon he would be playing them.

He reached a particular point in the canyon and positioned himself so he was in the deepest morning shadows. Sunny couldn't catch him unawares here, and he had a clear line of sight to a certain rock on the rim of the canyon. He took a laser light from his pocket, a pencil-thin tube about two inches long that, when clicked, emitted an extraordinarily bright finger of light.

He aimed it at the rock on the rim and began clicking, sending dashes of light in the code he and Zane had agreed on at the beginning of the plan. Every day he signalled Zane, both to let him know that everything was all right and that they shouldn't be rescued yet.

There was an answering flash, message received. No matter how closely he watched that rock, he never saw any movement, though he knew Zane would have immediately pulled back. He himself was damn good at moving around undetected, but Zane was extraordinary even for a SEAL. There was no one else on this earth Chance would rather have beside him in a fight than Zane.

That mission accomplished, Chance settled down in some cover where he could watch the trickle of water. Since the traps hadn't been productive overnight, he really did need to shoot something for supper. He was willing to starve to achieve his ends—but only if he had to. If a bunny rabbit showed its face, it was history.

As Sunny walked the canyon floor, picking up what sticks she could find, she studied the rock walls, looking for a fissure that might have escaped notice, an animal trail, anything that might point the way to freedom. If they only had some rock-climbing gear, she thought wistfully. A rope, cleats, anything. She had tried to anticipate any possible need when she packed her bag, but somehow being trapped in a box canyon hadn't occurred to her.

For the most part, the walls were perpendicular. Even when they slanted a little, the angle wasn't much off ninety degrees. Erosion from wind and rain had, over millions of years, cut grooves in the rock that looked like ripples in water. The only sign the canyon wasn't impregnable was the occasional little heap of rubble where smaller rocks had crumbled and fallen.

She had passed several of those small heaps before the light went on.

A fragile stirring of hope made her stomach tighten as she investigated one scattered pile of rock. It looked as if a larger boulder had fallen from the rim and shattered on impact. She picked up a fist-sized rock and rubbed her thumb over the surface, finding it gritty, the texture of sandpaper. Sandstone, she thought. It was a lovely pink color. It was also soft.

Just to be certain, she banged the rock down on a larger rock, and it broke into several pieces.

This site was no good; it was too steep. She walked along the wall, looking up at the rim and trying to find a place where the wall slanted back just a little. That was all she asked; just a little slant, enough that the angle wasn't so extreme.

There. One of the ripples curved backward, and when she picked her way through rocks and bushes to investigate she saw the opportunity for which she had been looking. She ran her hand over the rock, exulting in the sandpaper texture of it under her palm. Maybe, just maybe…

She ran back to the camp and grabbed the curling iron out of the bag. Chance hadn't asked, but the pistol wasn't the only weapon she carried. Quickly she unscrewed the metal barrel from the handle and removed a knife from the interior. It was a slender blade, made for slicing rather than hacking, but sharp and almost indestructible.

Her idea registered somewhere between being a long shot and just plain crazy, but it was the only idea she'd had that was even remotely possible. At least she would be doing *something*, rather than just waiting around for a rescue that might never happen.

She needed gloves to protect her hands, but she didn't have any. Hastily she opened the first-aid box and took out the roll of gauze. She wrapped the gauze around her palms and wove it in and around her fingers, then taped the loose ends. The result was crude but workable, she thought. She had seen the gloves rock climbers wore, with their fingers and thumbs left free; this makeshift approximation would have to do. She might wear blisters on her hands, anyway, but that was a small price to pay if they could get out of here.

Knife in hand, she went back to her chosen point of attack and tried to figure out the best way to do this. She needed another rock, she realized, one that wasn't soft. Anything that crumbled would be useless. She scouted around and finally found a pitted, dark gray rock that was about the size of a grapefruit, heavy enough to do the job.

Digging the point of the knife into the soft sandstone of the wall, she gripped the rock with her right hand and pounded it against the knife, driving the blade deeper. She jerked the blade out, moved it a little to the right, and pounded it in again. The next time she drove the knife in at a right angle to the original gouge, and hammered it downward. A chunk of sandstone broke loose, leaving a nice little gouge in the rock.

"This just might work," Sunny said aloud, and set herself to the task. She didn't let herself think how long it would take to carve handholds out of the rock all the way to the top, or if it was even possible. She was going to try; she owed it to Margreta, and to herself, to do everything she could to get out of this canyon.

Almost two hours later, the sharp crack of a pistol

shot reverberated through the canyon, startling her so much that she nearly fell. She clung to the rock, her cheek pressed against the rough surface. Her heart pounded from the close call. She wasn't that high, only about ten feet, but the canyon floor was jagged with rock, and any fall was certain to cause injuries.

She wiped the sweat from her face. The temperature was rising by the minute, and the rock was getting hotter and hotter. Standing with her toes wedged into the gouges she had hammered out of the rock, she had to lean inward against the rock to brace herself, because she had to have both hands free to wield the knife and the rock. She couldn't put nearly as much effort into it now, or the impact would jar her from her perch.

Panting, she reached over her head and blindly swung the rock. Because she had to press herself to the rock to keep her balance, she couldn't see to aim. Sometimes she hit the target and the knife bit into the rock; sometimes she hit her own hand. There had to be a better way to do this, but she couldn't think of one. She was an expert at working with what she had; she could do it this time, too. All she had to do was be careful, and patient.

"I can do this," she whispered.

Chance carried the skinned and cleaned rabbit back to the camp. He had also found a prickly pear cactus and cut off two of the stems, sticking himself several times as he removed the spines. The prickle pear was both edible and nutritious; it was usually fried, but he figured roasting would do just as well.

His temper had cooled. All right, so she had taken him in. He hadn't blown the plan; everything was still on track. All he had to do was remember not to be fooled by that oh-so-charming face she presented to the world and the plan would work just as he had expected. Maybe he couldn't make her love him, but he could make her think she did, and that was all he needed. A little trust, a little information, and he was in business.

He stepped beneath the overhang, grateful for the relief the shade afforded, and took off his sunglasses. Sunny wasn't here. He turned around and surveyed what he could see of the canyon but couldn't spot her. Her green T-shirt and beige jeans didn't exactly stand out in the terrain, he thought, and abruptly realized what effective camouflage her clothing was. Had she chosen it for that exact purpose? She must have; everything she carried in that bag had been geared toward survival, so why should her clothing be any different?

"Sunny!" he called. His voice echoed, then died. He listened, but there was no answer.

Damn it, where was she?

The fire had died down, which meant she hadn't tended it in quite a while. He bent down and added more sticks, then skewered the rabbit and set it on the spit, more to keep it away from insects than anything else. The fire was too low to cook it, but the smoke wafting over the meat would give it a good flavor. He wrapped the prickly pear stems in his handkerchief and walked back under the overhang to keep them out of the sun until he was ready to cook them.

The first thing he saw was the open first aid kit.

Alarm punched him in the gut. The paper wrapping had been torn off the roll of gauze; the tape was lying in the lid of the box, and it had also been used, because the end had been left free rather than stuck back to the roll.

Another detail caught his eyes. The curling iron had been taken apart; the two halves of it lay in the sand.

He swore viciously. Damn it, he should have remembered the curling iron and not assumed the pistol was the only weapon she had. She couldn't have hidden another pistol in the curling iron, but a knife would fit.

He didn't see any blood, but she must have injured herself somehow. Where in the hell was she?

"Sunny!" he roared as he stepped back out into the sun. Only silence answered him.

He studied the ground. Her footprints were everywhere, of course, but he saw where she had walked to her bag, presumably to get the first aid kit; then the prints led back out into the canyon. She was headed toward the plane.

He wasn't aware of reaching for his pistol. He was so accustomed to it that he didn't notice the weight of it in his hand as he followed her tracks, everything in him focusing on finding her.

If it hadn't been for the tracks, he would have missed her. She was almost at the far end of the canyon, past where the plane sat baking in the sun. The rock walls were scored with hundreds of cuts, and she was tucked inside one of them, clinging to the rock about a dozen feet off the ground.

Astonishment, anxiety, relief and anger all balled together in his gut. In speechless fury he watched her reach over her head and stab a wicked-looking blade into the soft rock, then, still keeping her face pressed against the hot stone, use another rock to try to pound the knife deeper. She hit her hand instead of the knife handle, and the curse she muttered made his eyebrows rise.

Strips of gauze were wound around her hands. He didn't know if she had wrapped her hands because she had hurt them, or if the gauze was an effort to keep them from being hurt. All he knew was that if she fell she would likely maim herself on the rocks, and that he really, *really* wanted to spank her.

He ruthlessly restrained the urge to yell at her. The last thing he wanted to do was startle her off her precarious perch. Instead, he stuck the pistol in his waistband at the small of his back and worked his way over until he was standing beneath her, so he could catch her if she fell.

He forced himself to sound calm. "Sunny, I'm right beneath you. Can you get down?"

She stopped with her right hand drawn back to deliver another blow with the rock. She didn't look down at him. "Probably," she said. "It has to be easier than getting up here."

He was fairly certain what she was doing, but the sheer magnitude of the task, the physical impossibility of it, left him stunned. Just for confirmation he asked, "What are you doing?"

"I'm cutting handholds in the rock, so we can climb out of here." She sounded grim, as if she also realized the odds against success.

His hands clenched into fists as he fought for control. He looked up at the towering wall, at the expanse stretching above her. The dozen feet she had climbed was only about one tenth of the distance needed—and it was the easiest tenth.

He put his hand on the rock and almost jerked back at the heat radiating from it. A new concern gnawed at him. He didn't yell at her that this was the stupidest idea he'd ever heard of, the way he wanted. Instead, he said, "Sweetheart, the rock's too hot. Come down before you're burned."

She laughed, but without her usual humor. "It's too late."

To hell with cajoling. "Throw the knife down and get off that damn rock," he barked in sharp command.

To his surprise, she dropped the knife, then the rock she held in her right hand, tossing both to the side so they wouldn't land near him. Every muscle in her body was taut with strain as she reached for the handholds she had cut and began to work her way down, feeling with her toes for the gouges. He stood directly beneath her, reaching up for her in case she fell. The muscles in her slender arms flexed, and he realized anew just how strong she was. One didn't get that kind of strength with a once-in-a-while jog or the occasional workout in a gym. It took dedication and time; he knew, because he kept himself in top physical condition. Her normal routine would be at least an hour of work, maybe two, every day. For all he knew, while he had been checking the traps she had been doing pushups.

For all the gut-deep burn of his anger, it was overridden by his concern as he watched her inch her way down the face of the rock. She was careful and took her time, despite the fact that he knew the rock was scorching her fingers. He didn't speak again, not wanting to distract her; he simply waited, not very patiently, for her to get within his reach.

When she did, he caught her feet and guided them to the next gouges. "Thanks," she panted, and worked her way down another foot.

That was enough. He caught her around the knees and scooped her off the rock. She shrieked, fighting for her balance, but now that he had her in his grip he wasn't about to let her go. Before she could catch her breath, he turned her and tossed her face down over his shoulder.

"Hey!" The indignant protest was muffled against his back.

"Just shut up," he said between his teeth as he dipped down to pick up her knife, then set off for the camp. "You scared the hell out of me."

"Good. You had too much hell in you, anyway." She clutched him around the waist to steady herself. He just hoped she didn't grab the pistol out of his waistband and shoot him, since it was so close to hand.

"Damn it, don't you dare joke about it!" Her upturned bottom was very close to his hand. Temptation gnawed at him. Now that he had her down, he was shaking, and he wanted some retribution for having been put through that kind of anxiety. He put his hand on her butt and indulged in a few moments of fantasy, which involved her jeans around her knees and her bent over his lap.

He realized he was stroking his palm over the round curves of her buttocks and regretfully gave up on his fantasy. Some things weren't going to happen. After he tended her hands and got through raising hell with her for taking such a risk, he fully intended to burn off his fright and anger with an hour or two on the blanket with her.

How could he still want her so much? This wasn't part of the job; he could live with it, if it had been. This was obsession, deep and burning and gut-twisting. He had tried to put a light face on it, for her benefit, but if she had been more experienced, she would have known a man didn't make love to a woman five times during the night just because she was available. At this rate, those three dozen condoms wouldn't last even a week.

He had already used six, and it might take two or three more to get him settled down after the scare she had given him.

The hard fact of it was, a man didn't make love to a woman that often unless he was putting his brand on her.

This wouldn't work. Couldn't work. He had to get himself under control, stay focused on the job.

He heard her sniffing as they neared the camp. "Are you *crazy?*" he demanded incredulously.

She sniffed again. "Don't be silly. What's that smell?" She inhaled deeply. "It smells like…food."

Despite himself, a smile quirked the corners of his mouth. "I shot a rabbit."

There was a small disruption on his shoulder as she twisted around so she could see the fire. Her squeal of delight almost punctured his eardrums, and his smile grew. He couldn't stop himself from enjoying her; he had never before met anyone who took such joy in life, who was so vibrantly alive herself. How she could be a part of a network devoted to taking lives was beyond his understanding.

He dumped her on the ground under the overhang and squatted beside her, taking both her hands in his and turning them up for his inspection. He barely controlled a wince. Her fingers were not only scorched from the hot rock, they were scraped raw and bleeding.

Fury erupted in him again, a flash fire of temper at seeing the damage she had done to herself. He surged to his feet. "Of all the stupid, lame-brained…! What in hell were you thinking? You weren't thinking at all, from the looks of it! Damn it, Sunny, you risked your life pulling this stupid stunt—!"

"It wasn't stupid," she shouted, shooting to her feet

to face him, her brilliant eyes narrowed. She clenched her bleeding hands into fists. "I know the risks. I also know it's my only hope of getting out of this damn canyon before it's too late!"

"Too late for what?" he yelled back. "Do you have a date this weekend or something?" The words were heavy with sarcasm.

"Yeah! It just so happens I do!" Breathing hard, she glared at him. "My sister is supposed to call."

Chapter 10

A sister? Chance stared at her. His investigation hadn't turned up any information about a sister. The Millers hadn't had any children of their own, and he had found adoption papers only on Sunny. His mind raced. "You said you didn't have any family."

She gave him a stony look. "Well, I have a sister."

Yeah, right. "You'd risk your life for a phone call?" Some terrorist act was being planned after all, he thought with a cold feeling in the pit of his stomach. That was why she'd been lugging the tent around. He didn't know how the tent fit into the scheme, but evidently she had been planning to drop out of sight.

"I would for this one." She wheeled away, every line of her body tense. "I have to try. Margreta calls my cell phone every week at the same time. It's how we know the other is still alive." She turned back to him and shouted, "If I don't answer that call, she'll think I'm dead!"

Whoa. Once again, the pieces of the puzzle that was Sunny had been scattered. Margreta? Was that a code name? He searched his memory, which was extensive, but couldn't find anything or anyone named Margreta. Sunny was so damned convincing....

"Why would she think you're dead?" he demanded. "You might just be in a place that doesn't have a signal—like here. What is she, some kind of nutcase?"

"I make certain I'm always somewhere that has a signal. And, no, she isn't a *nutcase!*" She threw the words back at him like bullets, her mouth twisted with fury at him, at the situation, at her own helplessness. "Her problem is the same as mine—we're our father's daughters!"

His pulse leaped. There it was, out in the open, just like that. He hadn't needed seduction; anger had done the job. "Your father?" he asked carefully.

Tears glittered in her eyes, dripped down her cheeks. She dashed them away with a furious gesture. "Our father," she said bitterly. "We've been running from him all our lives."

The pieces of the puzzle jumped about a little more, as if a fist had slammed down and jarred them. Easy, he cautioned himself. Don't seem too interested. Find out exactly what she means; she could be referring to his influence. "What do you mean, running?"

"I mean running. Hiding." She wiped away more tears. "Father dear is a terrorist. He'll kill us if he ever finds us."

Chance gently cleaned her hands with the alcohol wipes from the first aid kit, soothed the red places with burn ointment and the raw spots with antibiotic cream. The gauze she'd wrapped around her hands had protected her palms, but her fingers were a mess. Sunny felt a little bewildered. One minute they had been yelling at each other, the next she had been locked against him, his arms like a vise around her. His heart had been pounding like a runaway horse.

Since then he had been as tender as a mother with a child, rocking her in comfort, cuddling her, drying her tears. The emotional firestorm that had burned through her had left her feeling numb and disoriented; she let him do whatever he wanted without offering a protest, not that she had any reason to protest. It felt good to lean on him.

Satisfied with the care he had given her hands, he left her sitting on the rock while he added some fuel to the fire and turned the rabbit on the spit. Coming back under the overhang, he spread the blanket against the wall, scooped her into his arms, and settled on the blanket with her cradled against him. He propped his back against the wall, arranged her so she was draped half across his lap and lifted her face for a light kiss.

She managed a shaky smile. "What was that? A kiss to make it better?"

He rubbed his thumb over her bottom lip, his expression strangely intent as if studying her. "Something like that."

"I'm sorry for crying all over you. I usually handle things better than this."

"Tell me what's going on," he said quietly. "What's this about your father?"

She leaned her head on his shoulder, grateful for his strength. "Hard to believe, isn't it? But he's the leader of a terrorist group that has done some awful things. His name is Crispin Hauer."

"I've never heard of him," Chance lied.

"He operates mostly in Europe, but his network extends to the States. He even has someone planted in the FBI." She was unable to keep the raw bitterness out of her voice. "Why do you think I don't have a license for that pistol? I don't know who the plant is, how high he ranks, but I do know he's in a position to learn if the FBI gets any information Hauer wants. I didn't want to be in any database, in case he found out who adopted me and what name I'm using."

"So he doesn't know who you are?"

She shook her head. She had spent a lifetime keeping all her fear and worry bottled up inside her, and now she couldn't seem to stop it from spewing out. "My mother took Margreta and left him before I was born. I've never met him. She was five months pregnant with me when she ran."

"What did she do?"

"She managed to lose herself. America's a big place. She stayed on the move, changing her name, paying with cash she had taken from his safe. When I was born, she intended to have me by herself, in the motel room she'd taken for the night. But I wouldn't come, the labor just kept on and on, and she knew something was wrong. Margreta was hungry and scared, crying. So she called 911."

He wound a strand of golden hair around his finger. "And was there something wrong?"

"I was breech. She had a C-section. While she was groggy from the drugs, they asked her the father's name and she didn't think to make up a name, just blurted out *his*. So that's how I got into the system, and how he knows about me."

"How do you know he knows?"

"I was almost caught, once." She shivered against

him, and he held her closer. "He sent three men. We were in...Indianapolis, I think. I was five. Mom had bought an old car and we were going somewhere. We were always on the move. We got boxed in, in traffic. She saw them get out of their cars. She had taught us what to do if she ever told us to run. She dragged us out of the car and screamed 'Run!' I did, but Margreta started crying and grabbed Mom. So Mom took off running with Margreta. Two men went after them, and one came after me." She began shuddering. "I hid in an alley, under some garbage. I could hear him calling me, his voice soft like he was singing. 'Sonia, Sonia.' Over and over. They knew my name. I waited forever, and finally he went away."

"How did your mother find you again? Or was she caught?"

"No, she and Margreta got away, too. Mom taught herself street smarts, and she never went anywhere that she wasn't always checking out ways to escape."

He knew what that was like, Chance thought.

"I stayed in my hiding place. Mom had told us that sometimes, after we thought they were gone, the bad men would still be there watching, waiting to see if we came out. So I thought the bad men might be watching, and I stayed as still as I could. I don't think it was winter, because I wasn't wearing a coat, but when night fell I got cold. I was scared and hungry and didn't know if I'd ever see Mom again. I didn't leave, though, and finally I heard her calling me. She must have noticed where I ran and worked her way back when she thought it was safe. All I knew was that she'd found me. After that was when she decided it wasn't safe to keep us with her anymore, so she began looking for someone to adopt us."

Chance frowned. He hadn't found a record of any adoption but hers. "The same family took both of you?"

"Yes, but I was the only one adopted. Margreta wouldn't." Her voice was soft. "Margreta...remembers things. She had lost everything except Mom, so I guess she clung more than I did. She had a hard time adapting." She shrugged. "Having grown up the way I did, I can adjust to pretty much anything."

Meaning she had taught herself not to cling. Instead, with her sunny personality, she had found joy and beauty wherever she could. He held her closer, letting her cling to him. "But...you said he was trying to kill you. It sounds as if he was trying very hard to get you back."

She shook her head. "He was trying to get *Margreta* back. He didn't know me. I was just a means he could have used to force Mom to give Margreta back to him. That's all he would want with me now, to find Margreta. If I was caught, when he found out I don't know where she is, I'd be worthless to him."

"You don't know?" he asked, startled.

"It's safer that way. I haven't seen her in years." Unconscious longing for her sister was in her voice. "She has my cell phone number, and she calls me once a week. So long as I answer the call, she knows everything is all right."

"But you don't know how to get in touch with her?"

"No. I can't tell them what I don't know. I move around a lot, so a cell phone was the best way for us. I keep an apartment in Chicago, the tiniest, cheapest place I could find, but I don't live there. It's more of a decoy than anything else. I suppose if I live anywhere it's in Atlanta, but I take all the assignments I can get. I seldom spend more than one night at a time in one place."

"How would he find you now, since your name has

bccn changed? Unlcss hc knows who adopted you, but how could he find that out?'' Chance himself had found her only because of the incident in Chicago, when her courier package was stolen and he checked her out. As soon as he said it, though, he knew that the mole in the FBI—and he would damn sure find out who *that* was—had probably done the same checking. Had he gone as deep in the layers of bureaucracy as Chance had, to the point of hacking into those sealed adoption records? Sunny's cover might have been blown. He wondered if she realized it yet.

"I don't know. I just know I can't afford to assume I'm safe until I hear he's dead."

"What about your mom? And Margreta?"

"Mom's dead." Sunny paused, and he felt her inhale as if bracing herself. "They caught her. She committed suicide rather than give up any information on us. She had told us she would—and she did."

She stopped, and Chance gave her time to deal with the bleakness he heard in her voice. Finally she said, "Margreta is using another name, I just don't know what it is. She has a heart condition, so it's better if she stays in onc looation."

Margreta was living a fairly normal life, he thought, while Sunny was on the move, always looking over her shoulder. That was what she had known since birth, the way she had been taught to handle the situation. But what about the years they had spent with the Millers? Had her life been normal then?

She answered those questions herself. "I miss having a home," she said wistfully. "But if you stay in one place you get to know people, form relationships. I couldn't risk someone else's life that way. God forbid I should get married, have children. If Hauer ever found me—'' She broke off, shuddering at the thought of what Hauer was capable of doing to someone she loved in order to get the answers he wanted.

One thing didn't make sense, Chance thought. Hauer was vicious and crazy and cunning, and would go to any lengths to recover his daughter. But why Margreta, and not Sunny, too? ''Why is he so fixated on your sister?''

''Can't you guess?'' she asked rawly, and began shuddering again. ''That's why Mom took Margreta and ran. She found him with her, doing…things. Margreta was only four. He had evidently been abusing her for quite a while, maybe even most of her life. By then Mom had already found out some of what he was, but she hadn't worked up the nerve to leave. After she found him with Margreta, she didn't have a choice.'' Her voice dropped to an agonized whisper. ''Margreta remembers.''

Chance felt sick to his stomach. So in addition to being a vicious, murdering bastard, Hauer was also a pervert, a child molester. Killing was too good for him; he deserved to be dismembered—slowly.

Worn out by both physical labor and her emotional storm, Sunny drifted to sleep. Chance held her, content to let her rest. The fire needed more fuel, but so what? Holding her was more important. Thinking his way through this was more important.

First and foremost, he believed every word she'd said. Her emotions had been too raw and honest for any of it to have been faked. For the first time, all the pieces of the puzzle fit together, and his relief was staggering. Sunny was innocent. She had nothing to do with her father, had never seen him, had spent her entire life running from him. That was why she lugged around a tent, with basic survival provisions; she was ready to disappear at any given moment, to literally go to ground and live out in the forest somewhere until she thought it was safe to surface and rebuild her life yet again.

She had no way of contacting Hauer. The only way to get to him, then, was to use her as bait. And considering how she felt about her father, she would never, under any circumstances, agree to any plan that brought her to his attention.

He would have to do it without her agreement, Chance thought grimly. He didn't like using her, but the stakes were too high to abandon. Hauer couldn't be left free to continue wreaking his destruction on the world. How many innocent people would die this year alone if he wasn't caught?

There was no point in staying here any longer; he'd found out what he needed to know. Zane wouldn't check in again, though, until tomorrow morning, so they were stuck until then. He adjusted Sunny in his arms and rested his face against the top of her head. He would use the time to formulate his game plan—and to use as many of those condoms as possible.

"Get away from me," Sunny grumbled the next morning, turning her head away from his kiss. She pried his hand off her breast. "Don't touch me, you—you *mink*."

Chance snorted with laughter.

She pulled his chest hair.

"Ouch!" He drew back as far as he could in the small confines of the tent. "That hurt."

"Good! I don't think I can walk." Quick as a snake, her hand darted out and pulled his chest hair again. "This way, you can have as much fun as I'm having."

"Sunny," he said in a cajoling tone.

"Don't 'Sunny' me," she warned, fighting her way

into her clothes. Since they barely had room to move, he began dodging elbows and knees, and his hands slipped over some very interesting places. "Stop it! I mean it, Chance! I'm too sore for any more monkey business."

More to tease her than anything else, he zeroed in on an interesting place that had her squealing. She shot out of the tent, and he collapsed on his back, laughing— until she raised the tent flap and dashed some cold water on him.

"There," she said, hugely satisfied by his yelp. "One cold shower, just what you needed." Then she ran.

If she thought the fact that he was naked would hamper his pursuit, she found out differently. He snatched up a bottle of water as he passed by their cache of supplies and caught her before she had gone fifty yards. She was laughing like a maniac, otherwise she might have gotten away. He held her with one arm and poured the water over her head. It was ice-cold from having been left out all night, and she shrieked and sputtered and giggled, clinging to him when her legs went weak from so much laughter.

"Too sore to walk, huh?" he demanded.

"I w-wasn't walking," she said, giggling as she pushed her wet hair out of her face. Cold droplets splattered on him, and he shivered.

"Damn, it's cold," he said. The sun was barely up, so the temperature was probably in the forties.

She slapped his butt. "Then get some clothes on. What do you think this is, a nudist colony?"

He draped his arm around her shoulders, and they walked back to the camp. Her playfulness delighted him; hell, everything about her delighted him, from her wit to her willingness to laugh. And the sex—God, the sex was unbelievable. He didn't doubt she was sore, because *he* was. Last night had been a night to remember.

When she awakened yesterday afternoon she had been naturally melancholy, the normal aftermath of intense emotions. He hadn't talked much, letting her relax. She went with him to check the traps, which were still empty, and they had bathed together. After a quiet supper of rabbit and cactus they went to bed, and he had devoted the rest of the night to raising her spirits. His efforts had worked.

"How are your hands?" he asked. If she could pull his chest hairs and slap his butt, the antibiotic cream must have worked wonders.

She held them out, palms up, so he could see. The redness from the burns was gone, and her raw fingertips looked slick and shiny. "I'll wrap Band-Aids around them before I get started," she said.

"Get started doing what?"

She gave him a startled look. "Cutting handholds in the rock, of course."

He was stunned. He stared at her, unable to believe what he was hearing. "You're not climbing back on that damn wall!" he snapped.

Her eyebrows rose in what he now recognized as her "the-hell-you-say" look. "Yes, I am."

He ground his teeth. He couldn't tell her they would be "rescued" today, but no way was he letting her wear herself out hacking holes in rock or put herself at that kind of risk.

"I'll do it," he growled.

"I'm smaller," she immediately objected. "It's safer for me."

She was trying to protect him again. He felt like beating his head against a rock in frustration.

"No, it isn't," he barked. "Look, there's no way you can cut enough handholds for us to climb out of here in the next two days. You got, what, twelve feet yesterday? If you managed twelve feet a day—and you wouldn't get that much done today, with your hands the way they are—it would take you over a week to reach the top. That's if—*if*— you didn't fall and kill yourself."

"So what am I supposed to do?" she shot back. "Just give up?"

"Today you aren't going to do a damn thing. You're going to let your hands heal if I have to tie you to a rock, is that clear?"

She looked as if she wanted to argue, but he was a lot bigger than she was, and maybe she could tell by his expression that he meant exactly what he said. "All right," she muttered. "Just for today."

He hoped she would keep her word, because he would have to leave her alone while he went to the spot where he signaled Zane. He would just have to risk it, but there would be hell to pay if he came back to find her on that rock.

He quickly dressed, shivering, and they ate another cold breakfast of water and nutrition bar, since there wasn't anything left of the rabbit from the night before. Tomorrow morning, he promised himself, breakfast would be bacon and eggs, with a mountain of hash browns and a pot of hot coffee.

"I'm going to check the traps," he said, though he knew there wouldn't be anything in them. When he'd checked them the afternoon before, knowing they would be leaving here today, he had quietly released them so they couldn't be sprung. "Just tend to the fire and keep it smoking. You take it easy today, and I'll wash our clothes this afternoon.'' That was a safe promise to make.

''It's a deal,'' she said, but he could tell she was thinking about Margreta.

He left her sitting by the fire. It was a good ten-minute walk to the designated spot, but he hurried, unwilling to leave her to her own devices for so long. Taking the laser light from his pocket, he aimed it toward the rock on the rim and began flashing the pickup signal. Immediately Zane flashed back asking for confirmation, to make certain there wasn't an error. After all, they hadn't expected this to happen so fast. Chance flashed the signal again and this time received an okay.

He dropped the light back in his pocket. He didn't know how long it would take for Zane to arrange the pickup, but probably not long. Knowing Zane, everything was already in place.

He was walking back to the camp when the small twin-engine plane flew over. A grin spread across his face. That was Zane for you!

He began running, knowing Sunny would be beside herself. He heard her shrieking before he could see her; then she came into view, jumping in her glee as she came to meet him. ''He saw me!'' she screamed, laughing and crying at the same time. ''He waggled the wings! He'll come back for us, won't he?''

He caught her as she hurled herself into his arms and couldn't stop himself from planting a long, hard kiss on that laughing mouth. ''He'll come back,'' he said. ''Unless he thought you were just waving hello at him.'' The opportunity to tease her was too great to resist, considering she had pulled his chest hair and poured cold water on him. He'd retaliated for the cold water; this was for the hair-pulling.

She looked stricken, the laughter wiped from her face as if it had never been. "Oh, no," she whispered.

He didn't have the heart to keep up the pretense. "Of course he'll come back," he chided. "Waggling the wings was the signal that he saw you and would send help."

"Are you sure?" she asked, blinking back tears.

"I promise."

"I'll get you for this."

He had to kiss her again, and he didn't stop until she had melted against him, her arms locked around his neck. He hadn't thought he would be interested in sex for quite a while, not after last night, but she proved him wrong.

He huffed out a breath and released her. "Stop man-handling me, you hussy. We have to get packed."

The smile she gave him was brilliant, like the sun rising, and it warmed him all the way through.

They gathered their belongings. Chance returned her pistol to her, and watched her break it down and store the pieces in their hiding places. Then they walked back to the plane and waited.

Rescue came in the form of a helicopter, the blades beating a thumping rhythm in the desert air, the canyon echoing with the sound. It hovered briefly over them, then lowered itself like a giant mosquito. Sand whipped into their air, stinging them, and Sunny hid her face against his shirt.

A sixtyish man with a friendly face and graying beard hopped out of the bird. "You folks need some help?" he called.

"Sure do," Chance answered.

When he was closer, the man stuck out his hand. "Charlie Jones, Civil Air Patrol. We've been looking for you for a couple of days. Didn't expect to find you this far south.''

"I veered off course looking for a place to land. Fuel pump went out.''

"In that case, you're mighty lucky. That's rough territory out there. This might be the only spot in a hundred miles when you could have landed. Come on. I expect you folks are ready for a shower and some food.''

Chance held out his hand to Sunny, and she gave him that brilliant smile again as she put her hand in his and they walked to the helicopter.

Chapter 11

Sunny was almost dizzy with mingled relief and regret; relief because she wouldn't miss Margreta's call, regret because this time with Chance, even under such trying conditions, had been the happiest, most fulfilling few days of her life and they were now over. She had known from the beginning that their time together was limited; once they were back in the regular world, all the old rules came back into play.

She couldn't, wouldn't risk his life by letting him be a part of hers. He had given her two nights of bliss, and a lifetime of memories. That would have to be enough, no matter how much she was already aching at the thought of walking away from him and never seeing him again. At least now she knew what it was to love a man, to revel in his existence, and she was richer for it. She wouldn't have traded these few days with him for any amount of money, no matter the price in loneliness she would have to pay.

So she held his hand all during the helicopter flight to a small, ramshackle air field. The only building was made of corrugated metal, rounded at the top like a Quonset hut, with a wooden addition, housing the office, added to one side. If the addition had ever seen a coat of paint, the evidence of it had long since been blasted off by the wind-driven sand. After living under a rock for three days, Sunny thought the little field looked like heaven.

Seven airplanes, of various makes and vintage, were parked with almost military precision along one side of the air strip. Charlie Jones landed his helicopter on a concrete pad behind the corrugated building. Three men, one wiping his greasy hands on a stained red rag, left the building by the back door and walked toward them, ducking their heads against the turbulence of the rotor blades.

Charlie took off his headset and hopped out of the chopper, smiling. "Found 'em," he called cheerfully to the approaching trio. To Chance and Sunny he said, "The two on the left fly CAP with me. Saul Osgood, far left, is the one who spotted your smoke this morning and radioed in your position. Ed Lynch is the one in the middle. The one with the greasy hands is Rabbit Warren, the mechanic here. His real name's Jerome, but he'll fight you if you call him that."

Sunny almost laughed aloud. She controlled the urge, but she was careful not to look at Chance as they shook hands with the three men and introduced themselves.

"I couldn't believe it when I saw your bird in that little bitty narrow canyon," Saul Osgood said, shaking his head after Chance told them what had happened. "How you ever found it is a miracle. And to make a

dead stick landing—'' He shook his head again. ''Someone was sure looking out for you, is all I can say.''

''So you think it was your fuel pump went out, huh?''
Rabbit Warren asked as they walked into the hangar.

''Everything else checked out.''

''It's a Skylane, right?''

''Yeah.'' Chance told him the model, and Rabbit
stroked his lean jaw.

''I might have a pump for that. There was a feller in
here last year flying a Skylane. He ordered some parts
for it, then left and never did come back for 'em. I'll
check while you folks are refreshing yourselves.''

If ''refreshing'' themselves had anything to do with a
bathroom, Sunny was more than ready. Chance gave her
the first turn, and she almost crooned with delight at the
copious water that gushed from the faucet at a turn of
the handle. And a flush toilet! She was in heaven.

After Chance had his turn, they indulged in ice-cold
soft drinks from a battered vending machine. A snack
machine stood beside it, and Sunny surveyed the offer-
ings with an eager eye. ''How much change do you
have?'' she asked Chance.

He delved his hand into his front pocket and pulled
out his change, holding it out for Sunny to see. She
picked out two quarters and fed them into the machine,
punched a button, and a pack of cheese and crackers fell
to the tray.

''I thought you'd go for a candy bar,'' Chance said
as he fed more quarters into the machine and got a pack
of peanuts.

''That's next.'' She raised her eyebrows. ''You didn't
think I was going to stop with cheese and crackers, did
you?''

Ed Lynch opened the door to the office. ''Is there

anyone you need to call? We've notified the FAA and called off the search, but if you have family you want to talk to, feel free to use the phone.''

''I need to call the office,'' Sunny said, pulling a wry face. She had a good excuse—a very good one—for not making her delivery, but the bottom line was that a customer was unhappy.

Chance waited until she was on the phone, then strolled over to where Rabbit was making a show of looking for a fuel pump. His men were good, Chance thought; they had played this so naturally they should have been on the stage. Of course, subterfuge was their lives, just as it was his.

''Everything's good,'' Chance said quietly. ''You guys can clear out after Charlie takes us back to the canyon with the fuel pump.''

Rabbit pulled a greasy box from a makeshift shelf that was piled with an assortment of parts and tools. Over Chance's shoulder he eyed Sunny through the windowed door to the office. ''You pulled a real hardship assignment this time, boss,'' he said admiringly. ''That's the sweetest face I've seen in a while.''

''There's a sweet person behind it, too,'' Chance said as he took the box. ''She's not part of the organization.''

Rabbit's eyebrows went up. ''So all this was for nothing.''

''No, everything is still a go. The only thing that's changed is her role. Instead of being the key, she's the bait. She's been on the run from Hauer her entire life. If he knows where she is, he'll come out of hiding.'' He glanced around to make certain she was still on the phone. ''Spread the word that we're going to be extra careful with her, make sure she doesn't get hurt. Hauer has already caused enough damage in her life.''

And he himself was going to cause more, Chance thought bleakly. As terrified as she was of Hauer, when she learned Chance had deliberately leaked her location to the man she was going to go ballistic. That would definitely be the end of *this* relationship, but he'd known from the beginning this was only temporary. Like her, he wasn't in any position for permanent ties. Sunny's circumstances would change when her father was gone, but Chance's wouldn't; he would move on to another crisis, another security threat.

Just because he was her first lover didn't mean he would be her last.

The idea shot a bolt of pure rage through him. Damn it, she was *his*—he caught the possessive thought and strangled it. Sunny wasn't his; she was her own person, and if she found happiness in her life with some other man, he should be happy for her. She more than deserved anything good that came her way.

He wasn't happy. Her laughter, her passion—he wanted it all for himself. Knowing he couldn't have her was already eating a huge hole out of his insides, but she deserved far better than a mongrel with blood on his hands. He had chosen his world, and he was well-suited for it. He was accustomed to living a lie, to pretending to be someone he wasn't, to always staying in the shadows. Sunny was…sunny, both by name and by nature. He would enjoy her while he had her—by God, he'd enjoy her—but in the end he knew he would have to walk away.

Sunny ended the call and left the office. Hearing the door close, he turned to watch her approach, and he let himself savor the pleasure of just watching her.

She wrinkled her nose. "Everyone's glad the plane didn't crash, that I'm alive—but the fact that I didn't die makes it a little less forgivable that I didn't deliver the package on time. The customer still wants it, though, so I still have to go to Seattle.''

She came to him as naturally as if they had been together for years, and just as naturally he found himself slipping his arm around her slender waist. ''Screw 'em,'' he said dismissively. He lifted the box. ''Guess what I have.''

She beamed. ''The keys to the kingdom.''

''Close enough. Charlie's going to take me back to the plane so I can swap out the fuel pump. Do you want to go with me, or stay here and rest until I get back?''

''Go with you,'' she said promptly. ''I don't know anything about airplanes, but I can keep you company while you work. Are we coming back here, anyway?''

''Sure. This is as good a place to refuel as any.'' Plus she wouldn't find out they weren't in Oregon as he'd told her.

''Then I'll leave my bag here, if that's all right with Rabbit.'' She looked inquiringly at Rabbit, who nodded his head.

''That'll be just fine, ma'am. Put it in the office and it'll be as safe as a baby in the womb.''

Sunny walked away to get the bag. She felt safe, Chance realized, otherwise she would never let the bag out of her possession. Except for her worry for Margreta, these last few days she must have felt free, unburdened by the need to constantly look over her shoulder.

He had enjoyed their little adventure, too, every minute of it, because he had known they weren't in any danger. Sunny made him feel more alive than he ever had before, even when he was angry at her because she had just scared him half to death. And when he was inside her—then he was as close to heaven as he was ever likely to get. The pleasure of making love to her was so intense it was almost blinding.

He grinned to himself as he hefted his own overnight bag. No way was he leaving it here; after all, the condoms were in it. No telling what might happen when he and Sunny were alone.

The afternoon was wearing on when Charlie set the helicopter down in the canyon again. He looked up at the light with an experienced pilot's eye. "You think you have enough time to get that fuel pump put on before dark?"

"No problem," Chance said. After all, as he and Charlie both knew, there was nothing wrong with the fuel pump, anyway. He would tinker around for a while, make it look realistic. Sunny wasn't likely to stand at his elbow the entire time, and if she did he would distract her.

He and Sunny jumped out of the helicopter, and he leaned in to get his bag. "See you in a few hours."

"If you don't make it back to the airfield, we know where you are," Charlie said, saluting.

They ducked away from the turbulence as the helicopter lifted away. Sunny pushed her hair away from her face and looked around the canyon, smiling. "Home again," she said, and laughed. "Funny how it looks a lot more inviting now that I know we aren't stuck here."

"I'm going to miss it," he said, winking at her. He carried his bag and the box containing the fuel pump over to the plane. "But we'll find out tonight if a bed is more fun than a tent."

To his surprise, sadness flashed in her eyes. "Chance...once we're away from here..." She shook her head. "It won't be safe."

He checked for a moment, then very deliberately put

down the bag and box. Turning back to her, he put his hands on his hips. "If you're saying what I think you're saying, you can just forget about it. You aren't dumping me."

"You know what the situation is! I don't have a choice."

"*I* do. You're not just a fun screw who was available while we were here. I care about you, Sunny," he said softly. "When you look over your shoulder, you're going to see my face. Get used to it."

Tears welled in her brilliant eyes, filling them with diamonds. "I can't," she whispered. "Because I love you. Don't ask me to risk your life, because I can't handle it."

His stomach muscles tightened. He had set out to make her love him, or at least get involved in a torrid affair with him. He had succeeded at doing both. He felt humbled, and exhilarated—and sick, because he was going to betray her.

He had her in his arms before he was aware of moving, and his mouth was on hers. He felt desperate for the taste of her, as if it had been days since he'd kissed her instead of just hours. Her response was immediate and wholehearted, as she rose on her tiptoes to fit her hips more intimately to his. He tasted the salt of her tears and drew back, rubbing his thumbs across her wet cheeks.

He rested his forehead against hers. "You're forgetting something," he murmured.

She sniffed. "What?"

"I was a ranger, sweetheart. I'm a little harder to kill than your average guy. You need someone watching your back, and I can do it. Think about it. We probably made the news. When we get to Seattle, don't be surprised if there's a television camera crew there. Both our faces will be on television. Besides that, we were reported missing to the FAA, which is federal. Information would have been dug up on both of us. Our names our linked. If the mole in the FBI tumbles to who you are, your father's goons will be after me, anyway—especially if they can't find you.''

She went white. ''Television?'' She looked a lot like her mother; Chance had seen old photos of Pamela Vickery Hauer. Anyone familiar with Pamela would immediately notice the resemblance. As sharp as she was, Sunny also knew the danger of being on television, even a local newscast.

''We're in this together.'' He lifted her hand to his mouth and kissed her knuckles, then grinned down at her. ''Lucky for you, I'm one mean son of a bitch when I need to be—lucky for you, unlucky for them.''

Nothing she said would sway him, Sunny thought with despair late that night as she showered in the hotel suite he had booked them into for the night—a suite because it had more than one exit. He had been exactly right about the television news crew. Crews, she corrected herself. News had been slow that day, so every station in Seattle had jumped on the human-interest story. The problem was, so had both national news channels.

She had evaded the cameras as much as possible, but the reporters had seemed fixated on her, shouting questions at her instead of Chance. She would have thought the female reporters, at least, would be all over Chance, but he'd worn such a forbidding expression that no one had approached him. She hadn't answered any questions on camera, though at Chance's whispered suggestion she had given them a quick comment off-camera, for them to use as a filler on their broadcast.

Her one break was that, since it had been so late when they landed, the story didn't make even the late news. But unless something more newsworthy happened soon, the story would air in just a few hours over millions of breakfast tables countrywide.

She had to assume her cover had been blown. That meant leaving the courier service, moving—not that she had much to move; she had never accumulated many possessions—even changing her name. She would have to build a new identity.

She had always known it could happen, and she had prepared for it, both mentally and with actual paperwork. Changing her name wouldn't change who she was; it was just a tool to use to escape her father.

The real problem was Chance. She couldn't shake him, no matter how she tried, and she knew she was good at that kind of thing. She had tried to lose him at the airport, ducking into a cab when his back was turned. But he seemed to have a sixth sense where she was concerned, and he was sliding in the other door before she could give the driver the address where she had to deliver the courier package. He had remained within touching distance of her until they walked into the hotel room, and she had no doubt that, if she opened the bathroom door, she would find him sprawled across the bed, watching her.

In that, she underestimated him. Just as she began lathering her hair, the shower curtain slid back and he stepped naked into the tub with her. "I thought I'd conserve water and shower with you," he said easily.

"Hah! You're just afraid I'll leave if you shower by yourself," she said, turning her back on him.

A big hand patted her bottom. "You know me so well."

She fought a smile. Damn him, why did he have to be so well-matched to her in every way? She could, and had, run rings around most people, but not Chance.

She hogged the spray, turning the nozzle down to rinse her hair. He waited until she was finished with that, at least, then adjusted the nozzle upward so the water hit him in the chest. It also hit her full in the face. She sputtered and elbowed him. "This is *my* shower, and I didn't invite you. I get control of the nozzle, not you."

She knew challenging him was a mistake. He said, "Oh, yeah?" and the tussle was on. Before she knew it she was giggling, he was laughing, and the bathroom was splattered with water. She had played more with Chance than she had since she'd been a little girl; she felt lighthearted with him, despite her problems. Their wet, naked bodies slid against each other, and neither of them could get a good grasp on any body part. At least, she couldn't. She suspected he could have won the tussle at any time simply by using his size and strength and wrapping his arms around her, but he held back and played at her level, as if he were used to restraining his strength to accommodate someone weaker than himself.

His hands were everywhere: on her breasts, her bottom, sliding between her legs while she laughed and batted them away. One long finger worked its way inside her and she squealed, trying to twist away while excitement spiraled wildly through her veins. Their naked wrestling match was having a predictable effect on both of them. She grabbed for the nozzle and aimed the blast of water at his face, and while he was trying to deflect the spray she made her escape, hopping out of the tub and snatching up a towel to wrap around her.

He vaulted out of the tub and slammed the door shut just as she reached for it. "You left the shower running," she accused, trying to sidetrack him.

"I'm not the one who turned it on." He grinned and hooked the towel away from her.

"Water's getting all over the floor." She tried to sound disapproving.

"It needed mopping, anyway."

"It did not!" She pushed a strand of dripping wet hair out of her eyes. "We're going to be kicked out. Water will drip through the floor into the room below and we'll be kicked out."

He grabbed her and swung her around so she was facing the shower. "Turn it off, then, if you're worried."

She did, because she hated to waste the water, and it was making such a mess. "There, I hope you're satisfied."

"Not by a long shot." He turned her to face him, holding her lips against his and angling her torso away from him, so he could look his fill at her. "Have I told you today how damn sexy you are?"

"Today? You've never told me at all!"

"I have so."

"Have not. When?"

"Last night. Several times."

She tried not to be entranced by the way water droplets were clinging to his thick dark lashes. "That doesn't count. Everyone knows you can't believe anything a man says when he's in...uh—"

"You?" he supplied, grinning.

She managed a haughty look. "I was going to say 'extremis,' but I think that applies only to dying."

"Close enough." He looked down at her breasts, his expression altering and the laughter fading. Still holding

her anchored to him with one arm, he smoothed a hand
up her torso to cup her breasts, and they both watched
his long brown fingers curve around the pale globes.
"You're sexy," he murmured, a slow, dark note entering his voice. She knew that note well, having heard it
many times over the past two nights. "And beautiful.
Your breasts are all cream-and-rose colored, until I kiss
your nipples. Then they pucker up and turn red like
they're begging me to suck them."

Her nipples tightened at his words, the puckered tips
flushing with color. He groaned and bent his dark head,
water dripping from his hair onto her skin as he kissed
both breasts. She was leaning far back over his arm,
supported by his arm around her hips and her own desperate grasp on his shoulders. She didn't know how
much longer she would be able to stand at all. Her loins
throbbed, and she gasped for breath.

"And your ass," he growled. "You have the sweetest
little ass." He turned her around so he could stroke the
aforementioned buttocks, shaping his palms to the full,
cool curves. Sunny's legs trembled, and she grabbed the
edge of the vanity for support. The cultured marble slab
was a good six feet long, and a mirror covered the entire
wall behind it. Sunny barely recognized herself in the
naked woman reflected there, a woman whose wet hair
dripped water down her back and onto the floor. Her
expression was etched with desire, her face flushed and
her eyes heavy-lidded.

Chance looked up, and his gaze met hers in the mirror.
Electricity sparked between them. "And here," he whispered, sliding one hand around her belly and between
her legs. His muscled forearm looked unbelievably powerful against her pale belly, and his big hand totally covered her mound. She felt his fingers sliding between her

folds, rubbing her just as she liked. She moaned and collapsed against him, her legs going limp.

"You're so soft and tight," the erotic litany continued in her ear. "I can barely get inside you. But once I do— my heart stops. And I can't breathe. I think I'm going to die, but I can't, because it feels too good to stop." His fingers slid farther, and he pressed two of them inside her.

She arched under the lash of sensation, soaring close to climax as his fingers stretched her. She heard herself cry out, a strained cry that told him exactly how near she was to fulfillment.

"Not yet, not yet," he said urgently, sliding his fingers out of her and bending her forward. He braced her hands on the vanity. "Hold on, sweetheart."

She didn't know if he meant to the vanity, or to her control. Both were impossible. "I can't," she moaned. Her hips moved, undulating, searching for relief. "Chance, I can't—please!"

"I'm here," he said, and he was, dipping down and pushing his muscled thighs between her legs, spreading them. She felt his lower belly against her buttocks, then the smooth, hard entry of his sex. Instinctively she bent forward to aid his penetration, taking all of him deep within her. He began driving, and on the second hard thrust she convulsed, crying out her pleasure. His climax erupted a moment later, and he collapsed over her back, holding himself as deep as he could while he groaned and shook.

Sunny closed her eyes, fighting for breath. Oh God, she loved him so much she ached with it. She wasn't strong enough to send him away, not even for his own protection. If she had been really trying, she could have gotten away from him, but deep down she knew she couldn't give him up. Not yet. Soon. She would have to, to keep him safe.

Just one more day, she thought as tears welled. One more. Then she would go.

Chapter 12

Ten days later, Sunny still hadn't managed to shake him. She didn't know if she was losing her touch or if army rangers, even ex ones, were very, very good at not being shaken.

They had left Seattle early the next morning. Sunny was too cautious to fly back to Atlanta; as she had feared, the morning newscasts had been splashed with the "real-life romantic adventure" she and Chance had shared. His name was mentioned, but by some perverse quirk his face was never clearly shown; the camera would catch the back of his head, or while he was in a quarter profile, while hers was broadcast from coast to coast.

One of the a.m. news shows even tracked them down at the hotel, awakening them at three in the morning to ask if they would go to the local affiliate studios for a live interview.

"Hell, no," Chance had growled into the phone before he slammed it down into the cradle.

After that, it had seemed best they remove themselves from the reach of the media. They checked out of the hotel and took a taxi to the airport before dawn. The plane was refueled and ready to go. By the time the sun peeked over the Cascades they were in the air. Chance didn't file a flight plan, so no one had any way of finding out where they were going. Sunny didn't know herself until they landed in Boise, Idaho, where they refurbished their wardrobes. She always carried a lot of cash, for just such a situation, and Chance seemed to have plenty, too. He still had to use his credit card for refueling, so she knew they were leaving a trail, but those records would show only where they had last been, not where they were going.

Chance's presence threw her off her plan. She knew how to disappear by herself; Chance and his airplane complicated things.

From a pay phone in Boise, she called Atlanta and resigned her job, with instructions to deposit her last paycheck into her bank. She would have the money wired to her when she needed it. Sometimes, adrift from the familiar life she had fashioned for herself, she wondered if she was overreacting to the possibility anyone would recognize her. Her mother had been dead for over ten years; there were few people in the world able to see the resemblance. The odds had to be astronomical against one of those few people seeing that brief human-interest story that had been shown for only one day.

But she was still alive because her mother had taught her that any odds at all were unacceptable. So she ran, as she had learned how to do in the first five years of her life. After all, the odds were also against her getting pregnant, yet here she was, waiting for a period that hadn't materialized. They had slipped up twice, only twice: once in the canyon, and in the hotel bathroom in Seattle. The timing hadn't been great for her to get pregnant even if they hadn't used protection at all, so why hadn't her period started? It was due two days ago, and her cycle was relentlessly regular.

She didn't mention it to Chance. She might just be late, for one of the few times in her life since she'd starting having menstrual periods. She had been terrified when she thought they were going to crash; maybe her emotions had disrupted her hormones. It happened.

She might sprout wings and fly, too, she thought in quiet desperation. She was pregnant. There were no signs other than a late period, but she knew it deep down in her bones, as if on some level her body was communicating with the microscopic embryo it harbored.

It would be so easy just to let Chance handle everything. He was good at this, and she had too much on her mind to be effective. She didn't think he'd noticed how easily distracted she'd been these past few days, but then, he didn't know when her period had been due, either.

She had talked to Margreta twice, and told her she was going underground. She would have to arrange for a new cellular account under a different name, with a new number, and do it before the service she now had was disconnected. She had tried to tell Margreta everything that was going on, but her sister, as usual, kept the calls short. Sunny understood. It was difficult for Margreta to handle anything having to do with their father. Maybe one day they would be able to live normal lives, have a normal sisterly relationship; maybe one day Margreta would be able to get past what he had done to her and find some happiness despite him.

Then there was Chance. He had brought sunshine into her life when she hadn't even known she was living in shadows. She had thought she managed quite well, but it was as if B.C., Before Chance, had been in monochrome. Now, A.C., was in vivid technicolor. She slept in his arms every night. She ate her meals with him, quarreled with him, joked with him, made plans with him—nothing long term, but plans nevertheless. Every day she fell more and more in love with him, when she hadn't thought it possible.

Sometimes she actually pinched herself, because he was too good to be true. Men like him didn't come along every day; most women lived their entire lives without meeting a man who could turn their worlds upside down with a glance.

This state of affairs couldn't last much longer, this aimless drifting. For one thing, it was expensive. Chance wasn't earning any money while they were flying from one remote airfield in the country to another, and neither was she. She needed to get the paperwork for her new name, get a job, get a new cellular number—and get an obstetrician, which would cost money. She wondered how her mother had managed, with one frightened, traumatized child in tow, pregnant with another, and without any of the survival skills Sunny possessed. Pamela must have spent years in a state of terror, yet Sunny remembered her mother laughing, playing games with them, and making life fun even while she taught them how to survive. She only hoped she could be half as strong as her mother had been.

She was full of wild hopes these days. She hoped she hadn't been recognized. She hoped her baby would be healthy and happy. Most of all, she hoped she and Chance could build a life together, that he would be thrilled about the baby even though it was unplanned, that he truly cared about her as much as he appeared to. He never actually said he loved her, but it was there in his voice, in his actions, in his eyes and his touch as he made love to her.

Everything had to be all right. It had to. There was too much at stake now.

Sunny slept through the landing as Chance set the plane down in Des Moines. He glanced at her, but she was soundly asleep, like a child, her breathing deep and her cheeks flushed. He let her sleep, knowing what was coming to a head.

The plan was working beautifully. He had arranged for Sunny's face to be broadcast worldwide, and the bait had been taken immediately. His people had tracked two of Hauer's men into the country and maintained discreet but constant surveillance on them. Chance hadn't made it easy for anyone to follow him and Sunny; that would have been too obvious. But he had left a faint trail that, if the bloodhounds were good, they would be able to follow. Hauer's bloodhounds were good. They had been about a day behind them for about a week now, but until Hauer himself showed up, Chance made sure the hounds never caught up with him.

The news he'd been waiting for had finally come yesterday. Word in the underground of terrorist organizations was that Hauer had disappeared. He hadn't been seen in a few days, and there was a rumor he was in the States planning something big.

Somehow Hauer had slipped out of Europe and into America without being spotted, but now that Chance knew there was a mole in the FBI helping Hauer, he wasn't surprised.

Hauer was too smart to openly join his men, but he would be nearby. He was the type who, when Sunny was captured, would want to interrogate this rebellious daughter himself.

Chance would take him apart with his bare hands before he let that happen.

But he would have to let them think they had her, not knowing they were surrounded at all times, at a distance, by his men. Chance just hoped he himself wasn't shot at the beginning, to get him out of the way. If Hauer's men were smart, they would realize they could use threats to Chance to keep Sunny in line, and they had proven they were smart. This was the risky part, but he had taken all the safeguards he could without tipping his hand.

His interlude with Sunny would end tonight, one way or another. If all went well, they would both live through it, and she would be free to live her life out in the open. He just hoped that one day she wouldn't hate him, that she would realize he had done what he had to do in order to capture Hauer. Who knows? Maybe one day he would meet her again.

He guided the Cessna to a stop in its designated spot and killed the engine. Sunny slept on, despite the sudden silence. Maybe he'd cost her too much sleep and it had finally caught up with her, he thought, smiling despite his inner tension. He had glutted himself with sex for the past two weeks, as if subconsciously he had been trying to stockpile memories and sensations for the time when she was no longer there. But as often as he'd had her, he still wanted her. Again. More. He was half hard right now, just thinking about her.

Gently he shook her, and she opened her sleepy eyes with a look of such trust and love that his heart leaped. She sat up, stretching and looking around. "Where are we?"

"Des Moines." Puzzled, he said, "I told you where we were going."

"I remember," she said around a yawn. "I'm just groggy. Wow! That was some nap. I don't usually sleep during the daytime. I must not be getting enough sleep at night." She batted her eyelashes at him. "I wonder why."

"I have no idea," he said, all innocence. He opened the door and climbed out, turning around to hold his hands up for her. She clambered out, and he lifted her to the ground. Looking up at the wide, cerulean-blue sky, he stretched, too, twisting his back to get out the kinks. "It's a pretty day. Want to have a picnic?"

"A what?" She looked at him as if he were speaking a foreign language.

"A picnic. You know, where you sit on the ground and eat with your hands, and fight wild animals for your food."

"Sounds like fun. But haven't we already done that?"

He laughed. "This time we'll do it right—checkered tablecloth, fried chicken, the works."

"All right, I'm game. Where are we going to have this picnic? Beside the runway?"

"Smart-ass. We'll rent a car and go for a drive."

Her eyes began to sparkle as she realized he meant it. That was what he loved best about Sunny, her ability to have fun. "How much time do we have? What time are we leaving?"

"Let's stay for a couple of days. Iowa's a nice place,

and my tail could use some time away from that airplane seat.''

He handled his business with the airport, then went to a rental car desk and walked away with the keys to a sport utility.

''You rented a *truck?*'' Sunny teased when she saw the green Ford Explorer. ''Why didn't you get something with style, like a red sports car?''

''Because I'm six-three,'' he retorted. ''My legs don't fit in sports cars.''

She had bought a small backpack that she carried instead of the bulky carry-on she had been lugging around. She could get her toiletries and a change of clothes into the backpack, and that was enough for the single night they usually spent in a place. That meant her pistol was always with her, fully assembled when they weren't having to go through x-ray scanners, and he didn't protest. He always carried his own pistol with him, too, tucked into his waistband under his loose shirt. She put the backpack on the floorboard and climbed into the passenger seat, and began pushing buttons and turning knobs, every one she could reach.

Chance got behind the wheel. ''I'm afraid to start this thing now. There's no telling what's going to happen.''

''Chicken,'' she said. ''What's the worst that could happen?''

''I'm just thankful Explorers don't have ejection seats,'' he muttered as he turned the key in the ignition. The engine caught immediately. The radio blared, the windshield wipers flopped back and forth at high speed, and the emergency lights began blinking. Sunny laughed as Chance dived for the radio controls and turned the volume down to an acceptable level. She buckled herself into the seat, smiling a very self-satisfied smile.

He had a map from the rental car company, though he already knew exactly where he was going. He had gotten very specific directions from the clerk at the rental agency, so the clerk would remember where they had gone when Hauer's men asked. He had personally scouted out the location before putting the plan into motion. It was in the country, to cut the risk of collateral damage to innocent civilians. There was cover for his men, who would be in place before he and Sunny arrived. And, most important, Hauer and his men couldn't move in without being observed. Chance had enough men in place that an ant couldn't attend this picnic unless he wanted it there. Best of all, he knew Zane was out there somewhere. Zane didn't usually do fieldwork, but in this instance he was here guarding his brother's back. Chance would rather have Zane looking out for him than an entire army; the man was unbelievable, he was so good.

They stopped at a supermarket deli for their picnic supplies. There was even a red-checkered plastic cloth to go on the ground. They bought fried chicken, potato salad, rolls, cole slaw, an apple pie, and some green stuff Sunny called pistachio salad. He knew he wasn't about to touch it. Then he had to buy a small cooler and ice, and some soft drinks to go in it. By the time he got Sunny out of the supermarket, over an hour had passed and he was almost seventy bucks lighter in the wallet.

"We have apple pie," he complained. "Why do we need apples?"

"I'm going to throw them at you," she said. "Or better yet, shoot them off your head."

"If you come near me with an apple, I'll scream," he warned. "And pickled beets? Excuse me, but who eats pickled beets?"

She shrugged. "Someone does, or they wouldn't be on the shelves."

"Have *you* ever eaten pickled beets?" he asked suspiciously.

"Once. They were nasty." She wrinkled her nose at him.

"Then why in hell did you buy them?" he shouted.

"I wanted you to try them."

He should be used to it by now, he thought, but sometimes she still left him speechless. Muttering to himself, he stowed the groceries—including the pickled beets—in the back of the Explorer.

God, he was going to miss her.

She rolled down the window and let the wind blow through her bright hair. She had a happy smile on her face as she looked at everything they passed. Even service stations seemed to interest her, as did the old lady walking a Chihuahua that was so fat its belly almost kept its feet from touching the ground. Sunny giggled about the fat little dog for five minutes.

If it made her laugh like that, he thought, he would eat the damn pickled beets. But he'd damn sure eat something else afterward, because if he got shot, he didn't want pickled beets to be the last thing he tasted.

The late August afternoon was hot when he pulled off the road. A tree-studded field stretched before them. "Let's walk to those trees over there," he said, nodding to a line of trees about a hundred yards away. "See how they're growing, in a line like that? There might be a little creek there."

She looked around. "Shouldn't we ask permission?"

He raised his eyebrows. "Do you see a house anywhere? Who do we ask?"

"Well, all right, but if we get in trouble, it's your fault."

He carried the cooler and most of the food. Sunny slung her backpack on her shoulders, then took charge of the ground cloth and the jar of pickled beets. "I'd better carry these," she said. "You might drop them."

"You could take something else, too," he grunted. This stuff was heavy.

She stretched up to peek in the grocery bag. The apple pie was perched on top of the other stuff. "Nah, you won't drop the pie."

He grumbled all the way to their picnic site, more because she enjoyed it than any other reason. This was the last day she would ever tease him, or he would see that smile, hear that laugh.

"Oh, there *is* a creek!" she exclaimed when they reached the trees. She carefully set the jar of beets down and unfolded the ground cloth, snapping it open in that brisk, economical movement all women seemed to have, and letting it settle on the thick, overgrown grass. A light breeze was blowing, so she anchored the cloth with her backpack on one corner and the jar of beets on the another.

Chance set the cooler and food down and sprawled out on the cloth. "I'm too tired now to enjoy myself," he complained.

She leaned over and kissed him. "You think I don't know what you're up to? Next thing I know you'll get something in your eye, and I'll have to get really, really close to see it. Then your back will need scratching, and you'll have to take off your shirt. Before I know it, we'll both be naked and it'll be time to leave, and we won't have had a bite to eat."

He gave her a quizzical look. "You have this all planned out, don't you?"

"Down to the last detail."

"Suits me." He reached for her, but with a spurt of laughter she scooted out of reach. She picked up the jar of beets and looked at him expectantly.

He flopped back with a groan. "Oh, man. Don't tell me you expect me to try them *now.*"

"No, I want you to open the jar so *I* can eat them."

"I thought you said they were nasty."

"They are. I want to see if they're as nasty as I remember." She handed him the jar. "If you'll open them for me, I'll let you eat fried chicken and potato salad to build up your strength before I wring you out and hang you up to dry."

He sat up and took the jar. "In your dreams, little miss 'don't-touch-me-again-you-lech.'" He put some muscle behind the effort, twisting the lid free.

"I've been sandbagging," she said. "This time, don't even bother begging for mercy."

She reached for the jar. The loosened lid came off, and the jar slipped from her hands. He dived for it, not wanting beets all over everything. Just as he moved, the tree beside him exploded, and a millisecond later he heard the blast of the shot.

He twisted in midair, throwing himself on top of Sunny and rolling with her behind the cover of the tree.

Chapter 13

"Stay down!" Chance barked, shoving her face into the grass.

Sunny couldn't have moved even if she had wanted to, even if his two hundred-plus pounds hadn't been lying on top of her. She was paralyzed, terror freezing in her veins as she realized her worst nightmare had come true, her father had found them, and Chance was nothing more than an obstacle to be destroyed. That bullet hadn't been aimed at *her*. If she hadn't dropped the jar of beets, if Chance hadn't lunged for it, the slug that blew chunks of wood out of the tree would have blown off half his head.

"Son of a bitch," he muttered above her, his breath stirring her hair. "Sniper."

The earth exploded two inches from her head, clods of dirt flying in her face, tiny pieces of gravel stinging her like bees. Chance literally threw her to the side, rolling with her again; the ground dropped out from beneath her, and her stomach gave a sickening lurch. As suddenly as the fall began, it stopped. She landed hard in three inches of sluggish water.

He had rolled them into the creek, where the banks afforded them more cover. A twist of his powerful body and he was off her, his big pistol in his hand as he flattened himself against the shallow bank. Sunny managed to get to her knees, slipped on the slimy creek bottom, and clambered on her hands and knees to a spot beside him. She felt numb, as if her arms and legs didn't belong to her, yet they were working, moving.

This wasn't real. It couldn't be. How had he found them?

She closed her eyes, fighting the terror. She was a liability to Chance unless she got herself under control. She'd had close calls before and handled herself just fine, but she had never before seen the man she loved almost get killed in front of her. She had never before been pregnant, with so much to lose.

Her teeth were chattering. She clamped her jaw together.

Silence fell over the field. She heard a car drive by on the road, and for a wild moment she wondered why it didn't stop. But why would it? There was nothing the average passerby would notice, no bodies lying around on the highway, no haze of gun smoke hanging over the green grass. There was only silence, as if even the insects had frozen in place, the birds stopped singing; even the breeze had stopped rustling the leaves. It was as if nature held its breath, shocked by the sudden violence.

The shot had come from the direction of the road, but she hadn't seen anyone drive up. They had only just arrived themselves; it was as if whoever had shot at them had already been here, waiting. But that was impossible, wasn't it? The picnic was an impulse, and the location sheer chance; they could just as well have stopped at a park.

The only other explanation that occurred to her was if the shooter had nothing to do with her father. Maybe it was a crazy landowner who shot at trespassers.

If only she had brought her cell phone! But Margreta wasn't due to call her for several more days, and even if she had brought the phone, it would be in her backpack, which was still lying on the ground cloth. The distance of a few yards might as well be a mile. Her pistol was also in the pack; though a pistol was useless against a sniper, she would feel better if she had some means of protection.

Chance hadn't fired; he knew the futility of it even more than she did. His dark gold eyes were scanning the countryside, looking for anything that would give away the assailant's position: a glint of sunlight on the barrel, the color of his clothing, a movement. The extreme angle of the late afternoon sun picked out incredible detail in the trees and bushes, but nothing that would help them.

Only nightfall would help, she thought. If they could just hold out for...how long? Another hour? Two hours, at most. When it was dark, then they could belly down in the little creek and work their way to safety, either upstream or down, it didn't matter.

If they lived that long. The sniper had the advantage. All they had was the cover of a shallow creek bank.

She became aware that her teeth were chattering again. Again she clamped her jaw together to still the movement. Chance spared a glance at her, a split-second assessment before he returned to once again scanning the trees for the sniper. "Are you all right?" he asked, though he obviously knew she was all in one piece. He wasn't asking about her physical condition.

"S-scared spitless," she managed to say.

"Yeah. Me, too."

He didn't look scared, she thought. He looked coldly furious.

He reached out and rubbed her arm, a brief gesture of comfort. "Thank God for those beets," he said.

She almost cried. The beets. She had thoroughly enjoyed teasing him about the beets, but the truth was, when she saw them in the supermarket she had been overcome by an almost violent craving for them. She wanted those beets. She felt as if she could eat the entire jar of them. Could cravings start this early in a pregnancy? If so, then he should thank God not for the beets, but for the beginnings of life forming inside her.

She wished she had told him immediately when her period didn't come. She couldn't tell him now; the news would be too distracting.

If they lived through this, she thought fervently, she wouldn't keep the secret to herself a minute longer.

"It can't be Hauer's men," she blurted. "It's impossible. They couldn't be here ahead of us, because we didn't know we were coming here. It has to be a crazy farmer, or a—a jerk who thought it would be funny to shoot at someone."

"Sweetheart." He touched her arm again, and she realized she was babbling. "It isn't a crazy farmer, or a trigger-happy jerk."

"How do you know? It could be!"

"The sniper's too professional."

Just four words, but they made her heart sink. Chance would know; he had training in this sort of thing.

She pressed her forehead against the grassy bank,

fighting for the courage to do what she had to do. Her mother had died protecting her and Margreta; surely she could be as brave? She couldn't tell Hauer anything about Margreta, so her sister was safe, and if she could save Chance, then dying would be worth it....

Her child would die with her.

Don't make me choose, she silently prayed. *The child or the father.*

If it were just her, she wouldn't hesitate. In the short time she had known Chance—was it really just two weeks?—he had given her a lifetime of happiness and the richness of love. She would gladly give her life in exchange for his.

The life inside her wasn't really a child yet; it was still just a rapidly dividing cluster of cells. No organs or bones had formed, nothing recognizable as a human. It was maybe the size of a pin head. But the potential...oh, the potential. She loved that tiny ball of cells with a fierceness that burned through every fiber of her being, had loved it from the first startled awareness that her period was late. It was as if she had blinked and said, "Oh. Hello," because one second she had been totally unaware of its existence, and the next she had somehow known.

The child or the father. The father or the child.

The words writhed in her brain, echoing, bouncing. She loved them both. How could she choose? She couldn't choose; no woman should have to make such a decision. She hated her father even more for forcing her into this situation. She hated the chromosomes, the DNA, that he had contributed to her existence. He wasn't a father, he had never been a father. He was a monster.

"Give me your pistol." She heard the words, but the voice didn't sound at all like hers.

His head snapped around. "What?" He stared at her as if she had lost her mind.

"Give me the pistol," she repeated. "He—they—don't know we have it. You haven't fired back. I'll tuck it in the back of my jeans and walk out there—"

"The hell you will!" He glared at her. "If you think I—"

"No, listen!" she said urgently. "They won't shoot me. He wants me alive. When they get close enough for me to use the pistol I—"

"No!" He grabbed her by the shirt and hauled her close so they were almost nose to nose. His eyes were almost shooting sparks. "If you make one move to stand up, I swear I'll knock you out. Do you understand me? *I will not let you walk out there.*"

He released her, and Sunny sank back against the creek bank. She couldn't overpower him, she thought bleakly. He was too strong, and too alert to be taken by surprise.

"We have to do something," she whispered.

He didn't look at her again. "We wait," he said flatly. "That's what we do. Sooner or later, the bastard will show himself."

Wait. That was the first idea she'd had, to wait until dark and slip away. But if Hauer had more than one man here, the sniper could keep them pinned down while the other worked his way around behind them—

"Can we move?" she asked. "Up the creek, down the creek—it doesn't matter."

He shook his head. "It's too risky. The creek's shallow. The only place we have enough cover is flat against the bank on this side. If we try to move, we expose ourselves to fire.''

''What if there's more than one?''

''There is.'' He sounded positive. A feral grin moved his lips in a frightening expression. ''At least four, maybe five. I hope it's five.''

She shook her head, trying to understand. Five to two were deadly odds. ''That makes you happy?''

''Very happy. The more the merrier.''

Nausea hit the back of her throat, and she closed her eyes, fighting the urge to vomit. Did he think sheer guts and fighting spirit would keep them alive?

His lean, powerful hand touched her face in a gentle caress. ''Chin up, sweetheart. Time's on our side.''

Now wasn't the time for explanations, Chance thought. The questions would be too angry, the answers too long and complicated. Their situation was delicately balanced between success and catastrophe; he couldn't relax his guard. If he was correct and there were five men out there hunting them—and that was the only explanation, that one of his own men was a traitor and had given Hauer the location of their supposedly impromptu picnic—then they could, at any time, decide to catch him in a pincer movement. With only one pistol, and Sunny to one side of him, he couldn't handle an attack from more than two directions. The third one would get him—and probably Sunny, too. In a fire fight, bullets flew like angry hornets, and most of them didn't hit their target. If a bullet didn't hit its target, that meant it hit something—or someone—else.

His own men would have been stood down, or sent to a bogus location. That was why there hadn't been any return fire when he and Sunny were fired on—no one was there. For that to have happened, the traitor had to be someone in a position of authority, a team leader or higher. He would find out. Oh, yeah, he'd find out. There had been several betrayals over the years, but they hadn't been traceable. One such breach had almost cost Barrie, Zane's wife, her life. Chance had been trying to identify the bastard for four years now, but he'd been too smart. But this time it was traceable. This time, his men would know who had changed their orders.

The traitor must have thought it was worth blowing his cover, to have this opportunity to kill Chance Mackenzie himself. And he should be here in person, to see the job done. Hauer's two men would bring the count to three. Hauer made it four. The only way Hauer could have gotten into the country and moved about as freely and undetected as he had was with inside help—the FBI mole. If Chance were really lucky, the mole was here, too, bringing the count to five.

But they'd made a big mistake. They didn't know about his ace in the hole: Zane. They didn't know he was out there; that was an arrangement Chance had made totally off the record. If Zane wasn't needed, no one would ever know he was there. Chance's men were damn good, world class, but they weren't in Zane's class. No one was.

Zane was a superb strategist; he always had a plan, and a plan to back up his plan. He would have seen in an instant what was going down and been on the phone calling the men back into position from wherever they'd been sent. How long it took them to get here depended on how far away they were, assuming they could get here at all. And after the call Zane would have started moving, ghosting around, searching out Hauer and his men. Every minute that passed increased the odds in Chance's favor.

He couldn't explain any of that to Sunny, not now, not even to ease the white, pinched expression that made him ache to hold her close and reassure her. Her eyes were haunted, their sparkle gone. She had worked her entire life to make certain she was never caught off guard, and yet she had been; he himself had seen to it.

The knowledge was bitter in his mouth. She was terrified of the monster who had relentlessly hunted her all her life, yet she had been willing to walk out there and offer herself as a sacrifice. How many times in the short two weeks he'd known her had she put herself on the line for him? The first time had been when she barely knew him, when she swooped down to grab the snake coiled so close to his feet. She was terrified of snakes, but she'd done it. She was shaking with fear now, but he knew that if he let her, she would do exactly what she'd offered. That kind of courage amazed him, and humbled him.

His head swiveled restlessly as he tried to keep watch in all directions. The minutes trickled past. The sun slid below the horizon, but there was still plenty of light; twilight wouldn't begin deepening for another fifteen, twenty minutes. The darker it was, the more Zane was in his element. By now, he should have taken out at least one, maybe two—

A man stepped out from behind the tree under which Chance and Sunny had intended to have their picnic and aimed a black 9mm automatic at Sunny's head. He didn't say ''Drop it'' or anything else. He just smiled, his gaze locked with Chance's.

Carefully Chance placed his pistol on the grass. If the gun had been aimed at his own head, he would have taken the risk that his reflexes were faster. He wouldn't risk Sunny's life. As soon as he moved his hand away from the pistol, the black hole in the man's weapon centered between his eyes.

"Surprised?" the man asked softly. At his voice Sunny gasped and whirled, her feet sliding on the slippery creek bottom. Chance reached out and steadied her without taking his gaze from a man he knew very well.

"Not really," he said. "I knew there was someone."

Sunny looked back and forth between them. "Do you *know* him?" she asked faintly.

"Yeah." He should have been prepared for this, he thought. Knowing one of his own men was involved, he should have realized the traitor would have the skill to approach silently, using the same tree that helped shield them as his own cover. Doing so took patience and nerve, because if Chance had happened to move even a few inches to one side, he would have seen the man's approach.

"H-how?" she stammered.

"We've worked together for years," Melvin Darnell said, still smiling. Mel the Man. That was what the others called him, because he would volunteer for any mission, no matter how dangerous. What better way to get inside information? Chance thought.

"You sold out to Hauer," Chance said, shaking his head. "That's low."

"No, that's lucrative. He has men everywhere. The FBI, the Justice Department, the CIA…even here, right under your nose." Mel shrugged. "What can I say? He pays well."

"I misjudged you. I never thought you'd be the type to get a kick out of torture. Or are you chickening out and leaving as soon as he gets his hands on her?" Chance nodded his head toward Sunny.

"Nice try, Mackenzie, but it won't work. He's her father. All he wants is his little girl." Mel smirked at Sunny.

Chance snorted. "Get a clue. Do you think she'd be so terrified if all he wanted was to get to know her?"

Mel spared another brief glance in her direction. She was absolutely colorless, even her lips. There was no mistaking her fear. He shrugged. "So I was wrong. I don't care what he does with her."

"Do you care that he's a child molester?" Keep him talking. Buy time. Give Zane time to work.

"Give it up," Mel said cheerfully. "He could be Hitler's reincarnation and it still wouldn't change the color of his money. If you think I'm going to develop a conscience—well, you're the one who needs to get a clue."

There was movement behind Mel. Three men approaching, walking openly now, as if they had nothing to fear. Two were dressed in suits, one in slacks and an open-necked shirt. The one in slacks and one of the suits carried hand guns. The suit would be the FBI informant, the one in slacks one of Hauer's bloodhounds. The man in the middle, the one wearing the double-breasted Italian silk suit, his skin tanned, his light brown hair brushed straight back—that was Hauer. He was smiling.

"My dear," he said jovially when he reached them. He stepped carefully around the spilled beets, his nose wrinkling in distaste. "It is so good to finally meet you. A father should know his children, don't you think?"

Sunny didn't speak for a moment. She stared at her father with unconcealed horror and loathing. Beside her, Chance felt the fear drain out of her, felt her subtly relax. Extreme terror was like that, sometimes. When one

feared that something would happen, it was the dread
and anxiety, the anticipation, that was so crippling. Once
the thing actually happened, there was nothing left to
fear. He took a firm grip on her arm, wishing she had
remained petrified. Sunny was valiant enough when she
was frightened; when she thought she had nothing left
to lose, there was no telling what she would do.

"I thought you'd be taller," she finally said, looking
at him rather dismissively.

Crispin Hauer flushed angrily. He wasn't a large man,
about five-eight, and slender. The two men flanking him
were both taller. Chance wondered how Sunny had
known unerringly how to prick his ego. "Please get out
of the mud—if you can bring yourself to leave your
lover's side, that is. I recommend it. Head shots can be
nasty. You wouldn't want his brains on you, would you?
I hear the stain never comes out of one's clothes."

Sunny didn't move. "I don't know where Margreta
is," she said. "You might as well kill me now, because
I can't tell you anything."

He shook his head in mock sympathy. "As if I believe
that." He held out his hand. "You may climb out by
yourself, or my men will assist you."

There wasn't much light left, Chance thought. If
Sunny could keep delaying her father without provoking
him into violence, Zane should be here soon. With Hauer
out in the open, Zane must be positioning himself so he
could get all four men in his sights.

"Where's the other guy?" he asked, to distract them.
"There *are* five of you, aren't there?"

The FBI man and the bloodhound looked around, in
the direction of the trees on the opposite side of the road.
They seemed vaguely surprised that no one was behind
them.

Mel didn't take his attention from Chance. "Don't let him spook you," he said sharply. "Keep your mind on business."

"Don't you wonder where he is?" Chance asked softly.

"I don't give a damn. He's nothing to me. Maybe he fell out of the tree and broke his neck," Mel said.

"Enough," Hauer said, distaste for this squabbling evident in his tone. "Sonia, come out now. I promise you won't like it if my men have to fetch you."

Sunny's contemptuous gaze swept him from head to foot. Unbelievably, she began singing. And the ditty she sang was a cruel little song of the sort gradeschoolers sang to make fun of a classmate they didn't like. "Monkey man, monkey man, itty bitty monkey man. He's so ugly, he's so short, he needs a ladder to reach his butt."

It didn't rhyme, Chance thought in stunned bemusement. Children, crude little beasts that they were, didn't care about niceties such as that. All they cared about was the effectiveness of their taunt.

It was effective beyond his wildest expectation.

Mel Darnell smothered a laugh. The two other men froze, their expressions going carefully blank. Crispin Hauer flushed a dark, purplish red and his eyes bulged until white showed all around the irises. "You bitch!" he screamed, spittle flying, and he grabbed for the gun in the FBI mole's hand.

A giant red flower bloomed on Hauer's chest, accompanied by a strange, dull splat. Hauer stopped as if he had run into a glass wall, his expression going blank.

Mel had excellent reflexes, and excellent training. In that nanosecond before the sound of the shot reached them, Chance saw Mel's finger begin tightening on the trigger, and he grabbed for his own weapon, knowing he wouldn't be fast enough. Then Sunny hit him full force, her entire body crashing into him and knocking him sideways, her scream almost drowning out the thunderous boom of Mel's big-caliber pistol. She clambered off him almost as fast as she had hit him, trying to scramble up the grassy bank to get to Mel before he could fire another round, but Mel never had another opportunity to pull the trigger. Mel never had anything else, not even a second, because Zane's second shot took him dead center of the chest just as his first had taken Hauer.

Then all hell broke loose. Chance's men, finally back in position and with the threat to Chance and Sunny taken care of, opened fire on the remaining two men. Chance grabbed Sunny and flattened her in the creek again, covering her with his own body, holding her there until Zane roared a cease fire and the night was silent.

Sunny sat off to the side of the nightmarish scene, brightly lit now with battery-operated spotlights that picked out garish detail and left stark black shadows. From somewhere, one of the small army of men who suddenly swarmed the field had produced a bucket that he turned upside down for her, providing her with a seat. She was wet and almost unbearably cold, despite the warmth of the late August night. Her muddy clothes were clammy, so the blanket she clutched around her with nerveless fingers didn't do much to help, but she didn't release it.

She hurt, with an all-consuming agony that threatened to topple her off the bucket, but she grimly forced herself to stay upright. Sheer willpower kept her on that bucket.

The men around her were professionals. They were quiet and competent as they dealt with the five bodies that were laid out on the ground in a neat row. They were courteous with the local law enforcement officers who arrived *en force,* sirens blasting, blue lights strobing the night, though there was never any doubt who held jurisdiction.

And Chance was their leader.

That man, the one who had first held a gun on them, had called him "Mackenzie." And several times one or another of the locals had referred to him as Mr. Mackenzie; he had answered, so she knew there was no mistake in the name.

The events of the night were a chaotic blur in her mind, but one fact stood out: this entire scene was a setup, a trap—and she had been the bait.

She didn't want to believe it, but logic wouldn't let her deny it. He was obviously in charge here. He had a lot of men on site, men he commanded, men who could be here only if he had arranged it in advance.

Viewed in the light of that knowledge, everything that had happened since she met him took on a different meaning. She even thought she recognized the cretin who had stolen her briefcase in the Salt Lake City airport. He was cleaned up now, with the same quiet, competent air as the others, but she was fairly certain he was the same man.

Everything had been a setup. Everything. She didn't know how he'd done it, her mind couldn't quite grasp the sphere of influence needed to bring all of this off, but somehow he had manipulated her flights so that she was in the Salt Lake City airport at a certain time, for the cretin to grab her briefcase and Chance to intercept him. It was a hugely elaborate play, one that took skill and money and more resources than she could imagine.

He must have thought she was in cahoots with her

father, she thought with a flash of intuition. This had all happened after the incident in Chicago, which was undoubtedly what had brought her to Chance's notice. What had his plan been? To make her fall in love with him and use her to infiltrate her father's organization? Only it hadn't worked out that way. Not only was she not involved with her father, she desperately feared and hated him. So Chance, knowing why Hauer really wanted her, had adjusted his plan and used her as bait.

What a masterful strategy. And what a superb actor he was; he should get an Oscar.

There hadn't been anything wrong with the plane at all. She didn't miss the significance of the timing of their "rescue." Charlie Jones had just happened to find them first thing in the morning after she spilled her guts about her father to Chance the night before. He must have signaled Charlie somehow.

How easy she had been for him. She had been completely duped, completely taken in by his lovemaking and charm. He had been a bright light to her, a comet blazing into her lonely world, and she had fallen for him with scarcely a whisper of resistance. He must think her the most gullible fool in the world. The worst of it was, she was an even bigger fool than he knew, because she was pregnant with his child.

She looked across the field at him, standing tall in the glaring spotlights as he talked with another tall, powerful man who exuded the deadliest air she had ever seen, and the pain inside her spread until she could barely contain it.

Her bright light had gone out.

Chance looked around at Sunny, as he had been doing periodically since the moment she sank down on the overturned bucket and huddled deep in the blanket someone had draped around her. She was frighteningly white, her face drawn and stark. He couldn't take the time to comfort her, not now. There was too much to do, local authorities to soothe at the same time that he let them know he was the one in control, not they, the bodies to be handled, sweeps initiated at the agencies Mel had listed as having Hauer's moles employed there.

She wasn't stupid; far from it. He had watched her watching the activity around her, watched her expression become even more drawn as she inevitably reached the only conclusion she *could* reach. She had noticed when people called him Mackenzie instead of McCall.

Their gazes met, and locked. She stared at him across the ten yards that separated them, thirty feet of unbridgeable gulf. He kept his face impassive. There was no excuse he could give her that she wouldn't already have considered. His reasons were good; he knew that. But he had used her and risked her life. Being the person she was, she would easily forgive him for risking her life; it was the rest of it, the way he had used her, that would strike her to the core.

As he watched, he saw the light die in her eyes, draining away as if it had never been. She turned her head away from him—

And gutted him with the gesture.

Shaken, pierced through with regret, he turned back to Zane and found his brother watching him with a world of knowledge in those pale eyes. "If you want her," Zane said, "then don't let her go."

It was that simple, and that difficult. Don't let her go. How could he not, when she deserved so much better than what he was?

But the idea was there now. Don't let her go. He

couldn't resist looking at her again, to see if she was still watching him.

She wasn't there. The bucket still sat there, but Sunny was gone.

Chance strode rapidly across to where she had been, scanning the knots of men who stood about, some working, some just observing. He didn't see that bright hair. Damn it, she was just here; how could she disappear so fast?

Easily, he thought. She had spent a lifetime practicing.

Zane was beside him, his head up, alert. The damn spotlights blinded them to whatever was behind them. She could have gone in any direction, and they wouldn't be able to see her.

He looked down to see if he could pick up any tracks, though the grass was so trampled by now that he doubted he would find anything. The bucket gleamed dark and wet in the spotlight.

Wet?

Chance leaned down and swiped his hand over the bucket. He stared at the dark red stain on his fingers and palm. Blood. Sunny's blood.

He felt as if his own blood was draining from his body. My God, she'd been shot, and she hadn't said a word. In the darkness, the blood hadn't been noticeable on her wet clothing. But that had been...how long ago? She had sat there all that time, bleeding, and not told anyone.

Why?

Because she wanted to get away from him. If they had known she was wounded, she would have to be bundled up and taken to a hospital, and she wouldn't be able to escape without having to see him again. When

Sunny walked, she did it clean. No scenes, no excuses, no explanations. She just disappeared.

If he had thought it hurt when she turned away from him, that was nothing to the way he felt now. Desperate fear seized his heart, froze his blood in his veins. ''Listen up!'' he boomed, and a score of faces, trained to obey his every command, turned his way. ''Did anyone see where Sunny went?''

Heads shook, and men began looking around. She was nowhere in sight.

Chance began spitting out orders. ''Everyone drop what you're doing and fan out. Find her. She's bleeding. She was shot and didn't tell anyone.'' As he talked, he was striding out of the glare of the spotlights, his heart in his mouth. She couldn't have gone far, not in that length of time. He would find her. He couldn't bear the alternative.

Chapter 14

Chance blindly paced the corridor outside the surgical waiting room. He couldn't sit down, though the room was empty and he could have had any chair he wanted. If he stopped walking, he thought, he might very well fall down and not be able to stand again. He hadn't known such crippling fear existed. He had never felt it for himself, not even when he looked down the barrel of a weapon pointed at his face—and Mel's hadn't been the first—but he felt it for Sunny. He'd been gripped by it since he found her lying facedown in the grassy field, unconscious, her pulse thready from blood loss.

Thank God there were medics on hand in the field, or she would have died before he could get her to a hospital. They hadn't managed to stop the bleeding, but they had slowed it, started an IV saline push to pump fluid back into her body and raise her plummeting blood pressure, and gotten her to the hospital still alive.

He had been shouldered aside then, by a whole team

of gowned emergency personnel. "Are you any relation to her, sir?" a nurse had asked briskly as she all but manhandled him out of the treatment room.

"I'm her husband," he'd heard himself say. There was no way he was going to allow the decisions for her care to be taken out of his hands. Zane, who had been beside him the entire time, hadn't revealed even a flicker of surprise.

"Do you know her blood type, sir?"

Of course he didn't. Nor did he know the answers to any of the other questions posed by the woman they handed him off to, but he was so numb, his attention so focused on the cubicle where about ten people were working on her, that he barely knew anyone was asking the questions, and the woman hadn't pushed it. Instead, she had patted his hand and said she would come back in a little while when his wife was stabilized. He had been grateful for her optimism. In the meantime, Zane, as ruthlessly competent as usual, had requested that a copy of their file on Sunny be downloaded to his wireless Pocket Pro, so Chance would have all the necessary information when the woman returned with her million and one questions. He was indifferent to the bureaucratic snafu he was causing; the organization would pay for everything.

But the shocks had kept arriving, one piling on top of the other. The surgeon came out of the cubicle, his green paper gown stained red with her blood. "Your wife regained consciousness briefly," he'd said. "She wasn't completely lucid, but she asked about the baby. Do you know how far along she is?"

Chance had literally staggered and braced his hand against the wall for support. "She's pregnant?" he asked hoarsely.

"I see." The surgeon immediately switched gears. "I think she must have just found out. We'll do some tests and take all the precautions we can. We're taking her up to surgery now. A nurse will show you where to wait." He strode away, paper gown flapping.

Zane had turned to Chance, his pale blue eyes laser sharp. "Yours?" he asked briefly.

"Yes."

Zane didn't ask if he was certain, for which Chance was grateful. Zane took it for granted Chance wouldn't be mistaken about something that important.

Pregnant? How? He pinched the bridge of his nose, between his eyes. He knew how. He remembered with excruciating clarity how it felt to climax inside her without the protective sheath of a condom dulling the sensation. It had happened twice—just twice—but once was enough.

A couple of little details clicked into place. He'd been around pregnant women most of his life, with first one sister-in-law and then another producing a little Mackenzie. He knew the symptoms well. He remembered Sunny's sleepiness this afternoon, and her insistence on buying the beets. Those damn pickled beets, he thought; her craving for them—for he was certain now that was why she'd wanted them—had saved his life. Sometimes the weird cravings started almost immediately. He could remember when Shea, Michael's wife, had practically wiped that section of Wyoming clean of canned tuna, a full week before she missed her first period. The sleepiness began soon in a pregnancy, too.

He knew the exact day when he'd gotten her pregnant. It had been the second time he'd made love to her, lying on the blanket in the late afternoon heat. The baby would be born about the middle of May...if Sunny lived.

She had to live. He couldn't face the alternative. He loved her too damn much to even think it. But he had seen the bullet wound in her right side, and he was terrified.

"Do you want me to call Mom and Dad?" Zane asked.

They would drop everything and come immediately if he said yes, Chance knew. The whole family would; the hospital would be inundated with Mackenzies. Their support was total, and unquestioning.

He shook his head. "No. Not yet." His voice was raw, as if he had been screaming, though he would have sworn all his screams had been held inside. If Sunny…if the worst happened, he would need them then. Right now he was still holding together. Just.

So he walked, and Zane walked with him. Zane had seen a lot of bullet wounds, too; he'd taken his share. Chance was the lucky one; he'd been cut a few times, but never shot.

God, there had been so much blood. How had she stayed upright for so long? She had answered questions, said she was all right, even walked around a little before one of the men had found that bucket for her to sit on. It was dark, she had a blanket wrapped around her—that was why no one had noticed. But she should have been on the ground, screaming in pain.

Zane's thoughts were running along the same path. "I'm always amazed," he said, "at what some people can do after being shot."

Contrary to what most people thought, a bullet wound, even a fatal one, didn't necessarily knock the victim down. All cops knew that even someone whose heart had been virtually destroyed by a bullet could still attack and kill *them,* and die only when his oxygen-starved brain died. Someone crazed on drugs could absorb a truly astonishing amount of damage and keep on fighting. On the other side of the spectrum were those who suffered relatively minor wounds and went down as if they had been poleaxed, then screamed unceasingly until they reached the hospital and were given enough drugs to quiet them. It was pure mind over matter, and Sunny had a will like titanium. He only hoped she applied that will to surviving.

It was almost six hours before the tired surgeon approached, the six longest hours of Chance's life. The surgeon looked haggard, and Chance felt the icy claw of dread. No. No—

"I think she's going to make it," the surgeon said, and smiled a smile of such pure personal triumph that Chance knew there had been a real battle in the O.R. "I had to remove part of the liver and resection her small intestine. The wound to the liver is what caused the extensive hemorrhage. We had to replace almost her complete blood volume before we got things under control." He rubbed his hand over his face. "It was touch and go for a while. Her blood pressure bottomed out and she went into cardiac arrest, but we got her right back. Her pupil response is normal, and her vitals are satisfactory. She was lucky."

"Lucky," Chance echoed, still dazed by the combination of good news and the litany of damage.

"It was only a fragment of a bullet that hit her. There must have been a ricochet."

Chance knew she hadn't been hit while he'd had her flattened in the creek. It had to have happened when she knocked him aside and Darnell fired. Evidently Darnell had missed, and the bullet must have struck a rock in the creek and fragmented.

She had been protecting him. Again.

"She'll be in ICU for at least twenty-four hours, maybe forty-eight, until we see if there's a secondary infection. I really think we have things under control, though." He grinned. "She'll be out of here in a week."

Chance sagged against the wall, bending over to clasp his knees. His head swam. Zane's hard hand gripped his shoulder, lending his support. "Thank you," Chance said to the doctor, angling his head so he could see him.

"Do you need to lie down?" the doctor asked.

"No, I'm all right. God! I'm great. She's going to be okay!"

"Yeah," said the doctor, and grinned again.

Sunny kept surfacing to consciousness, like a float bobbing up and down in the water. At first her awareness was fragmented. She could hear voices in the distance, though she couldn't make out any words, and a soft beeping noise. She was also aware of something in her throat, though she didn't realize it was a tube. She had no concept of where she was, or even that she was lying down.

The next time she bobbed up, she could feel smooth cotton beneath her and recognized the fabric as sheets.

The next time she managed to open her eyes a slit, but her vision was blurry and what seemed like a mountain of machinery made no sense to her.

At some point she realized she was in a hospital. There was pain, but it was at a distance. The tube was gone from her throat now. She vaguely remembered it being removed, which hadn't been pleasant, but her sense of time was so confused that she thought she remembered the tube being there after it was removed. People kept coming into the small space that was hers, turning on bright lights, talking and touching her and doing intimate things to her.

Gradually her dominion over her body began to return, as she fought off the effects of anesthesia and drugs. She managed to make a weak gesture toward her belly, and croak out a single word. "Baby?"

The intensive care nurse understood. "Your baby's fine," he said, giving her a comforting pat, and she was content.

She was horribly thirsty. Her next word was "Water," and slivers of ice were put in her mouth.

With the return of consciousness, though, came the pain. It crept ever nearer as the fog of drugs receded. The pain was bad, but Sunny almost welcomed it, because it meant she was alive, and for a while she had thought she might not be.

She saw the nurse named Jerry the most often. He came into the cubicle, smiling as usual, and said, "There's someone here to see you."

Sunny violently shook her head, which was a mistake. It set off waves of agony that swamped the drugs holding them at bay. "No visitors," she managed to say.

It seemed as if she spent days, eons, in the intensive care unit, but when she asked Jerry he said, "Oh, about thirty-six hours. We'll be moving you to a private room soon. It's being readied now."

When they moved her, she was clearheaded enough to watch the ceiling tiles and lights pass by overhead. She caught a glimpse of a tall, black-haired man and quickly looked away.

Settling her into a private room was quite an operation, requiring two orderlies, three nurses and half an hour. She was exhausted when everything, including herself, had been transferred and arranged. The fresh bed was nice and cool; the head had been elevated and a pillow tucked under her head. Sitting up even that much made her feel a hundred percent more normal and in control.

There were flowers in the room. Roses, peach ones, with a hint of blush along the edges of their petals, dispensed a spicy, peppery scent that overcame the hospital scents of antiseptics and cleaning fluids. Sunny stared at them but didn't ask who they were from.

"I don't want any visitors," she told the nurses. "I just want to rest."

She was allowed to eat Jell-O, and drink weak tea. On the second day in the private room she drank some broth, and she was placed in the bedside chair for fifteen minutes. It felt good to stand on her own two feet, even for the few seconds it took them to move her from bed to chair. It felt even better when they moved her back to the bed.

That night, she got out of bed herself, though the process was slow and unhappy, and walked the length of the bed. She had to hold on to the bed for support, but her legs remained under her.

The third day, there was another delivery from a florist. This was a bromeliad, with thick, grayish green leaves and a beautiful pink flower blooming in its center. She had never had houseplants for the same reason she had never had a pet, because she was constantly on the move and couldn't take care of them. She stared at the bromeliad, trying to come to grips with the fact that she could have all the houseplants she wanted now. Everything was changed. Crispin Hauer was dead, and she and Margreta were free.

The thought of her sister sent alarm racing through

her. What day was it? When was Margreta due to call? For that matter, where was her cell phone?

On the afternoon of the fourth day, the door opened and Chance walked in.

She turned her head to look out the window. In truth, she was surprised he had given her this long to recover. She had held him off as long as she could, but she supposed there had to be a closing act before the curtain could fall.

She had held her inner pain at bay by focusing on her physical pain, but now it rushed to the forefront. She fought it down, reaching for control. There was nothing to be gained by causing a scene, only her self-respect to lose.

"I've kept your cell phone with me," he said, walking around to place himself between her and the windows, so she had to either look at him or turn her head away again. His conversational opening had guaranteed she wouldn't turn away. "Margreta called yesterday."

Sunny clenched her fists, then quickly relaxed her right hand as the motion flexed the IV needle taped to the back of it. Margreta would have panicked when she heard a man's voice answer instead of Sunny's.

"I talked fast," Chance said. "I told her you'd been shot but would be okay, and that Hauer was dead. I told her I'd bring the phone to you today, and she could call again tonight to verify everything I said. She didn't say anything, but she didn't hang up on me, either."

"Thank you," Sunny said. He had handled the situation in the best possible way.

He was subtly different, she realized. It wasn't just his clothing, though he was now dressed in black slacks and a white silk shirt, while he had worn only jeans, boots, and casual shirts and T-shirts before. His whole demeanor was different. Of course, he wasn't playing a raffish, charming charter pilot any longer. He was himself now, and the reality was what she had always sensed beneath the surface of his charm. He was the man who led some sort of commando team, who exerted enormous influence in getting things done his way. The dangerous edge she had only glimpsed before was in full view now, in his eyes and the authority with which he spoke.

He moved closer to the side of the bed, so close he was leaning against the rail. Very gently, the touch as light as gossamer, he placed his fingertips on her belly. "Our baby is all right," he said.

He knew. Shocked, she stared at him, though she realized she should have known the doctor would tell him.

"Were you going to tell me?" he asked, his golden-brown eyes intent on her face, as if he wanted to catch every nuance of expression.

"I hadn't thought about it one way or the other," she said honestly. She had just been coming to terms with the knowledge herself; she hadn't gotten around to forming any plans.

"This changes things."

"Does it really," she said, and it wasn't a question. "Was *anything* you told me the truth?"

He hesitated. "No."

"There was nothing wrong with the fuel pump."

"No."

"You could have flown us out of the canyon at any time."

"Yes."

"Your name isn't Chance McCall."

"Mackenzie," he said. "Chance Mackenzie."

"Well, that's one thing," she said bitterly. "At least your first name was really your own."

"Sunny…don't."

"Don't what? Don't try to find out how big a fool I am? Were you really an army ranger?"

He sighed, his expression grim. "Navy. Naval Intelligence."

"You arranged for all of my flights to be fouled up that day."

He shrugged an admittance.

"The cretin was really one of your men."

"A good one. The airport security people were mine, too."

She creased the sheet with her left hand. "You knew my father would be there. You had it set up."

"We knew two of his men were trailing us, had been since the television newscast about you aired."

"You arranged that, too."

He didn't say anything.

"Why did we fly all over the country? Why didn't we just stay in Seattle? That would have been less wear and tear on the plane."

"I had to make it look good."

She swallowed. "That day…the picnic. Would you have made love—I mean, had sex—with me with your men watching? Just to make it look good?"

"No. Having an affair with you was necessary, but…private."

"I suppose I should thank you for that, at least. Thank you. Now get out."

"I'm not going anywhere." He sat down in the bedside chair. "If you've finished with the dissection, we need to make some decisions."

"I've already made one. I don't want to see you again."

"Sorry about that, but you aren't getting your wish. You're stuck with me, sweetheart, because that baby inside you is mine."

Chapter 15

Sunny was released from the hospital eight days after the shooting. She could walk, gingerly, but her strength was almost negligible, and she had to wear the nightgown and robe Chance had bought her, because she couldn't stand any clothing around her middle. She had no idea what she was going to do. She wasn't in any condition to catch a flight to Atlanta, not to mention that she would have to travel in her nightgown, but she had to find somewhere to stay. Once she knew she was being released, she got the phone book and called a hotel, made certain the hotel had room service, and booked herself a room there. The hotel had room service; until she was able to take care of herself again, a hotel was the best she could do.

In the hospital she had, at first, entertained a fragile hope that Margreta would come to stay with her and help her until she was recovered. With their father dead, they didn't have to hide any longer. But though Margreta had sounded happy and relieved, she had resisted Sunny's suggestion that she come to Des Moines. They had exchanged telephone numbers, but that was all—and Margreta hadn't called back.

Sunny understood. Margreta would always have problems relating to people, forming relationships with them. She was probably very comfortable with the long-distance contact she had with Sunny, and wanted nothing more. Sunny tried to fight her sadness as she realized she would never have the sister she had wanted, but melancholy too easily overwhelmed her these days.

Part of it was the hormonal chaos of early pregnancy, she knew. She found herself tearing up at the most ridiculous things, such as a gardening show she watched on television one day. She lay in her hospital bed and began thinking how she had always wanted a flower garden but had never been able to have one, and presto, all of a sudden she was feeling sorry for herself and sitting there like an idiot with tears rolling down her face.

Depression went hand in glove with physical recovery, too, one of the nurses told her. It would pass as she got stronger and could do more.

But the biggest part of her depression was Chance. He visited every day, and once even brought along the tall, lethal-looking man she had noticed him talking to the night she was injured. To her surprise, Chance introduced the man as his brother, Zane. Zane had shaken her hand with exquisite gentleness, shown her photos of his pretty wife and three adorable children, and spent half an hour telling her yarns about the exploits of his daughter, Nick. If even half of what he said about the child was true, the world had better brace itself for when she was older.

After Zane left, Sunny was even more depressed. Zane

had what she had always wanted: a family he loved, and who loved him in return.

When he visited, Chance always avoided the subject that lay between them like a coiled snake. He had done what he had done, and no amount of talking would change reality. She had to respect, reluctantly, his lack of any attempt to make excuses. Instead, he talked about his family in Wyoming, and the mountain they all still called home, even though only his parents lived there now. He had four brothers and one sister, a dozen nephews—and one niece, the notorious Nick, whom he obviously adored. His sister was a horse trainer who was married to one of his agents; one brother was a rancher who had married the granddaughter of an old family enemy; another brother was an ex-fighter pilot who was married to an orthopedic surgeon; Zane was married to the daughter of an ambassador; and Joe, his oldest brother, was General Joseph Mackenzie, chairman of the Joint Chiefs of Staff.

That couldn't all be true, she thought, yet the tales had a ring of truth to them. Then she remembered that Chance was a consummate actor, and bitterness would swamp her again.

She couldn't seem to pull herself out of the dismals. She had always been able to laugh, but now she found it difficult to even smile. No matter how she tried to distract herself, the knowledge was always there, engraved on her heart like a curse that robbed her life of joy: Chance didn't love her. It had all been an act.

It was as if part of her had died. She felt cold inside, and empty. She tried to hide it, tried to tell herself the depression would go away if she just ignored it and concentrated on getting better, but every day the grayness inside her seemed to spread and deepen.

The day she was released, the escort finally arrived with a wheelchair and Sunny called a taxi to meet them at the entrance in fifteen minutes. She gingerly lowered herself into the wheelchair, and the escort obligingly placed the small bag containing her few articles of clothing and her backpack on her lap, then balanced the bromeliad on top.

"I'm sure I have to sign some papers before I'm released," Sunny said.

"No, I don't think so," the woman said, checking her orders. "According to this, you're all ready to go. Your husband probably handled it for you."

Sunny bit back the urge to snap that she wasn't married. He hadn't mentioned it, and in truth she hadn't given a thought to how she would pay for her hospital care, but now that she thought about it, she realized Chance had indeed handled all of that. Maybe he thought the least he could do was pick up her tab.

She was surprised he wasn't here, since he'd been so adamant about being a part of the baby's life, and persistent in visiting. For all she knew, she thought, he had been called away on some mysterious spy stuff.

She underestimated him. When the escort rolled her to the doors of the patient discharge area, she saw a familiar dark green Ford Explorer parked under the covered entrance. Chance unfolded his long length from behind the steering wheel and came to meet her.

"I've already called a taxi," she said, though she knew it was a waste of breath.

"Tough," he said succinctly. He took her clothes and the bromeliad and put them in the back of the Explorer, then opened the passenger door.

Sunny began to inch herself forward in the wheelchair seat, preparatory to standing; she had mastered the art when seated in a regular chair, but a wheelchair was trickier. Chance gave her an exasperated look, then leaned down and scooped her up in his powerful arms, handling her weight with ease as he deposited her in the Explorer.

"Thank you," she said politely. She would at least be civil, and his method had been much less painful and time-consuming than hers.

"You're welcome." He buckled the seat belt around her, making certain the straps didn't rub against the surgical incision, then closed the door and walked around to slide under the steering wheel.

"I've booked a room in a hotel," she said. "But I don't know where it is, so I can't give you directions."

"You aren't going to a hotel," he growled.

"I have to go somewhere," she pointed out. "I'm not able to drive, and I can't handle negotiating an airport, so a hotel with room service is the only logical solution."

"No it isn't. I'm taking you home with me."

"No!" she said violently, everything in her rejecting the idea of spending days in his company.

His jaw set. "You don't have a choice," he said grimly. "You're going—even if you kick and scream the whole way."

It was tempting. Oh, it was tempting. Only the thought of how badly kicking would pull at the incision made her resist the idea.

The dime didn't drop until she noticed he was driving to the airport. "Where are we going?"

He gave her an impatient glance. "I told you. Hell, Sunny, you know I don't live in Des Moines."

"All right, so I know where you don't live. But I *don't* know where you *do* live." She couldn't resist adding, "And even if you had told me, it would probably be a lie."

This time his glance was sulfuric. "Wyoming," he said through gritted teeth. "I'm taking you home to Wyoming."

She was silent during the flight, speaking only when necessary and then only in monosyllables. Chance studied her when her attention was on the landscape below, his sunglasses hiding his eyes. They had flown around so much during the time they'd been together that it felt natural to once again be in the plane with her, as if they were where they belonged. She had settled in with a minimum of fussing and no complaints, though he knew she had to be exhausted and uncomfortable.

She looked so frail, as if a good wind would blow her away. There wasn't any color in her cheeks or lips, and she had dropped a good ten pounds that she didn't need to lose. The doctor had assured him that she was recovering nicely, right on schedule, and that while her pregnancy was still too new for any test to tell them anything about the baby's condition, they had taken all precautions and he had every confidence the baby would be fine.

As thrilled as he was about the baby, Chance was more worried that the pregnancy would sap her strength and slow her recovery. She needed all the resources she could muster now, but nature would ensure that the developing child got what it needed first. The only way he could be confident she was getting what *she* needed was if he arranged for her to be watched every minute, and coddled and spoiled within an inch of her life. The best place for that was Mackenzie's Mountain.

He had called and told them he was bringing Sunny

there, of course. He had told them the entire situation, that she was pregnant and he intended to marry her, but that she was still mad as hell at him and hadn't forgiven him. He had set quite a task for himself, getting back in Sunny's good graces. But once he had her on the Mountain, he thought, he could take his time wearing her down.

Mary, typically, was ecstatic. She took it for granted Sunny would forgive him, and since she had been prodding him about getting married and giving her more grandchildren, she probably thought she was getting everything she wanted.

Chance was going to do everything he could to see that she did, because what she wanted was exactly what he wanted. He'd always sworn he would never get married and have children, but fate had stepped in and arranged things otherwise. The prospect of getting married scared him—no, it terrified the hell out of him, so much so that he hadn't even broached the subject to Sunny. He didn't know how to tell her what she needed to know about him, and he didn't know what she would do when she found out, if she would accept his proposal or tell him to drop dead.

The only thing that gave him hope was that she'd said she loved him. She hadn't said it since she found out how he'd set her up, but Sunny wasn't a woman who loved lightly. If there was a spark of love left in her, if he hadn't totally extinguished it, he would find a way to fan it to life.

He landed at the airstrip on Zane's property, and his heart gave a hard thump when he saw what was waiting for them. Even Sunny's interest was sparked. She sat up straighter, and for the first time since she'd been shot he saw a hint of that lively interest in her face. "What's going on?" she asked.

His spirits lifting, he grinned. "Looks like a welcoming party."

The entire Mackenzie clan was gathered by the airstrip. Everyone. Josh and Loren were there from Seattle with their three sons. Mike and Shea and their two boys. Zane and Barrie, each holding one of the twins. And there was Joe, decked out in his Air Force uniform with more rows of fruit salad on it than should be allowed. How he had carved time out of his schedule to come here, Chance didn't know—but then, Joe could do damn near anything he wanted, since he was the highest ranking military officer in the nation. Caroline, standing beside him and looking positively chic in turquoise capri pants and white sandals—and also looking damn good for her age—had probably had a harder time getting free. She was one of the top-ranked physicists in the world. Their five sons were with him, and John, the oldest, wasn't the only one this time who had a girlfriend with him. Maris and Mac stood together; Mac had his arm draped protectively around Maris's slight frame. And Mom and Dad were in the middle of the whole gang, with Nick perched happily in Wolf's arms.

Every last one of them, even the babies, held a balloon.

"Oh, my," Sunny murmured. The corners of her pale mouth moved upwards in the first smile he had seen in eight days.

He cut the motor and got out, then went to the other door and carefully lifted Sunny out. She was so bemused by the gathering that she put her arm around his neck.

That must have been the signal. Wolf leaned down and set Nick on her feet. She took off toward Chance like a shot, running and skipping and shrieking his name in the usual litany. "UncaDance, UncaDance, Unca-*Dance!*" The balloon she was holding bobbed like a mad thing. The whole crowd started forward in her wake.

In seconds they were surrounded. He tried to introduce everyone to Sunny, but there was too much of a hubbub for him to complete a sentence. His sisters-in-law, bless them, were laughing and chattering as if they had known her for years; the men were flirting; Mary was beaming; and Nick's piping voice could be heard above everyone. "Dat's a weally, weally pwetty dwess." She fingered the silk robe and beamed up at Sunny.

John leaned down and whispered something in Nick's ear. *"Dress,"* she said, emphasizing the *r.* "Dat's a weally, weally pwetty *dress.*"

Everyone cheered, and Nick glowed.

Sunny laughed.

Chance's heart jumped at the sound. His throat got tight, and he squeezed his eyes shut for a second. When he opened them, Mary had taken control.

"You must be exhausted," she was saying to Sunny in her sweet, Southern-accented voice. "You don't have to worry about a thing, dear. I have a bed all ready for you at the house, and you can sleep as long as you want. Chance, carry her along to the car, and be careful with her."

"Yes, ma'am," he said.

"Wait!" Nick wailed suddenly. "I fordot de sign!"

"What sign?" Chance asked, gently shifting Sunny so he could look down at his niece.

She fished in the pocket of her little red shorts and pulled out a very crumpled piece of paper. She stretched up on her tiptoes to hand it to Sunny. "I did it all by myself," she said proudly. "Gamma helped."

Sunny unfolded the piece of paper.

"I used a wed cwayon," Nick informed her. "Because it's de pwettiest."

"It certainly is," Sunny agreed. She swallowed audibly. Chance looked down to see the paper shaking in her hand.

The letters were misshapen and wobbly and all different sizes. The little girl must have labored over them for a long time, with Mary's expert and patient aid, because the words were legible. "'Welcome home Sunny,'" Sunny read aloud. Her face began to crumple. "That's the most beautiful sign I've ever seen," she said, then buried her face against Chance's neck and burst into tears.

"Yep," Michael said. "She's pregnant, all right."

It was difficult to say who fell more in love with whom, Sunny with the Mackenzies, or the Mackenzies with her. Once Chance placed her in the middle of the king-sized bed Mary had made up for her—he didn't tell her it was his old bedroom—Sunny settled in like a queen holding court. Instead of lying down to sleep, she propped herself up on pillows, and soon all of the women and most of the younger kids were in there, sitting on the bed and on the floor, some even in chairs. The twins were working their way from one side of the bed to the other and back again, clutching the covers for support and babbling away to each other in what Barrie called their "twin talk." Shea had Benjy down on the floor, tickling him, and every time she stopped he would shriek, "More! More!" Nick sat cross-legged on the bed, her "wed cwayon" in hand as she studiously worked on another sign. Since the first one had been such a resounding success, this one was for Barrie, and she was embellishing it with lopsided stars. Loren, being a doctor, wanted the details of Sunny's wound and present condition. Caroline was doing an impromptu fashion consultation, brushing Sunny's hair and swirling it on top of her head, with some very sexy tendrils curling loose on her slender neck. Maris, her dark eyes glowing, was telling Sunny all about her own pregnancy, and Mary was overseeing it all.

Leaving his family to do what they did best, weave a magic spell of warmth and belonging, Chance walked down to the barn. He felt edgy and worried and a little panicked, and he needed some peace and quiet. When everything quieted down tonight, he had to talk to Sunny. He couldn't put it off any longer. He prayed desperately that she could forgive him, that what he had to tell her didn't completely turn her against him, because he loved her so much he wasn't certain he could live without her. When she had buried her face against him and cried, his heart had almost stopped because she had turned *to* him instead of away from him.

She had laughed again. That sound was the sweetest sound he'd ever heard, and it had almost unmanned him. He couldn't imagine living without being able to hear her laugh.

He folded his arms across the top of a stall door and rested his head on them. She had to forgive him. She had to.

"It's tough, isn't it?" Wolf said in his deep voice, coming up to stand beside Chance and rest his arms on top of the stall door, too. "Loving a woman. And it's the best thing in the world."

"I never thought it would happen," Chance said, the

words strained. "I was so careful. No marriage, no kids. It was going to end with me. But she blindsided me. I fell for her so fast I didn't have time to run."

Wolf straightened, his black eyes narrowed. "What do you mean, 'end with you'? Why don't you want kids? You love them."

"Yeah," Chance said softly. "But they're Mackenzies."

"You're a Mackenzie." There was steel in the deep voice.

Tiredly, Chance rubbed the back of his neck. "That's the problem. I'm not a real Mackenzie."

"Do you want to walk in the house and tell that little woman in there that you're not her son?" Wolf demanded sharply.

"*Hell*, no!" No way would he hurt her like that.

"You're my son. In all the ways that matter, you're mine."

The truth of that humbled Chance. He rested his head on his arms again. "I never could understand how you could take me in as easily as you did. You know what kind of life I led. You may not know the details, but you have a good general idea. I wasn't much more than a wild animal. Mom had no idea, but you did. And you still brought me into your home, trusted me to be around both Mom and Maris—"

"And that trust was justified, wasn't it?" Wolf asked.

"But it might not have been. You had no way of knowing." Chance paused, looking inward at the darkness inside him. "I killed a man when I was about ten, maybe eleven," he said flatly. "That's the wild kid you brought home with you. I stole, I lied, I attacked other kids and beat them up, then took whatever it was they had that I wanted. That's the kind of person I am. That kid will always live inside me.''

Wolf gave him a sharp look. ''If you had to kill a man when you were ten, I suspect the bastard deserved killing.''

''Yeah, he deserved it. Kids who live in the street are fair game to perverts like that.'' He clenched his hands. ''I have to tell Sunny. I can't ask her to marry me without her knowing what she'll be getting, what kind of genes I'll be passing on to her children.'' He gave a harsh laugh. ''Except I don't know what kind of genes they are. I don't know what's in my background. For all I know my mother was a drugged-out whore and—''

''Stop right there,'' Wolf said, steel in his voice.

Chance looked up at him, the only father he had ever known, and the man he respected most in the world.

''I don't know who gave birth to you,'' Wolf said. ''But I do know bloodlines, son, and you're a thoroughbred. Do you know what I regret most in my life? Not finding you until you were fourteen. Not feeling your hand holding my finger when you took your first step. Not getting up with you in the night when you were teething, or when you were sick. Not being able to hold you the way you needed holding, the way all kids need holding. By the time we got you I couldn't do any of that, because you were as skittish as a wild colt. You didn't like for us to touch you, and I tried to respect that.

''But one thing you need to know. I'm more proud of you than I've ever been of anything in my life, because you're one of the finest men I've ever known, and you had to work a lot harder than most to get to where you are. If I could have had my pick of all the kids in the world to adopt, I still would have chosen you.''

Chance stared at his father, his eyes wet. Wolf Mac

kenzie put his arms around his grown son and hugged him close, the way he had wanted to do all these years. "I would have chosen you," he said again.

Chance entered the bedroom and quietly closed the door behind him. The crowd had long since dispersed, most to their respective homes, some spending the night here or at Zane's or Michael's. Sunny looked tired, but there was a little color in her cheeks.

"How do you feel?" he asked softly.

"Exhausted," she said. She looked away from him. "Better."

He sat down beside her on the bed, taking care not to jostle her. "I have some things I need to tell you," he said.

"If it's an explanation, don't bother," she shot back. "You used me. Fine. But *damn* you, you didn't have to take it as far as you did! Do you know how it makes me feel that I was such a fool to fall in love with you, when all you were doing was playing a game? Did it stroke your ego—"

He put his hand across her mouth. Above his tanned fingers, her gray eyes sparked pure rage at him. He took a deep breath. "First and most important thing is: I love you. That wasn't a game. I started falling the minute I saw you. I tried to stop it but—" He shrugged that away and got back to the important part. "I love you so much I ache inside. I'm not good enough for you, and I know it—"

She swatted his hand aside, scowling at him. "What? I mean, I agree, after what you did, but—what do you mean?"

He took her hand and was relieved when she didn't pull away from him. "I'm adopted," he said. "That

part's fine. It's the best. But I don't know who my bi-
ological parents are or anything about them. They—
she—tossed me into the street and forgot about me. I
grew up wild in the streets, and I mean literally in the
streets. I don't remember ever having a home until I was
about fourteen, when I was adopted. I could come from
the trashiest people on the planet, and probably do, otherwise they wouldn't have left me to starve to death in
the gutter. I want to spend the rest of my life with you,
but if you marry me, you have to know what you'll be
getting.''

''What?'' she said again, as if she couldn't understand
what he was telling her.

''I should have asked you to marry me before,'' he
said, getting it all out. ''But—hell, how could I ask anyone to marry me? I'm a wild card. You don't know what
you're getting with me. I was going to let you go, but
then I found out about the baby and I couldn't do it. I'm
selfish, Sunny. I want it all, you and our baby. If you
think you can take the risk—''

She drew back, such an incredulous, outraged look on
her face that he almost couldn't bear it. ''I don't believe
this,'' she sputtered, and slapped him across the face.

She wasn't back to full strength, but she still packed
a wallop. Chance sat there, not even rubbing his stinging
jaw. His heart was shriveling inside him. If she wanted
to hit him again, he figured he deserved it.

''You fool!'' she shouted. ''For God's sake, my father
was a *terrorist!* That's the heritage *I'm* carrying around,
and you're worried because you *don't know who your
parents were?* I wish to hell I didn't know who my father was! I don't believe this! I thought you didn't love
me! Everything would have been all right if I'd known
you love me!''

Chance uttered a startled, profound curse, one of Nick's really, really bad words. Put in those terms, it did sound incredibly trivial. He stared at her lovely, outraged face, and the weight lifted off his chest as if it had never been. Suddenly he wanted to laugh. "I love you so much I'm half crazy with it. So, will you marry me?"

"I have to," she said grumpily. "You need a keeper. And let me tell you one thing, Chance Mackenzie, if you think you're still going to be jetting all over the world getting stabbed and shot at while you get your adrenaline high, then you'd better think again. You're going to stay home with me and this baby. Is that understood?"

"Understood," he said. After all, the Mackenzie men always did whatever it took to keep their women happy.

Epilogue

Sunny was asleep, exhausted from her long labor and then the fright and stress of having surgery when the baby wouldn't come. Her eyes were circled with fatigue, but Chance thought she had never been more beautiful. Her face, when he laid the baby in her arms, had been exalted. Until he died, he would never forget that moment. The medical personnel in the room had faded away to nothing, and it had been just him and his wife and their child.

He looked down at the wrinkled, equally exhausted little face of his son. The baby slept as if he had run a marathon, his plump hands squeezed into fierce little fists. He had downy black hair, and though it was difficult to judge a newborn's eye color, he thought they might turn the same brilliant gray as Sunny's.

Zane poked his head in the door. "Hi," he said softly. "I've been sent to reconnoiter. She's still asleep, huh?"

Chance looked at his wife, as sound asleep as the baby. "She had a rough time."

"Well, hell, he weighs ten pounds and change. No wonder she needed help." Zane came completely into the room, smiling as he examined the unconscious little face. "Here, let me hold him. He needs to start meeting the family." He took the baby from Chance, expertly cradling him to his chest. "I'm your uncle Zane. You'll see me around a lot. I have two little boys who are just itching to play with you, and your aunt Maris—you'll meet her in a minute—has one who's just a little older than you are. You'll have plenty of playmates, if you ever open your eyes and look around."

The baby's eyelids didn't flicker open, even when Zane rocked him. His pink lips moved in an unconscious sucking motion.

"You forget fast how little they are," Zane said softly as he smoothed his big hand over the baby's small round skull. He glanced up at Chance and grinned. "Looks like I'm still the only one who knows how to make a little girl."

"Yeah, well, this is just my first try."

"It'll be your last one, too, if they're all going to weigh ten pounds," came a voice from the bed. Sunny sighed and pushed her hair out of her eyes, and a smile spread across her face as she spied her son. "Let me have him," she said, holding out her arms.

There was a protocol to this sort of thing. Zane passed the baby to Chance, and Chance carried him to Sunny, settling him in her arms. No matter how often he saw it, he was always touched by the communion between mother and new baby, that absorbed look they both got as if they recognized each other on some basic, primal level.

''Are you feeling well enough for company?'' Zane asked. ''Mom's champing at the bit, wanting to get her hands on this little guy.''

''I feel fine,'' Sunny said, though Chance knew she didn't. He had to kiss her, and even now there was that flash of heat between them, even though their son was only a few hours old. She pulled back, laughing a little and blushing. ''Get away from me, you lech,'' she said, teasing him, and he laughed.

''What are you going to name him?'' Zane demanded. ''We've been asking for months, but you never would say. It can't stay a secret much longer.''

Chance trailed his finger down the baby's downy cheek, then he put his arms around both Sunny and the baby and held them close. Life couldn't get much better than this.

''Wolf,'' he said. ''He's little Wolf.''

* * * * *

INTIMATE MOMENTS®
™ *Silhouette®*

presents a riveting 12-book continuity series:
a Year of loving dangerously

Where passion rules and nothing is what it seems...

When dishonor threatens a top-secret agency,
the brave men and women of SPEAR are prepared to
risk it all as they put their lives—and their hearts—
on the line.

Available September 2000:

NIGHT OF NO RETURN
by Eileen Wilks

Hard-edged Alex Bok fought valiantly to keep his emotions
in check when a dangerous undercover assignment reunited
him with the virginal beauty he found irresistible. Could he
accomplish his mission...*and* surrender his heart to love?

*Available only from Silhouette Intimate Moments
at your favorite retail outlet.*

Silhouette®
Where love comes alive™

Visit Silhouette at www.eHarlequin.com   SIMAYOLD4

Beloved author

JOAN
ELLIOTT PICKART

reprises her successful miniseries

THE
BABY BET

with the following delightful stories:

On sale June 2000
TO A MacALLISTER BORN
Silhouette Special Edition® #1329
The Bachelor Bet's Jennifer Mackane proves more than
a match for marriage-wary Jack MacAllister.

On Sale July 2000
THE BABY BET: HIS SECRET SON
Silhouette Books®
A secret son stirs up trouble for patriarch
Robert MacAllister and the clan.

On sale October 2000
BABY: MacALLISTER-MADE
Silhouette Desire® #1326
A night of passion has bachelor Richard MacAllister awaiting
the next bouncing MacAllister bundle!

And coming to Special Edition® in 2001:
HER LITTLE SECRET.

Available at your favorite retail outlet.

Where love comes alive™

**Don't miss
an exciting opportunity
to save on the purchase of
Harlequin and Silhouette books!**

Buy any two Harlequin or
Silhouette books and save
$10.00 off future Harlequin
and Silhouette purchases

OR

buy any three
Harlequin or Silhouette books
and save **$20.00 off** future
Harlequin and Silhouette purchases.

*Watch for details
coming in October 2000!*

PHQ400

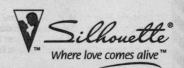

If you enjoyed what you just read,
then we've got an offer you can't resist!

Take 2 bestselling love stories FREE!
Plus get a FREE surprise gift!

COMING NEXT MONTH